THE LOST MEMORIES OF CALLUM BRECKER

MARILYN BORDELON

SPECTRUM BOOKS

CONTENTS

.

To Celia and Angelika. Thank you for always believing in me.
I love you forever and ever after that.

PART ONE
Seven Stale Years

CHAPTER 1

AMBROSE

"Are you sure that you should do this, Ambrose?" the bodyguard asked in a thick Italian accent. "You don't have to. We can stay in."

"I don't have to go to this bar? You don't say!" Ambrose responded, a hint of annoyance breaking through. "It's been a whole fucking year since the attack. I'm not going to hole up on the grounds my entire life. It's fine. I'm fine. Let's get going."

Ambrose opened the car door and then froze. "Wait a minute, where's Checo?" he was surprised that he hadn't noticed he wasn't with them earlier. Where Ambrose was, Checo was sure to be. He had been his personal bodyguard since Ambrose was eighteen when things... well, when his life became what it was today. Slight panic bubbled in his chest, not helped by the face Antonio made.

"Sir," he started, loosening his tie as if it were suddenly tight enough to choke him. Ambrose didn't know Antonio as well as he knew Checo, but he knew him enough to understand that was a tell.

"What happened to Checo?" he demanded, losing patience.

"That's just it, sir," António swallowed. "We have no idea. He's... he's gone."

"And I'm just hearing of this now because?" he said, as he swallowed down his panic. Showing weakness to anyone was not acceptable. Not for him.

"I thought you knew. It's been days, sir."

With a curse, he punched the headrest in front of him. The driver didn't even bat an eye, just another day in his life.

Ambrose was angry, but mostly at himself. He had been overly preoccupied the past few days with Sean. Angry and humiliated. Humiliated that chasing tail led him to totally miss the fact that the only man he trusted in the entire world was gone and had been missing for literally days. The worst part of it all was he was just chasing tail; Sean meant little to nothing to him but was just an easy and convenient lay every time he came from Boston to update the family on certain business.

Ambrose sighed, slumping back in the seat. "Any idea at all? What does Marco say?"

Antonio didn't respond. He looked pained.

"Tell me now, Antonio, or I swear to God, you will regret it."

"He thinks... he thinks he may have abdicated to the Campano side."

Ambrose laughed. It wasn't joyful; it was manic and terrifying, causing both Antonio and the driver to become uneasy. This laugh, they knew, preceded extremely unpleasant things.

"No way," Ambrose said finally, between laughs, "there is no way. Text Marco and tell him to get a search party together. Someone took him to get to me. We need to figure this out."

Antonio nodded, though anyone could see that he didn't believe it; he believed that Checo abdicated. It was hardly uncommon. But he shot the command over to Marco and then returned his attention to his boss. "So, does that mean we will head back?"

Ambrose, chin in his hand, looking longingly out the window before slowly shaking his head said, "No. If I stopped living every time something like this happened, I might as well shoot myself in the head right now. I just want to go to a fucking bar. Stop whining and open my door."

Antonio was out of the car and opening the door for his boss in moments. "This place is packed, sir. I advise that you carry."

Ambrose patted his chest. Underneath his three-piece suit was the Glock that he was rarely without.

"Don't tail me too closely," he demanded as he headed towards the line of people filing into Cosmos. A line that he skipped entirely, the bouncer nodding and letting him in right away, Antonio close at his heels.

A descendant of the five families, the son of a prominent Mafia man did not wait in line for anything. One very minuscule positive to any of it.

Ambrose was cocooned in a mess of loud music, flashing lights, and dancing bodies, a strange sort of comfort. It was a distraction, a way for him to pretend that he was just a regular Floridian, getting trashed on a Friday night, his only worry getting back to work on Monday in one piece.

Antonio spoke in his earpiece, temporarily smashing the illusion. "I am to your left by the bathroom hall. I have an ample view. Enjoy yourself sir, and I'm just an earbud away if you need me."

Ambrose didn't respond, instead he headed straight for the bar. He pushed his way through the crowd and then motioned for the bartender, pulling out his phone while he waited. It was going to be quite the wait, so he sent a hopeful text to Checo. Maybe, just maybe, this was all a misunderstanding.

"What can I get you?" The bartender shouted over the noise, and Ambrose's fingers froze over the keyboard. Time seemed to stop, and he felt like he was the only person in the bar—in the entire world. He would know that voice anywhere. Slowly, ever so slowly, he looked up and met the gaze of a young man, one man he could never forget.

Callum Brecker.

He looked almost the same as he had at seventeen, rich brown curls framing a round face, tempting freckles spattered over his nose and cheeks, and those big eyes the color of the ocean during a storm.

Something twisted inside Ambrose.

He wanted to turn and run, but then he realized with a start that there was no recognition on Callum's face. His eyebrows pinched expectantly as he waited for Ambrose to respond, a polite smile on his face.

Again, something twisted inside Ambrose. How could Callum not recognize him when all Ambrose could think about the past seven years was him?

Him, him, him.

Coming out was a stupid idea, after all.

CHAPTER 2

CALLUM

Callum waited for the strange man to give him his drink order, slowly losing his patience. Who came to a nightclub in Florida in a three-piece suit? Just another entitled rich kid, that's who. Not for the first time that day, Callum wondered what prompted him to move to Boca Raton.

"Sorry," the man said finally. Callum pinched his brows together at the sound of the voice as familiarity niggled at the back of his mind. He cringed a little in actual pain as he tried to remember how he might know this man.

Surely, he would remember a face like that. Sharp cheekbones, dark eyes, thick wavy hair, a little outgrown. Callum knew that there were a lot of Italians living in this area, so he was used to serving them. But this man was beautiful. A face he would remember, a face anyone would remember.

And to top it off, the man was looking at him as if he *should* remember.

Could... could he have possibly been someone Callum had known during his time in Kansas? There was a mental block in his brain. A specialist said it resulted from the trauma of that year, and anything from those last few years of high school was a complete and total blur. As if his memory had been wiped away.

But what were the odds? Unlikely. Besides, he may not remember much, but the people around him told him enough for him to know that if this was someone from those years, he did not *want* to remember.

He waited.

"I—I'll just have a gin and tonic, please," the man said in a rich, smooth voice. Disappointment was clear on his face. Callum smiled at him sympathetically and got to work making his drink.

"What's your name?" the man hedged.

For a plethora of reasons, Callum lied. "It's Jake."

The man's lip quirked slightly before Callum recalled his own manners and asked, "and who are you?"

"Ambrose," the man responded, slowly and purposefully. "Ambrose Romano."

Callum stilled in the middle of passing the man his drink. He wasn't even sure why. The name clicked in his head, turning and turning. Familiarity knocked, begging to be let through the block.

Ambrose was grinning slightly at him as if he understood what was happening.

But then it was gone. There was nothing there when Callum tried to remember the name. He sighed, his fingers lightly brushing against the man's as he took his drink.

Something about it all just begged to be remembered.

***

His aunt was exactly where he had left her when he left for his shift; on the lazy boy in the apartment living room, her eyes gazing at nothing.

She startled briefly when Callum walked in and offered him a small smile. "How was work?"

"Fine," Callum told her, leaning over to kiss her forehead. "How was your evening, Aunt Sia?"

"Fine," she echoed.

"Did you... did you sit here the whole time?" he asked as gently as he could. There was no judgment in his voice; if he could, he'd probably do the same. His aunt had it worse; she had no mental block, protecting her from the memories of it all. She remembered every little detail.

He had once begged her to tell him everything. What were the details surrounding Mick's death? Why did Lucas practically drop out of their lives? Why did everyone he knew look at him with a mixture of pity and loathing? She refused. She claimed it was a blessing that he had this block. That he could, maybe, live some semblance of a life still.

How could he? He may have this block, hazing out the details of that year, but he remembered Mick, her son, his cousin, the most wonderful person who had ever existed. And he knew that Mick died tragically. Murder. A murder that, for reasons unknown to him, could never be resolved. He remembered Lucas, Mick's brother, and all the years of their friendship, their brotherhood, leading up to the mental block.

He knew enough to know that whatever happened involved him, and was tragic. He begged his therapist to ask his aunt to tell him, but she simply sided with Sia.

"Why do you need to know?" she had said. "It makes no difference in the recovery process. You've suffered untold trauma and your brain is only trying to protect you. To recover, you do not need to know details. You only need to power through."

"Why did we move to Florida?" he asked suddenly, taking a seat on their little couch.

His aunt looked at him strangely, as if she was debating what to say. "Because we needed to get away."

"Why Florida though? And Boca Rotan of all places. It's expensive and crowded."

"And safe and beautiful," she responded quietly.

Callum pinched his eyebrows. There was always something she wasn't saying, always something she was holding back. He debated, for a moment, mentioning the name of the man from the bar. To see if recognition would flash on her features and if she would try to pretend it away.

But something stopped him.

Maybe he didn't want to be lied to again.

Or.

Maybe he wanted the truth to stay hidden.

His aunt slept on the chair that night again. Callum wondered if she had even gotten off it at all in the past forty-eight hours. It had been seven years since the tragedy. Seven years since Mick died. And still she was but a husk of a human... barely a human at all, in fact.

He wished the truth could be taken from her too, somehow.

***

He woke up Saturday around noon. He had to be back at the club at five pm, so he decided to use the extra hours to grocery shop for his aunt and to tidy up their little apartment.

She was still asleep when he grabbed the keys from the bar and headed out to their shared Toyota Camry. They used to have a Tesla, but he wasn't sure what happened, why they downgraded to this old junker. In fact, his aunt used to be incredibly well off. She took Callum in when his parents died when he was thirteen and unofficially adopted him into their life. They started off in Portland, Oregon before her work brought them to Wichita, Kansas, and then they ended up here. Well, what was left of the four of them. He could remember that their life was luxurious, so much so that it was almost easy.

He shook his head, climbing into the driver's seat. Wouldn't it be nice if his brain could have just shut out the entire past? Losing his parents, finding his aunt and his cousins, building a beautiful life with him, only to lose that, too.

As he drove, he recalled the night his aunt found him.

Callum ignored the knock on the door, cowering behind the sofa, as close to the dying embers of the fire that he could get. The electricity was shut off weeks ago, and he had to scrounge for kindling himself when he was brave enough to go outside.

He knew this couldn't last forever. His parents were dead, and this was their house; the bank would sell it sooner or later and the new owners would likely not want a thirteen-year-old boy attached to the deal.

Fresh tears fell onto his cheeks as the knocking continued. He wasn't crying for the loss of his parents. Maybe he was awful, but he didn't cry about them at all. They never really cared about him. They put anything and everything in their lives before him. In fact, he felt like he was a total burden to them his entire life. When they died, it was shocking, but it was like a weight had been lifted. It was like relief. No one to burden anymore. No one to disappoint with his very existence.

"Callum, if you are in there, please," a voice called from the other side of the front door. He froze. He recognized the voice; his mother's sister, Sia. She lived somewhere in New York and had a terrible relationship with his mom. She didn't even come to the funeral. Why was she here now?

"Please," she said again, and Callum found himself getting up and going to the door against his better judgment. There was a distinct desperation in her voice that made him sad.

He opened the door. He had only ever seen Sia when he was much younger and in pictures on Facebook. She was tall, so much so that he had to tilt his head up to look at her. Well, he was below average in height, so that was not entirely uncommon.

Holding on to each of her hands were two boys wrapped up nicely to protect them from the cold. He knew he had cousins, but he couldn't remember their names.

Relief washed over his aunt's face, and she dropped to her knees on the porch to be more to Callum's level.

"Callum, oh my god, Callum, look at you, aren't you freezing?!" she pulled over her own coat, wrapping him tightly. The smaller of the two boys unwrapped his scarf and handed it to his mom. She smiled at him and then wrapped it around Callum.

He had never seen a smile so beautiful. The way his aunt just smiled at her son and then even at him had him fighting back tears. His mother had never looked at him like that. Never.

"W-won't you be cold?" he stammered.

She ushered them all inside the house, tsking. "Don't you worry about me. Oh, Callum, have you been staying in this house? It's freezing! Was there no one to take care of you? I called social services, and they didn't even know about you!" she shook her head. "That Malina." The last part was mumbled under her breath and laced with anger.

Malina was his mother's name.

"I don't know anyone here," Callum admitted. "I was not in school because my mom said they brainwashed kids there."

The older boy chuckled at that. He was maybe a year older

than Callum. Their dad was Japanese; he knew this because his mom was awful about it, and both boys seemed to favor their dad's genetics over their moms. They had rich skin and dark hair, dark slanted eyes. The little one kept smiling at Callum.

Callum nervously smiled back.

"Well, Callum," his aunt said as she looked around the room, a sadness in her eyes, "you have us now. We are your family. This is Mick," she said, patting the younger boy's head, "and this is Lucas. They are your cousins."

Callum wanted to crawl back behind the sofa. Mick was all smiles, but Lucas was more wary, maybe even shy. All eyes were on him, and they were full of pity and scrutiny.

"Hi," Callum said, with a small wave. His voice cracked on the word, and he took a shuddering breath. He knew he couldn't cry in front of Lucas. He wanted to look strong.

His aunt shook her head. Her eyes were watery, like she was struggling to hold back tears herself. "I'm so sorry, Callum," she said. "You must miss them so much."

"I don't," he said before he could think any better of it. They all looked rather shocked by it, so he hurried to add, "They were never around much. I... I hardly knew them."

His aunt sighed. "I wish I had known. I am so sorry, Callum. Is it okay if you come with us? It's... it's just us three. Their dad left a while back. We could be a family. We could be a good family. Let me take care of you."

Mick nodded in vigorous agreement, and even Lucas offered a small, encouraging smile.

Callum was overwhelmed. He had nowhere else to go, but he didn't want to impose, "I—I don't want to be a burden," he said, eyes down, staring at his old shoes.

He heard his aunt suck in a breath and then her arms were around him and she was definitely crying, which broke his resolve and had him crying too.

"Burden, Callum? You could never be a burden. You are ours now, and we are going to love you unconditionally. We are going to love you every day."

A tiny hand rested on his own hand and Mick peaked around his mother's back. "You can share my PlayStation," he said with a big smile, as if that was all the encouragement anyone needed.

In a way, it was. Callum smiled back. "Okay."

Callum pulled up to Whole Foods and parked his car. He didn't get out right away, though. Remembering that day when he first met Mick was always acutely bittersweet. Mick had become his best friend, a part of his soul. To not know his end... a blessing or a curse?

He meandered aimlessly through the grocery store, empty basket in hand. His thoughts kept drifting to the man from last night and how desperately familiar he seemed while being a complete stranger.

After a while, he left the grocery store empty-handed. He sat in the car for a while, spacing out, before heading back to the apartment. He could get groceries another day. Right now, his head was pounding in a way it hadn't in quite a while. Fuzzy, hazy memories tried to push their way through.

When he walked in, he was surprised to see his aunt was out of the chair and cooking. She looked up when he opened the door and scolded, "Where were you? Did you have any tea yet?"

He shook his head. "Not yet," and a panicked, strained look flitted across his aunt's features, barely perceptible. She pushed over a mug of hot tea. "I'm sorry," she said, "It's the first time I have forgotten to give you some in seven years."

"Don't cry," Callum said, panicked when he noticed her lip was quivering, "it's no big deal. Look, I'll drink it now."

He never really understood the big deal. Ever since Mick died, she insisted that they have tea together every morning. She would make it and bring it to him, and they would just sit together, sipping on the tea in silence. It was like a comforting ritual to her and he was sure she needed it more than him, so he went along with it, making sure to never miss a day. "I'm sorry. We both slept in. Come on, we can sit now and drink it. It's okay, better late than never, right?"

She nodded and pushed over a plate piled with scrambled eggs and bacon. "Exactly right," she responded with a strange look in her eyes.

CHAPTER 3

AMBROSE

"Antonio tells me you ran into an old friend," Tomas stated.

"Dad, Antonio has a big mouth," Ambrose responded, shooting said person a warning look. Antonio ignored it, continuing to stare straight ahead as if we weren't in the room. Like the other three bodyguards currently in his father's study.

Tomas pursed his lips in thought before shaking his head. He was balding and what little hair that was left was grey. He used to be fit and lean but had been filling out lately. Especially after... well. After everything. "I knew it was trouble to bring them to Florida."

Ambrose practically flew out of his seat, leaning over the desk so his face was inches away from his father's. "You knew he was here? You *brought* him here? After everything!"

Tomas made a motion with his hand and Marco was there, pulling Ambrose back into his seat. "Be respectful. He may be your father, but he is your boss first."

The words almost made him flinch, but he caught himself. Weakness was especially forbidden in front of his father.

"I'm sorry, sir," Ambrose said to his father. "I... got carried away."

Ambrose straightened his suit jacket, his heart pounding wildly at this revelation.

"I didn't want to tell you because I was sure we would never cross paths. We only came to Boca Raton last year... It doesn't matter, though. He doesn't remember anything."

That was like a knife to the chest, pain all over again. "I saw that. What happened?"

Tomas eyed his son warily, before leaning back in his chair, kicking his feet up and crossing them at the ankles over his desk, "Dissociative amnesia," he said and when he continued, effectively sounding like a copy and paste from Google. "It's when a person has a mental block to certain times and events due to stress and trauma. He's a special case that Callum. He truly cannot remember anything from that entire year. And even some things before and after," he paused, "probably for the best. You know. For his sake."

Ambrose wanted to punch his dad right in the face. There was a time when his father was his favorite person in the world, when he looked up to him and was always by his side. That ended seven years ago. Now he harbored a barely hidden hate for the man and everything he caused.

But he only smiled, fake and tight. "I guess. So, you stay in touch with Sia then? Is that a double standard?"

Marco cleared his throat in warning and Ambrose had to restrain from rolling his eyes all the way to the back of his head. Tomas only chuckled. "Don't be petty. We do not keep in touch, unless absolutely necessary. She *was* my lawyer for ten plus years. There are some things that I need to speak with her about, here and there. Besides, I check up on your precious little Callum every now and again. I keep them safe. You should be grateful."

This time, Ambrose's smile was cruel. "I should be grateful?"

His father nodded. "Callum should be dead, Ambrose. Plain and simple. He knew too much. I spared his life for your sake."

Ambrose barked out a laugh. "It was easy for you to do, seeing as he can't remember a fucking thing about any of us. He couldn't even recognize me at all! Don't act like you did anyone a favor. You were let off the hook because of *dissociative amnesia.*"

Tomas held out a hand, stopping Marco from approaching Ambrose to teach him a lesson. "Son. You are upset. I can imagine seeing Callum was hard, especially since he doesn't remember you. Don't lash out at me. I explicitly warned you time and again to not get involved with Callum. Who can you blame but yourself?"

"I suppose I could blame you," he replied, crossing an ankle over his knee. "Since, ya know, you are the Lastra lapdog."

This time, his father didn't stop Marco, and the bodyguard's fist landed firmly on Ambrose's jaw. He didn't take it personally; he actually rather liked Marco. This was just his job. He winced a little, but straightened up in his chair. Marco dipped his chin in his direction before taking his place back to the right of his father.

What a strange position Marco had to be in. He deferred to both Tomas and Ambrose, but Tomas had seniority, which meant that Marco literally had to punch his boss in the face sometimes. Ambrose held in the urge to chuckle.

Instead, he looked at his father as unlovingly as he could possibly manage. "If you wanted to keep me away from him, bringing him to Florida, to the same damn city as us, was a big mistake. Of course, I would run into him, eventually."

"Stay away from him," his father clipped. "If you care about him at all, Ambrose, stay away. I had to bring them here. After the attack last year... something happened back home too. Don't panic–don't interrupt. Let me finish. Sia was targeted. So, I moved them here to give them some protection. I figured I could keep you away. It's a big city and you don't go out much."

Ambrose conceded with a crisp nod. Despite his father being a jackass and the reason for this all, he wasn't wrong about one thing. It was safest for Callum to remain in the dark. It was safest for him to never remember or to never get involved with him again.

Painful though.

Ambrose wanted nothing more than to go right back to that nightclub and shake Callum until he could remember who he was. And then... kiss him senseless or punch him or... just...

Hug him.

"I hate you, Dad," Ambrose whispered so that only his father could hear.

He might have imagined it, but his father almost looked hurt before schooling his feature to his typical nonchalance.

"That's okay," his father whispered back. "I do not need your love. I only demand your obedience."

***

Ambrose motioned for Antonio to step up closer so he could talk to him. He was strolling the grounds, Antonio tailing him. It seemed unnecessary to Ambrose once—to have a bodyguard on their own property—but the attack last year showed him the truth. That a bodyguard was always necessary. Besides, the grounds attached to their mansion went on for miles and miles, only gated for the first mile.

"Yes, sir," Antonio said when he fell into place alongside him. He was unofficially his personal bodyguard at that point, at least until they found Checo.

"Any update?"

Antonio cleared his throat, tugging at his tie again. "No sir. He really has disappeared. We... we have sent a convoy to the Campano estate in Boston."

Ambrose rolled his eyes. "That is completely unnecessary. He would never betray me."

The guard said nothing.

Ambrose felt annoyance rising. Checo had been with the family for so long. He knew Ambrose inside out and backwards and vice versa. They were brothers. Ambrose would trust him with anything.

But he steered the conversation to the next topic. "Did... did you know about Callum and his aunt?"

"Sir... I am sorry," he replied, and had the decency to look it. "A lot of us were briefed. We were to keep you away from his work. He must have recently gotten employment at The Cosmo, otherwise I would have dissuaded you."

"You tried to, anyway."

Antonio nodded. "After... after the attack. Well, we are all a little nervous. We don't know who those men were working with to this day. Until we do, we have every reason to be on higher alert than usual."

The attack. It was always the fucking attack. A year ago, several buildings on their estate, including three guards' quarters and the servant home, were burnt to the ground and twenty of their employees were murdered. It happened deep in the night and by the time Ambrose and his father were alerted in the main estate, when they rushed out, the front yard was littered with limbs and body parts, sprayed with blood spelling out: *Stay in your lane, Lastra lap dogs.*

It could have been a plethora of people. Any member of the Mafia had as many enemies as they could count. His father always suspected the Campano branch, but there had been a tentative peace between the five families and their descendants, so it was simply a wild guess.

Whoever it was, they weren't the brightest, at least if anyone cared to ask Ambrose. Stay in your lane was a rather cryptic message. What was it specifically that was making this particular enemy angry? Last year, the Lastra family and their relatives started branching out, expanding their sharking to beyond their usual perimeters. But that was not uncommon; the five families were always expanding. As long as they respected each other's territory, they were fine.

Perhaps another gang, then?

Leonardo Lastra had been making big steps in expanding into the illegal drug business. Perhaps the other gangs felt that they were encroaching.

Ambrose shook his head. He tried not to care or to get overly involved in the workings of the Mafia, but it was hard. This was his life, after all, and as the only child of Tomas he would inherit this estate one day, he would become the head of their portion. He would be what he detested; one of Leonardo Lastra's many lap dogs.

"Let's go out again," he said to Antonio.

Antonio balked.

"Not to The Cosmo, obviously," Ambrose snapped, his patience wearing thin. "Somewhere else. Anywhere else. I just want to go out."

His guard nodded. "I'll gather a team. Your father has decided that you will be accompanied by three men now if you wish to leave the grounds."

"Three? *Che diavolo!* That is a little extreme."

Antonio responded. "We cannot be too careful, sir."

***

As he got ready to go out, Ambrose allowed himself a little walk down memory lane.

"There's a new kid, coming from Portland," Liam was saying to the group. "Well, three of them. But one of them is going to be a senior like us. His name is Lucas."

Ambrose grinned. "Portland? Why would they ever move from Oregon to Wichita, Kansas? Poor souls."

"Apparently their mom is a big-wig lawyer and got some work here," Liam responded.

This got Ambrose's attention. He had overheard his dad telling Marco that the lawyer would be in next week. Could this be them? Would he be going to school with the children of his father's employees? Likely a coincidence. Still, he was intrigued.

He was leaning against his Jeep, surrounded by his three friends: Liam, Asther and Rose, in the parking lot of the school. They were having a quick cigarette before the start of their final year.

"I'll have to talk to this Lucas," Ambrose said, taking a long drag and watching the smoke leave through his nostrils.

"Why?" Liam whined. "Just leave them be. We have a good thing going on."

Rose chuckled. "You could at least pretend you aren't an overly jealous friend. It's borderline obsessive. You don't like any of us talking to anyone. Ever."

Liam made a face.

"It's fine," Ambrose teased his friend, "no matter what Liam, we will still love you."

Asther rolled his eyes. "Will we?" He adjusted his skirt, putting out his cigarette on the hood of Ambrose's car. "Your clinginess gets on my nerves."

Liam threw an arm around his friend and said, "You like it" at the same time Ambrose said, "Hey, be mindful of my Jeep!"

A few minutes later, they were walking into the school together, like they had the past three years.

"Meet you at lunch!" Rose said with a wave before ducking off to her first class. Liam left too, but Asther and Ambrose both had Spanish first period, so they headed to the class together.

On the way, Ambrose spotted a new face at the lockers. He seemed nervous, stuffing his bag into the cubby, and pulling out some books. He had brown curly hair, a little outgrown, and when he turned his face slightly, Ambrose saw a scattering of freckles.

He wanted to approach. So he did.

Shane got to him before he did, though.

"What's up, new kid?" Shane asked, ruffling those curls and not very gently. "Are you... wait," he pulled his hand away, pretending to be disgusted, "are you a fag?"

The new kid stilled at the same time Ambrose did. Shane was nothing more than a big bully and Ambrose had always suspected he was at least mildly homophobic, but he'd never witnessed him do something like this.

"W—why would you say that?" the boy stammered. His eyes didn't meet Shane's, they stayed on his shoes.

Shane laughed. "Your jeans are tighter than my mom's Spanx, dude!"

Ambrose took this as his moment, pushing past Shane and leaning up on the new kid's locker, crossing his ankles. "Pretty fucking weird that you know how tight your moms Spanx are, isn't it?"

Shane paled. He was easily twice Ambrose's size and towered a few inches above Ambrose's own generous six feet. But most people in school knew that messing with Ambrose was like playing with fire. A rumor started a few years back that he was connected to a gang after a kid who had tried to bully him showed up weeks later with a missing hand. No one could prove anything, but still... there was that fear. No one wanted to test those waters.

The rumor was basically the truth, though Ambrose had not wanted any of it. He was indeed part of the Lastra branch of the US Italian Mafia and Dawson had bullied him at the beginning of ninth year, his first year at Wichita. Ambrose had made the mistake of telling his dad and then Dawson disappeared from class. When he showed up later, he was missing his left hand.

Ambrose stopped telling his dad about anything that happened at school and secretly deposited money into Dawson's parent's bank account; more than enough to cover *the hospital fees.*

"Ambrose, I was just... you know, hazing the new kid," Shane stated innocently.

"You used a really naughty f-word," Ambrose said in a patronizing tone, a bright smile on his face, "and not the fun one, either."

"It's okay," the new kid interjected. "Really."

Ambrose made a shooing motion with his hand, and Shane didn't need to be told twice. He bolted.

Ambrose turned to face the boy, leaning his shoulder against the locker again, "He won't mess with you again," Ambrose assured him.

"I think he was just teasing," the kid said. He kept his eyes lowered, like his shoes were fascinating. They really weren't, though; they were just regular black Converse. Ambrose liked them well enough, but everyone had a pair. This boy was obviously very anxious. Maybe slightly anti-social.

"Eh, he shouldn't say things like that though, you know, it's not very forward of him. I know this is Kansas, but we still try," Ambrose smiled at the boy, but it was lost to him as he wouldn't look up.

"Hey, kid, are you the new senior, Lucas?"

The boy bit his lower lip nervously. "No. I—I'm his cousin. I'm a junior. I should be a senior, but I missed a lot of school... anyway, sorry, it's not important. I'm Callum."

Callum.

"Nice to meet you," Ambrose said, offering his right hand.

"I'm Ambrose." He cocked his head to the left. "This is Asther."

Callum tentatively took his hand and shook it. He even glanced up at him for the briefest of moments. He had shocking eyes, deep blue, like a stormy ocean. He had lots of freckles across his nose and cheeks, too.

He was... really fucking beautiful.

"Nice to meet you, Ambrose, Asther," Callum said, almost timidly.

"If you are gay," Ambrose went on, "don't worry. Most people here are super chill. They won't bully you for it or anything." He chuckled. "I mean, look at Asther. Everyone loves him and he comes to school in skirts half the time."

"Oh. I... I'm not gay," Callum stammered. "I mean... yeah, I'm pretty sure I'm not gay."

Ambrose wanted to laugh until he realised the boy wasn't joking. Something like disappointment stupidly, settled into Ambrose. He only smiled in return.

"I mean, cool. You can be whatever you want. What's your first class?"

"Uhm," Callum pulled a crumpled paper from his jeans pocket. They really were tight jeans, delightfully so, showing off his lean legs, "Spanish IV."

Ambrose smiled again. "Oh, same as us. You've taken Spanish before?"

Callum nodded, then shook his head. "Well... I taught myself when... I was bored."

Ambrose flung an arm around Callum's shoulders, absolutely delighted. Callum seemed to stiffen, like he didn't know what to do in a situation like this. "That's awesome, dude. You'll like Ms. Gomez, she's super dope. We just call her Alice and she's an excellent teacher."

"Nice," Callum said, his voice small, his eyes trained to the floor, even as they walked.

Ambrose smiled at the memory. Then he poured himself a glass of whiskey, gulped it down and one go and left his room, joining Antonio and the other two recently assigned bodyguards.

"Let's go," Ambrose said, straightening his tie, "get me out of this house."

Chapter 4

Callum

Saturday nights were the busiest at Cosmo. And that was saying a lot, as every other night they were jam-packed. But Saturdays were especially anxiety-inducing for Callum as the club was at full capacity the entire night; people left only for more people to be ushered in from the line outside.

It was pretty ironic that Callum worked for a place that was essentially his worst nightmare. But beggars can't be choosers and he took the easiest and first job that he could after being laid off at the University.

"Ready Callum?" his co-worker and boss, Becky, asked as she took a final look around the club. "Max is opening the door in t-minus two minutes."

"I'm ready," Callum said, about as excited as a college student heading in for finals.

Becky rolled her eyes and playfully nudged him. "Come on, show them you deserve those tips!"

He nodded. There were ten bartenders, two more than any other night, and eight bouncers, all taking up their positions as Max went to open. The first surge of people would be coming, and the first surge was usually the worst.

Callum took a deep breath. Six of them worked the bar and the other four walked the club, though they rotated every few hours. Callum especially hated when he had to walk the area.

An hour later and he was already sweating as he made his one hundredth and whatever drink. The girl who ordered it was pretty and a little flirty, but he was too stressed to notice and care.

Grace came over to him, handing him a tray of jello shots. "Time to switch, buddy. Go get 'em."

His heart sank, but he took the tray and squished his way out from the bar into the throngs of people. The club was designed so that the bar was off to the side with a little room for a small crowd, and then there were two steps that led down to the rest of the club and the dance floor.

VIP was on the second floor and consisted of small private rooms. Those required separate servers and, thankfully, Callum very rarely had to work the VIP area. But as he found himself in the middle of a throng of dancers, exchanging Jello-shots for dollar bills, drowning in a pool of body odor and horny college students, he wondered if perhaps the relative peace of the VIP would be preferable.

"Heyyyy, you are so cute," a girl told him, handing him a five in exchange for a few jell-o shots. "Can you dance?" she asked, as she practically snorted the first shot before passing the others off to her friends. "Or is that, like, against the rules?"

Callum smiled at her. "Against the rules, sorry," he lied,

before moving on. It was only a few minutes before his tray was empty and he headed back to the bar to top it up.

"Hey," Becky approached him apologetically, which was never a good sign. "One of the VIP servers had to leave. Emergency or whatever. Can you cover? We have it handled down here for now. Please?"

Callum groaned. "Do I have to?"

She nodded. "I'm sorry, I know you don't like the VIP area, but I need you up there ASAP. It's not too bad tonight, a few football players' groups and some dude claiming he was in Game of Thrones. Dude, I've seen every episode. He must have been like a walker or something because I have never seen him before in my life."

Callum smiled, slightly. "Okay. Wouldn't want to pass up on an autograph from a White Walker, would I?"

"That's the spirit!" she exclaimed, handing him the tacky gold apron that he would switch out with his black to show that he was VIP for the night. "Go on up. And Callum, try to have some fun. There really are worse ways to spend your Saturday nights."

***

Ambrose turned the whiskey glass around in his hand, watching the dregs of the amber liquid, spacing out. There was a man in his lap, dark-skinned, buff, and beautiful in a Greek God sort of way, but the arm Ambrose had wrapped around his waist was lazy and bored; he stopped stroking his side a long time ago.

His thoughts were somewhere else, in a different club on the other side of the city.

The man, his name was Blake, at least Ambrose was ninety percent sure, turned a little in his lap, angling his face up for another kiss.

Ambrose angled his own face away. "Sorry," he said, "not feeling it anymore. I'm... tired."

Blake shrugged. He got off and exited the private room, not even slightly disappointed. *Flattering,* Ambrose thought.

"Antonio, bring me a cigarette."

Antonio moved from his spot against the wall and handed Ambrose the pack of Newports. He lit one up before offering one to his guard, who politely declined as always.

"Checo would smoke with me," Ambrose stated, half-teasing, half-bitter.

"I'm sorry, sir."

Ambrose shook his head. It was only himself and his three guards in the VIP room now that he basically kicked Blake out and he was bored. He sighed. "Let's go."

He stood up, a plan forming. It had been a long time since he had done something risky like this, but... he was desperate to go back to Cosmo. He wasn't going to approach Callum or anything. He just wanted to look. Maybe he was a masochist and just wanted the pain.

"I need to use the restroom," he said when they reached the

main floor. This club had individual rooms, not stalls, exactly what Ambrose needed.

Antonio and Fonsi took up position on either side of the door and the third guard headed out to have their driver pull up. Ambrose shut the bathroom door and, as quietly as he could, locked it. It went against protocol and internally he cringed, hoping with all his might that they didn't hear the lock.

Moments passed and nothing.

He got to work as quietly as he could, prying open the window. It was tough work to make it up on the ledge in his suit, and to do it quietly, but after a few minutes, he was out in the humid Florida air.

He walked for a bit before calling an Uber. His nerves were frayed. He looked from left to right as he waited. When the Uber arrived and he climbed into the back seat, he still couldn't settle. Was this a mistake? Could the Uber driver be working for one of their enemies? He hadn't realized how much anxiety he had about going out since the attack until now. He took a deep breath. The Uber driver was young and too chatty.

His nerves were in full force when they pulled up to Cosmo. What was he doing? The texts were already streaming in from Antonio, and he had five missed calls. He knew the first place they would look was Cosmo, so he had to hurry.

He approached the bouncer at the door.

"Romano," he told him. It was stupid to announce who he was without his bodyguards for protection, but he knew they would be showing up at any moment, so he risked it. "VIP room, please. With a good view of the bar."

The bouncer nodded, relaying it to someone through his earpiece as he let Ambrose through. Ambrose was immediately met by a woman in her mid-forties.

"Ahh, honored guest, we are so delighted to have you visit our establishment," she oozed. "My name is Becky. Let me show you to your VIP room. Is it just you then?"

"Three others will be here shortly," he told her as she led him to the stairs. He followed her up and then she ushered him into a small room with a booster seat taking up the entire back wall and a table in front. Curtains offered privacy. She pulled them closed, stepping out after saying, "I'll send your server right over."

Ambrose removed his tie and unbuttoned the top buttons. He removed his suit, laying them all neatly on the cushioned booth. He took a seat. After the server came and got his drink order, he would wander to the rail and see if Callum was even working tonight. Chances were that he wasn't since he worked last night. Or... Ambrose didn't actually know. He knew nothing about regular jobs like this.

He pulled out his phone in a moment of guilt and dialed Antonio.

"Sir, where are you?" Antonio's voice was breathless, like he had been running. "Please tell me you didn't go to Cosmo."

"I can't tell you that. But it's fine. I got a VIP room, and I told them you were coming to join me. Please don't be annoyed or upset. I just want to look." As he said it, he realized how desperate and pathetic he must seem. "Just trust me. I'm in VIP room three. I'll see you soon."

Before Ambrose hung up, he heard Antonio sigh heavily, resigned.

"Hello, sir. What can I start you off to drink tonight?"

At the sound of the voice, Ambrose reared his head up, panic clearly on his face. He hadn't even thought of the possibility that Callum might serve VIP and yet there he was, right in front of him.

"Oh," Callum said with a slight smile, "you were here last night."

It took Ambrose a moment before he could respond. He remembered him, but only from last night. It hurt all over again, worse than a knife-wound, and Ambrose knew exactly what those felt like. He wanted to stare at Callum, to take him in, this twenty-five-year-old version of the boy he had loved so much. To memorize every part of him and to find all the little changes that seven years left on him.

He cleared his throat. "Yes, last night. The service was so great I had to come back." He kept his voice light—teasing—while inside his chest was being torn into tiny pieces. "I'll just have a gin and tonic. Keep them coming. And three waters for my guests. They'll be here soon."

They'd be there soon, and Antonio was going to throw a fit when he saw who their personal server happened to be. But Ambrose was still his boss—one day would be his head boss—and he couldn't do anything about it until Tomas asked for a report.

Maybe Ambrose would get lucky, and Tomas would skip that part this time. *Ha. ha-ha,* he thought bitterly.

Callum was quick, returning in minutes with the drinks. He set them all at the table, pushing the gin and tonic gently towards Ambrose. "Can I get you an appetizer? Anything else?"

You can remember me, Ambrose pleaded in his mind. *You can promise to never remember me.*

Callum shifted a little uncomfortably and Ambrose realized he had been staring and hadn't responded, "I—I'm sorry," Callum was saying, "I—if I should recognize you and I don't, I'm sorry. I have a... condition and I can't remember some things from certain years in my life. I'm sorry."

It was almost exactly what Ambrose wanted to hear, but there was some stupid, naïve part of him that was disappointed that Callum could ever forget him, trauma or not. Ambrose liked to think that no matter what, he would never be able to forget Callum. He knew, realistically, that was not how trauma and mental illness worked. Still. Yet.

"No, no," he said aloud, though it hurt him to say the next words, "I mistook you for someone else last night. The lighting down there was dark, and I was drinking. You just looked so much like someone I used to know. I'm sorry if I made you uncomfortable."

Callum breathed a sigh of relief. "Oh, good."

Yes, good. If Ambrose said it enough perhaps, he would believe it. That this was the right thing to do. That he shouldn't pull Callum close to him and tell him everything, kiss him until he had to remember. Kiss him until he made those little noises that drove Ambrose mad in the best way. Kiss him until they were just Ambrose and Callum again, from seven years ago, the best of friends, the best of lovers.

That's when his bodyguards showed up. Antonio took one look at Callum and panic became evident on his face. Ambrose almost laughed.

"There you boys are," he said. "Come. Sit. I got you waters."

They obeyed immediately, though Ambrose could easily tell they were all disgruntled and annoyed with him. He would be too, of course. The fear he must have instilled in them in the moments they couldn't find him. They surely saw their lives flash before their eyes. This prompted Ambrose to say, genuinely, "I am sorry."

"It's not your place to ever apologize to us," Antonio responded, though he looked pleased by the gesture.

Callum stood at the opening of the room, awkwardly. "Is there anything else?" he asked. "There's a buzzer right under the lip of the table. Just hit it whenever you need me." He smiled. It was a familiar smile to Ambrose, the one he knew Callum employed when he was uncomfortable, awkward, or upset. One he had once thought would never be directed at him ever again.

"Thank you, *Jake,*" Ambrose said with a mischievous grin,

"that's all for now."

Confusion flashed across Callum's face before it dawned on him and he nodded, exiting the room.

"Jake?" Antonio asked. He was seated in the booth as Ambrose had instructed, but all three of them were sitting stiff and upright like statues. It was making Ambrose uncomfortable just to look at them.

Ambrose swirled his glass. "Yeah. He said his name was Jake last night."

"Probably smart."

Ambrose nodded. His eyes drifted to the opening where Callum had left. His mind drifted to Callum.

"Well, how was your first day?"

Callum turned to find Ambrose walking toward him. He was headed to Lucas' car, Mick at his side.

"It was good," Callum responded. It was pretty non-eventful actually, except for whatever it was that happened that morning with Shane. But Ambrose had been right. Shane was in two of Callum's other classes and he solidly ignored him in both. In fact, when Ambrose had approached him at the lockers, it was like Shane had been terrified. Callum didn't get it. Ambrose was tall, but Shane was taller, where Ambrose was lean and lanky, Shane was all brawn and muscles. Shane could easily take Ambrose. Something else was going on.

"Who's this little guy?" Ambrose asked with a grin, inclining his head towards Mick. Mick puffed. "I'm in year eleven!"

"Shit, I'm sorry dude!" Ambrose looked embarrassed. "Short definitely runs in the family, I see."

Callum was five foot six, Mick was five foot five.

Still, Mick had to mention, "My brother Lucas is tall! He's five eleven."

"Oh, I see," Ambrose said. "I wanted to meet him, but we didn't have any classes together today. Can you introduce me?"

"Introduce who?" Lucas said, coming from behind, his book bag slung lazily over his shoulder.

"That's Lucas," Mick declared proudly. "Lucas, this is..."

"Ambrose," Callum filled in. "He's in year twelve. You might have some classes together, eventually."

Lucas took Ambrose's hand. He wasn't friendly on the best of days, and Callum felt himself feeling strangely nervous and apprehensive. He wasn't sure why he cared. Maybe because Ambrose had been the only person who approached him that day, besides Shane. But Ambrose had been friendly and welcoming. He smiled a lot, which was kind of creepy, but you got used to it after the twentieth time or so.

"Ambrose Romano?" Lucas asked.

"Ahh, heard of me?"

Lucas nodded, furrowing his brow. So he chose unfriendly then. "A thing or two."

Ambrose only chuckled. "Don't believe everything you hear."

Lucas huffed. "Yeah, no kidding. There were some really tall tales."

Ambrose laughed again. "Oh great. Did you hear the one that blames me for Dawson's missing hand?"

Callum blanched. He had met Dawson earlier, and he did have a missing hand. To his surprise, though, Lucas actually laughed. "Yeah. Gosh, who did you piss off to create such nasty rumors about you?"

"I honestly have no idea. But I must have done a real number."

"That sucks for Dawson," Mick said, "to lose a hand. I can't imagine. He's really nice. He's in my English class."

Callum noticed that Ambrose made a strange face when Mick said that Dawson was nice. But he could have imagined it because he responded to Mick. "Yeah, he's honestly great. He manages really well. He's super positive about it, too."

But Callum couldn't help that suddenly Ambrose's smile was laced with something a little cruel.

"Anyway, I won't keep you, boys. First day is exhausting, I know I just want to go home and crash. See you tomorrow, okay? You should have lunch with us!"

He walked away, shooting them one last smile.

"I like him," Mick said as they walked to their car together.

"Even though he called you short?" Callum asked with a sly grin. Mick was especially sensitive about his height, the only physical trait he seemed to inherit from his mom. He often bemoaned the fact that Lucas got to be tall and he was stuck being so short.

"Everyone has their shortcomings," Mick deadpanned.

Callum grinned. "I think I like him too."

They piled into Lucas' Corolla. It was a gift from his mom for starting his senior year. She said Callum and Mick would get a car when they started their senior year too. It seemed that Sia was doing really well with whoever her new client was here in Wichita. She couldn't tell the boys who it was due to an intense client confidentiality agreement, but whoever it was, they paid her well.

As Mick would say, "We truly do live in the lap of luxury, out here in the middle of nowhere Kansas."

"What about you, Lucas?" Mick asked as he buckled in. "Did you like him? Did you make friends? I made a friend! Asther. He's super cool. I thought he was gay or trans even because he was wearing a skirt and nail polish, but he's actually completely straight. Like super into girls. He's super cool. I want to be just like him."

Callum turned in the passenger seat to get a good look at Mick. "I met him. He's friends with Ambrose. I'm really glad you made a friend, Mick."

Lucas was always pretty quiet when he was in the driver's seat; ultra-focused on the road, but he responded, "That's great. Yeah, there were a few chill people today. Going to school in Kansas is a lot less traumatizing than I thought it would be."

Callum nodded. He remembered when Aunt Sia had told them all around the dinner table back in Oregon, that she got a job in Kansas, and they were moving in time for the beginning of the school year. Callum's first thought had been, I hope I'm going with them.

It had already been years since his aunt had taken him in. It was rough going at first, especially because Lucas took a good while to warm up to the idea that he suddenly had another brother in the house, practically the same age as him. Mick was great right away, and Callum soon discovered that his little cousin was literally the kindest, most genuine person, probably on the entire planet. And it took a while, but he learned that Lucas had a tough exterior, but underneath all that he was a loyal, caring person with an intense fear of abandonment and being alone. They grew close in their own way. That's why his first thought was what it was. He didn't want to be left behind. He wanted to stay with them forever.

Lucas must have had the same thought because the first thing he said after his mom told them was, "Callum is staying with us, right?"

At that moment, Callum loved him so much.

"Yeah," Callum said then to Mick and to Lucas, "Kansas won't be so bad. I think it might actually be fun."

"Hey," Wyatt hissed at Callum, motioning him over to the little cubby that was the server's space on the VIP floor. "Come here."

Callum had only met Wyatt this evening because he exclusively served the VIP floor, so he never had reason to be on the ground floor. Callum already really, really didn't like him.

"What's up?" he asked him.

"Do you know who you are serving there?" Wyatt asked him, a smug smile on his face.

"Yeah, Ambrose Romano." Callum deadpanned.

Wyatt rolled his eyes. "But do you know *who* he is?"

"A rich kid?"

"You're impossible. Seriously, we need to fix you. But yeah, he is rich because he's the son of Tomas freaking Romano. Who happens to be a relative of the Lastra branch of the mother fucking *Mafia*. He's actually a real-life Mafia. Like that's why he has those terrifying guards with him."

Callum tilted his head. Something familiar tugged at his brain. He felt the headache coming on again.

Maybe that's why Ambrose had seemed familiar last night and today. He probably saw him on the news or in a paper.

"Interesting," was all he said, inflectionless.

"Seriously?" Wyatt asked, chomping extra loudly on his gum. "Interesting is all you have to say about that? You might be about to get the tip of your life! Bri had one of the Mafia guys last week and he tipped her like five hundos. For real."

"What's a hundo?" Callum asked. He knew perfectly well what it was. He had been in high school once, after all, but he had the urge to make Wyatt feel like an idiot.

"Where did you even come from?" Wyatt responded with a laugh, tussling Callum's hair. "You are seriously adorable."

There was little that annoyed Callum more than people tussling his hair. It happened way more than it should; maybe because he was so short, or because of the curls or the freckles, or all of it combined. He ducked his head. "Well, I better get back to it then. Don't want to get on the bad side of someone in the *mother fucking Mafia.*"

He slipped out of the cubby. The Mafia. It could be true. He knew that this part of Florida had Mafia activity, actually famously so. He also knew Wyatt was a dramatic ass, even though he only met him a few hours ago.

He walked back to the VIP room, the curtains falling back around him. Ambrose was playing cards with two of the men, the third one standing imposingly by the curtains.

"Ahh, Jake," Ambrose said, looking up from his cards with a smile. He always said Jake with a little inflection, as if he knew it was a fake name.

"Is there anything you need? Another gin and tonic?"

Ambrose nodded. "Yes, please. And..." he seemed to think on it for a moment, but finally asked, "do you know anything about hearts? I think my friend here is trying to cheat."

Callum pinched his brows together. He had a strange sense of déjà vu. "Hmm. No. I only know that it's a card game, but that's about the extent of my knowledge."

Ambrose's face fell. Callum swore it did.

"Oh. No problem. Thanks. I'll take that gin and tonic then."

Callum ducked out of the room to grab the drink.

Had he ever played hearts before? Seeing them there, it was all too... familiar. He rubbed at his temples, his headache pounding at this point.

Something about Ambrose's presence kept giving Callum these strange feelings. It couldn't be because he was so attractive? Or could it? Callum had never been one who was drawn to people because of looks. In fact, he was certain at this point that he was demi-sexual and needed a full connection with someone before the desire to be intimate occurred.

Did he know Ambrose? Had Ambrose been in that gap year of memory loss?

Mafia.

He brought the drink back and set it on the table. He stared at the cards for a moment and then two. Something was there in his mind and it was right about to surface.

Just when he was about to grasp a memory, the pain became too much and his eyes lolled to the back of his head; he stumbled forward, and darkness met him on the way down.

"Do you know how to play Hearts, Callum?" Ambrose asked. They had finished up lunch and were just lounging at their table with Rose and Liam. Ambrose had a deck of cards in his hand and was fanning them from one hand to the next.

"I don't know any card games," Callum admitted.

Rose's eyes got really big. "Not even, like, crazy eights?"

"What's that?"

Liam shook his head. "What did you do as a kid?"

Ambrose shot Liam a look, but Callum only shrugged. He was ultra-sensitive about this topic once upon a time, but lately, he didn't really care. The first day of school had only been a little over a week ago, but he felt a tiny bit of camaraderie with this group. He'd never had friends before. Sure, Mick and Lucas, but they were family. So, it was a little easier for him to say, "Nothing. There was no one around to play games with."

"Ahh, shit man," Ambrose said. "That sucks. I'm sorry. I can teach you hearts if you like. We like to play with four, but Asther is out for the day. Wanna give it a go?"

"Sure," Callum answered.

Ambrose grinned from ear to ear. "Good. Asther is actually a shit player, so don't even feel stressed. You have really tiny shoes to fill."

Callum chuckled. "Okay. But I'm telling him you said that."

Ambrose held his hand over his heart and scoffed. "You wound me, Callum Brecker. You. Wound. Me."

CHAPTER 5

AMBROSE

"Is he okay?" Ambrose asked the nurse, probably for the thirtieth time that hour.

"I cannot let you see him," she said through tight lips. "And I cannot discuss his condition with you. His aunt will be here soon. You can ask her."

Antonio tugged on his elbow. "We absolutely have to go before she gets here."

Ambrose shot him a look.

"I'll make sure you are updated on his condition," Antonio said. "I swear it. We can't do anything here, anyway. Let's go."

Ambrose sighed; his shoulders slumped. "Fine."

In the car, he shook his head. "I should never have gone to that club. This is all my fault. I think he was overwhelmed. I looked up Dissociative Amnesia. I think he was trying to remember, but his brain was trying to protect him, and it just got to be too much."

Antonio looked pained. He shifted uncomfortably in the seat next to Ambrose, but said nothing.

"Anything on Marco?"

"No sir. Not even a slight paper trail yet."

Ambrose bit his lip and shook his head. The more time passed, the more doubt crept in. Maybe he did abdicate. Maybe he went to the Campano family and gave all their information. Maybe they were all about to be in big fucking trouble.

"Don't worry too much, sir," Antonio went on, "we'll find him, dead or alive. You'll get closure somehow."

Ambrose ran a hand through his hair. He needed a haircut. This made him think of Callum. His hair was always on the longer side, effortlessly beautiful, even if it was slightly messy. Ambrose recalled Callum's face when he came back into the room, the way he had stared at the cards, the way his eyebrows had pinched together, how he visibly looked like he was forcing the memories to surface.

Ambrose had purposefully asked him about hearts. He had purposefully had the guards play with him. Now he felt incredibly guilty as he thought of Callum dropping to the floor, his features twisted in a grimace of pain.

He wanted to scream. The worst thing in the world was watching someone you cared about hurting and you could do nothing about it.

CHAPTER 6

CALLUM

Callum's vision slowly came to focus. He was in a hospital room, his aunt seated next to him, her cold hand in his. When she saw that she was awake, she gave him a sad smile. He hadn't seen her smile in years, but this only made him miss it more.

"You poor thing. The doctor said you were dehydrated and stressed, and you passed out because of it."

"I—I don't think that's it," Callum said, pulling himself up on his elbows.

She looked anywhere but in his eyes. "What do you mean?"

"Someone came to my work. I had this intense feeling of déjà vu and I kept trying to remember. It was all too much. I think..."

"Who was it that came to your work?" she asked and there was a dangerous edge to her voice; the most emotion he had heard from her in who knows how long.

"Ambrose. Uhm Romano, I believe."

She clenched the sides of her chair. "Quit your job," she demanded. "Get a new one."

"Why?" Callum had no intention of quitting his job, especially now. He was more convinced now than ever that Ambrose had been a part of his life during that year.

His aunt shook her head. Her hair was almost completely grey at this point, and he could see more wrinkles on her face. She was relatively young and should technically have had several more years before this kind of ageing showed. "He's someone you stay far away from. Do you understand?"

He had never seen her so angry, and he felt mildly terrified, but also angry. "No. I don't understand. How could I? I'm treated like a child, and no one tells me anything. Just tell me. Tell me, or maybe I'll ask Ambrose. I just want to know something... anything. My god, it's been seven years. I just want to know how Mick died. Where Lucas disappeared to. What the fuck happened."

His aunt flinched. Before she could respond, the doctor came in, smiling at Callum. "Good to see you're awake. I'll have the nurse start the discharge, but you need to make sure to drink water!"

Callum stared at her. She looked at his aunt and something wordless passed between them.

"Okay," he said, even though he realized they were all lying to him, even the doctor. Maybe he really would ask Ambrose. If he could find him again, then he would ask him.

It took hours before they were actually discharged, and his aunt helped him to their car.

When they were buckled and on their way, she said softly, "I really can't tell you anything, Callum. Don't you think I want to? Don't you think it's hell for me to carry this all on my own? If anything, I'm selfish and I want you to know so we can share the pain together. You don't understand. Dissociative Amnesia is a blessing. It literally saved your life."

Callum said nothing.

She reached a hand over and patted his knee before returning it to the steering wheel. Her voice was sharp when she continued. "If you go looking for answers, you only put your life in danger. But that isn't all. You put my life in danger... and Lucas' too." Her lips quivered the way they always did when her missing son came up.

Callum felt pity for her, his anger dissipating.

"Okay," he finally said, "okay."

"I can tell you that Ambrose and his family played a big part in everything that happened. I can tell you that the best thing for all of us is if you stay away from him."

"Is..." Callum thought back to what Wyatt had said and asked softly, "Is Ambrose in the... Mafia?"

For a long time, his aunt said nothing. Callum felt ridiculous for even asking. It sounded so juvenile and stupid out loud. This wasn't the Godfather of Vincenzo; this was real life. But after a while his aunt said, her hands tight on the steering wheel, "Callum. For your own good, steer clear of that topic and never ask questions like that again."

CHAPTER 7

AMBROSE

Ambrose stood with ten men behind him, his father on the stairs leading up to the mansion, in front of them.

"Do I need to be included in this?" Ambrose called up to his father. "The men can take care of it fine on their own." *Like the last ten times, he mumbled to himself.*

His father shook his head, crossing his arms. "I'm not as young as I used to be and definitely not as fit. But they need to see our faces, need to remember who they are dealing with. You will go in my place."

It was his least favorite thing to do. Visiting the families who were late to pay on their loans was a sickening part of the job and one he actively tried to avoid. There was something especially terrible about beating the shit out of an old man who borrowed money to save his family from starving or a desperate woman who had to take out a loan to get away from her abusive husband.

"Don't be weak," his father had snapped when he'd told him of his concerns years ago. "They shouldn't take out a loan if they cannot honor the deal. What should we do? Let them get away with it, let people walk all over us? We answer to the Lastras or have you forgotten? It's better them to be beaten than us. *Capisce?*"

"*Si,*" Ambrose had lied.

"Besides," his father continued now, a bite in his tone, "you caused a lot of trouble last night."

Antonio, the little bitch, Ambrose thought, suddenly and acutely missing Checo. He only stuffed his hands into his pockets; today he wore skinny jeans and a black t-shirt in case he needed to employ any fighting.

God, forbid.

"Go, take care of it, and then report back to me. We have some things to discuss."

***

Antonio was currently punching a middle-aged man senseless.

"Please," the man begged, "please, just give me more time."

When they were on their way to the man, Ambrose had gone over his file. The man had borrowed money because he had lost all of it to a scammer, promising to make him rich, who posed as a stockbroker. He had a wife who, according to the file, he cherished more than anything. They had been married for twenty years.

Ambrose looked away, out the window of the man's humble little house. He kept his hands stuffed in his pockets and his shoulders slouched; feigning casualty when in fact he wanted to throw up.

A woman came running in from the adjoining room, minutes later. She was his wife, Ambrose knew from the photos, and she was tear-stained, wringing her hands in exasperation and fear.

"Please," she pleaded, "please. I will help. I will do anything! I can work off some of the debt while my husband gets the rest of the money. Just please stop."

"Amelia, get the fuck out!" the man shouted at his wife, panic in his eyes, a more desperate panic that wasn't there before.

Ambrose's heart sank. The foolish man had shown his weakness. Antonio nodded at one of their men at the door and in the blink of an eye, his gun was out, and he shot the woman in the arm. She screamed and her husband screamed, as the two men that were holding him let him go. He rushed over to her, crying and trying to stop the blood. Ambrose knew it looked worse than it was. It was a warning. But still, he pitied them so much in that moment.

"The next time, the bullet gets her heart," Antonio said as he pulled out his handkerchief and wiped the blood off his hands. "You have forty-eight hours. If you value your wife, you'll figure something out."

They left the house and its blood stained the carpets. There was just as much a chance that the man wouldn't be able to get the money. It was quite a hefty sum. That meant, in forty-eight hours, Ambrose would be back here, watching a completely innocent woman die for the sins of her husband.

CHAPTER 8

CALLUM

"Someone's here to see you," Becky told Callum the next week, tilting her head to the end of the bar. A man was seated, in jeans and a t-shirt, sipping on a whiskey. He had rich brown skin and long wavy hair, but nothing screamed familiarity, so Callum let out a sigh of relief.

He couldn't quit his job, no matter how much his aunt begged, but he promised he would avoid Ambrose at all costs if he saw him again. Some small part of him was willing to let that be a lie, but, thankfully or not, the opportunity never arose, and Ambrose never came back.

"Can I help you?" he asked, approaching the man.

"You can," the man responded with a bright smile. "I have a favor to ask, if I may be so bold."

"Ask away," Callum responded amicably, fingers crossed for a big tip.

The man slid him a card. It was black, with red writing, only an address and nothing else.

"Come here after work," the man said, "it's too loud in here and this is important."

Callum raised a brow. "What is it?"

The man smiled again. It was off-putting, not a warming smile in any way. "You'll want to know what I have to say. It's about Lucas. Come alone."

***

The night seemed to drag on forever. Callum's hands were sweaty, and it had nothing to do with the humidity or the heat in the club. He knew he would be every kind of stupid if he went to the address on the card and especially if he went alone. But the man knew something about Lucas. The man knew who Lucas was. Callum... had to do it.

Lucas had disappeared after the events that took place, without a word to his aunt or to him. It was like everything about him was wiped from the earth; like no one with the name Lucas Sato ever existed. No amount of police searches could turn him up. No one could ever find him and after the first few years, everyone just sort of gave up.

Aunt Sia said it was for the best. If they couldn't find him, then no one could, and that meant he was exactly where she wanted him to be. Safe. But now Callum wasn't so sure. Someone, whoever this man was, knew about Lucas. He could be in danger. He could have been in danger this whole time. The very thought had Callum sweating more.

But he made up his mind.

He would go, no matter how stupid that made him. He

would do it for Lucas. Lucas, who was there for him all those twelve years ago.

"Callum, aren't you hungry?" his aunt asked. They were seated in his aunt's cozy little kitchen, a few days after his aunt had found him.

He was starving. He had spent a week without food and his aunt happened to be an especially good cook. But the first day back at her home, he ate what she made and then ended up spending the entire night puking.

Only Lucas knew, and he promised he wouldn't say anything. Callum felt like such a burden already. His aunt didn't ask for this and yet, suddenly, she had a whole new mouth to feed, a new boy to take care of. He was determined to be as little trouble as possible for her.

When he didn't answer, she just smiled. "Have a few bites at least, and then you can go play."

Ten minutes and four bites later, he was up in the room he shared with Mick in the adjoining bathroom. It had only been four bites and yet he couldn't stop throwing up. A throbbing headache followed, and he sank to the floor, hugging the base of the toilet. He was starving. The very thought of food made him nauseous. He wanted to eat so badly.

"Hey," Lucas slipped in, shutting the door behind him and crouching next to Callum. He pried Callum's hands from the toilet and helped him sit up. "I think we should tell Mom."

Callum shook his head. "Oh, no, please. She's so busy with

work and I'm already adding to it all. Please."

Lucas sighed. "You act like you're a burden."

"Aren't I?" Callum's voice was small.

Lucas's eyes went wide before he shook his head, a disgusted look on his face. "I'm sorry you had two shit parents who made you feel that way. I used to think I had it rough with an asshole dad. But I'm counting my blessings now." He reached over and patted Callum awkwardly on the back. "Look, you're not a burden. You're family. You don't have to tiptoe around us. We help each other out. Trust me, Mom deals with Mick on the daily. She knows what it's like to have her hands full."

Callum cracked a tiny smile. Lucas was only teasing. Mick was like this unlimited pool of energy, but Callum had only known him a few days and already knew that you couldn't not love Mick.

"Let me talk to Mom," Lucas said, "so you don't have to. I can do it."

Callum didn't say anything. He nervously pulled at the sleeves of his shirt. He loved it here with them, even in this short time, and he didn't want to leave. What if his aunt bit off more than she could chew and when she realized he had all these problems, she would then kick him to the curb? He wouldn't be able to handle it. That was the thing that would break him.

"Hey," Lucas said, scooting a little closer, "do you trust me?"

Callum nodded without hesitation and then realized it was true; that for the first time in his life, he trusted someone. So *he said, "Okay. You can talk to her. If you are sure?"*

Lucas grinned. Callum had a family in him, and it was the most wonderful feeling in the world.

CHAPTER 9

CALLUM

When he arrived at the address, he saw that it was a storage block. He wandered over to number 451 and stopped in front of the door. He felt strange knocking on the door. He wasn't an idiot. He had a good idea that he was walking into something that was not good at all. A storage trailer? He probably wasn't about to be served tea and have a friendly chat.

So why wasn't he turning back, walking away?

Because...

It didn't really matter. There was nothing for Callum when there was no Lucas or Mick. The past seven years of his life had felt so acutely empty and pointless, paired with the memory loss, it was almost torturous. There was more. He had a life at one point that was good. He knew it; it meant something once but he couldn't even remember. If there was even the smallest chance that he would walk into this trailer and find any information on Lucas or even the life that he could not remember, he had to try.

The man from the club came to the door and motioned for Callum to enter, then shut the door. It was bright in the trailer and Callum noticed immediately that it wasn't for storage but turned into a little living space. A bed was at the far end, recently slept in, and a small table and single chair on the opposite end. Papers were strewn everywhere, open books and lots of trash. There was a big black bag beside the table, the size of a body, and Callum's imagination went wild.

The man was in sweats and a white tee, his hair mussed as if he had just woken up. He smiled, lazily. "Glad you made it. Go ahead and sit anywhere."

There was really only the bed and a chair, but Callum said nothing, gingerly sitting on the edge of the chair. Everything was so messy and chaotic in this small space, and he felt a headache coming on.

"So..." he said. "How do you know my cousin?"

The man flopped onto his bed, using an elbow to lean on, the picture of casual and comfort. It rubbed Callum the wrong way. This was serious and important to him.

"Straight to business then, I like it," he grinned. "When's the last time you heard from ole Lucas?"

Callum pinched his brows at the informality. "Years ago. Are you familiar with him?"

"Very," the man said, jumping up from the bed. "In fact, how about I bring him out?"

Callum's eyes immediately went to the bag as he felt his stomach sink, his fists clench. The man noticed it and laughed. "Lucas!" he called. "Lucas, come on in now."

Callum went still. Sure enough, the door swung open, and

a man walked into the room. It only took Callum a few moments to confirm that it was, in fact, Lucas. Without even thinking, before he could register the look of anger and hate on Lucas's face, he bounded up from the chair and rushed to him, wrapping him in a hug.

"Lucas, oh my god, Lucas! Where were you? What happened? Lucas... Lucas... Lucas."

After moments, Callum realized Lucas was stiff, not returning the embrace, and completely silent. He pulled away to look at his cousin. He had a scar starting at his hairline and going down his right cheek to his jaw. He was taller somehow; his dark hair styled the same way it had been when they were younger.

His eyes, though, were dark and looking at Callum with nothing but hate. The other man had gotten up and was behind Callum now.

"What's happening?" Callum asked, "Lucas, what's wrong?"

Lucas laughed in disbelief, his eyes going wide. "What's wrong? Are you fucking serious with that?" Lucas tipped his head, a signal, and then before Callum could react, the other man grabbed him and in the span of a few moments had him cuffed, dragging him back to the chair.

"What the fuck?" Callum snapped, angry and confused. "Lucas, tell him to stop!"

The man roughly pushed him to the chair and then opened the bag. It wasn't for a body, after all. Callum understood that it still might be. The man grabbed some thick rope from the bag and wrapped it around Callum, securing him to the chair.

"Lucas, please," Callum said, looking up at his cousin. He was too confused and disoriented to even think about struggling. Lucas was *here*. He was alive and well. Aside from the scar, he looked perfectly healthy. He was right *here*. After all this time.

But he had his arms crossed, and his hateful eyes pinned on Callum. When he spoke, his eyes softened briefly. "As long as you answer our questions, Callum, we will let you go. Fine. Unharmed."

Unharmed? His cousin, the one who defended him from bullies, who saved his life, who wouldn't even harm a fly.

"Okay," Callum swallowed, mind buzzing. "What is it you want from me?"

The man came around and stood beside Lucas, also crossing his arms. The next words out of his cousin's mouth had him even more confused.

"Give us the address of the Romano's secret estate. The one you spent that week at in Kansas. That's it. That's all, and you can go."

"I... Romano's?" Callum asked, the name ringing a bell. He heard it recently, hadn't he? The rope was digging into his wrists, the pain making it hard to think. Up until now, he hadn't truly panicked, even when he was being bound. Not when Lucas was in the room. Because no matter what, Lucas wouldn't hurt him. That's what he believed.

But then it dawned on him.

He didn't know Lucas anymore or what happened for an entire year of their lives. Suddenly, the situation seemed a lot more dire, and he started to feel the panic bubbling inside him.

"Yes," Lucas spat, "Ro—ma—no's. As in Ambrose Romano. As in your fucking lover boy."

Now Callum had to laugh. He laughed for several moments before he stopped, suddenly and abruptly. Did Lucas mean Ambrose from the club? The same man whose mere presence caused him to pass out from trying to remember. Because he knew that somehow there was *something* to remember.

"I know him," Callum breathed, "I know Ambrose...?"

This time, it was Lucas who laughed. "Are you asking me if you know him? The boy you couldn't keep your hands off long enough to realize he was fucking ruining our lives!"

Callum's head was pounding, his breath coming out in short and fast little spurts.

"Lucas," he begged, "I can't remember."

Tell me, he wanted to beg, *tell me who he was. What happened to Mick? What happened to* you? *Tell me before I explode.*

But Lucas was punching him. Callum hardly felt it or registered any pain from the hits because his head was hurting and spinning too much. He was trying to remember something that he knew was right there at the cusp of his mind, something that was important, astronomically so.

"You fucking shit!" Lucas was saying, landing punch after punch after punch. "You can't remember?! You don't get to fucking pretend like none of it happened. It was all—your—fault. You shit!"

After an eternity, the other man dragged Lucas off. "Hey, come on. We need him awake. We need him to talk."

Lucas calmed down after a while. Blood was dripping from Callum's mouth, nose, and head. He felt like his heart was breaking as he stared up at his cousin through hazy vision, his cousin staring down at him.

"But..." Callum spoke, "I really don't remember."

He felt the blackout coming, so he tried to explain. "I can't remember some... things... it's called... Diss..."

But Lucas' fist found his face again, and Callum couldn't hold on. He slumped forward in the chair with a pained cry before everything went dark.

When he came to, his vision was hazy. He was still slumped over in the chair and could hear angry voices going back and forth. He stayed still, keeping his eyes shut, and listened. His heartbeat was as loud as a drum in his ears and his head was spinning.

His aunt was probably losing her mind with worry. His aunt! Could she know that Lucas was here? Had she known all along where her son was, and the secret was simply kept from him and only him?

"We don't need to keep hurting him," Callum was surprised to hear Lucas say, his voice tinged with shame. "I lost my temper earlier. It was just... overwhelming to see him after all this time. It brought back all those emotions."

He heard the other man spit. "Look, we do what it takes to get the information. Put your sentiments aside. Think of your brother, of Rose, of your life that was ruined because of these monsters."

"I know," Lucas agreed with a sigh. "I really do know. But Callum... none of it is really his fault. Not truly. He was manipulated. He was a stupid boy in love, and he let that blind him."

In love.

Callum suddenly felt angry. What was it that happened in that year and why was his aunt so meticulously keeping it from him? In love? Callum had never been in love. At this point, he even thought he was incapable of romantic feelings, in his mid-twenties without any romantic involvements.

"Who the fuck cares? He's got Ambrose wrapped around his finger! Trust me, Ambrose talked about Callum like he actually hung the fucking moon! And now he's living in the same state, in the same town? It's not a coincidence. He's here for Callum, he must be."

"I thought you said that Ambrose had an arrangement with his father and wouldn't have anything to do with Callum?" Lucas said through clenched teeth.

"Ambrose is a fucking hot-headed brat," the other man snarled. "That arrangement was killing him. He was only doing it *for* Callum, but it would appear his selfishness won out after all."

Lucas sighed again.

Callum couldn't see him, but he knew he was probably passing a hand over his face, the way he used to do when he was frustrated. It gave him a strange feeling of homesickness, of missing him more acutely than he ever had.

"L—Lucas," he called hoarsely.

"Shit," Lucas came into view, kneeling so he was eye level with Callum. He just looked at him, his features warring between shame, relief, anger, love, and that hatred too.

"Lucas, I—I really don't know what's going on," Callum said. "Please believe me."

"Just tell us. God, Callum, just tell us what we need to know and then we can end all of this. All of it, Cal! Imagine how many lives we could save! Think of Mick, for fuck's sake!"

The mention of Mick had Lucas getting really angry again, and it had Callum's head pounding. *Remember, remember, fucking remember,* he thought over and over again. Lucas had no idea about Callum's condition and Callum had a feeling the only way he was getting out of here in one piece was if he could give them some answers.

The other man came over and dragged Lucas into a standing position. "I knew you should have just left this to me," he said, but this time there was some gentleness in his voice, maybe even a little pity. "You should leave. I promise I won't kill him."

"Please," Callum said. He knew if Lucas stepped out, if he left, things would get eternally worse. And he didn't want him to go. What if seven years would pass again? What if he lost him again? He just wanted to hear his voice, see his face a little longer so he could never forget. No matter what. "Don't leave, Lucas."

Lucas looked at Callum, his features at war again with every emotion. His eyes had a suspicious shine to them and his fists were clenched tight at his sides.

Some things would never change.

He hated crying in front of anyone. He would never do it. Even now, seven years later, he was doing everything he could to fight back the tears.

"I'll go," he finally told the other man with a sigh, "you're right, I'll go. But don't you dare go too far."

Callum's heart sank. The other man reached forward and squeezed Lucas's shoulder affectionately. "I promise," he said gently, and they held each other's gazes for a beat longer than necessary.

Lucas didn't spare Callum another look as he walked out.

"Lucas!" Callum shouted or tried. His voice was hoarse and his throat was sore, so it came out more like a mangled cry. "Where are you going? What is happening?! Lucas, come back!" he sounded desperate. He *was* desperate. He didn't even care what capacity Lucas was in his life; even Lucas punching him was better than no Lucas at all. The years not knowing where he was were such torture, and he didn't know if he could do it all over again, if he could stand not knowing. Where Lucas was and why he hated him. "Come back," he said, even as Lucas shut the door behind him and was gone. "Come back."

"He's gone," the other man said and any gentleness in his

voice reserved for Callum's cousin was gone, replaced by an iciness that had Callum dreading and fearing for his life, "and we are gonna spend some quality time together, you and I."

He reached into the black bag and pulled out a knife, long and sharp.

His smile was terrifying. "So, tell me. Maybe you don't recall the exact address. Give me a general location. Fucking tell me where their secret estate is and then you can get out, poof! Just like that."

"I doubt that," Callum said, boldly and stupidly.

"I keep my promises," the man said with conviction, "especially when they are made to Lucas."

"I can't tell you shit," Callum snapped, overcome with anger, annoyed at everything but mostly himself for even coming in the first place, "because I literally don't remember a damn thing from a whole year of my life. I don't even know Ambrose, the first time I saw him was last week at my club."

The man laughed. "Isn't that rich?"

Hours later, Callum was drenched in his own blood. Question after question was asked by the man, but every time he tried to explain his condition, he got a laugh and some new form of torture. After a while, he just gave up trying.

He closed his eyes and prayed that he would die before there was any more pain.

Pain.

More awareness begged to be let through, more memories were knocking right at the surface.

So much pain.

But as he tried and tried to grasp them, they filtered through him, like wisps of sunlight, untouchable.

Let me die, then, he begged.

As his consciousness began to slip again, he heard the man curse, "Fucking hell, seriously!"

He heard the door being kicked down, loud and quick. The man was trying to hide Callum, pulling the chair to a corner and mumbling about a blanket. Voices filtered in before he could, and then chaos ensued. Callum heard fighting, fists hitting faces and there were even some gunshots.

The last words he heard before he sank into darkness again were, "Checo, you must have a death wish."

CHAPTER 10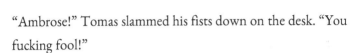

AMBROSE

"Ambrose!" Tomas slammed his fists down on the desk. "You fucking fool!"

Ambrose didn't flinch, but he couldn't hide the surprise on his face. His father rarely raised his voice at him anymore; he used his lackeys to do anything unpleasant. He racked his brain for reasons his father could be so upset. When he called for him, he was expecting it to be another trip into town to collect some debts, but then his father dismissed Antonio. They had only been completely alone like this, without their guards, one other time. And Ambrose would carry both the emotional and physical scar of that day forever.

"Follow me," his father said, voice clipped as he tried to rein in his anger. He led Ambrose to the bookshelf at the far end of his office and pulled on his favorite book, Catch 22. The shelves swung open, and they descended a staircase, Ambrose more worried now. He was rarely brought into the secret basement, and when he was, it was never a good thing.

Today was a day full of these rarities, and it was not shaping up to be a good one.

He recalled the time his father commanded Marco to break his arm, a lesson. For the life of him, Ambrose couldn't even remember what his crime had been. Maybe it was the time he voiced his displeasure about being in the Mafia. Maybe it was nothing at all. Did a father need a reason to teach his son a lesson?

His father led him down the dank hall to the door at the very end, pushing the thick metal door inward. What Ambrose saw inside made him instantly lose his breath.

"Oh my god," he breathed, finally finding his words. "Is—is he dead?" his whole world tilted to the side; he saw stars in his vision. His chest hurt. "Dad, is he dead?"

He tried to make his legs move forward or backwards or anywhere, but he was frozen because lumped on the ground was Callum, bruised, bloody, and broken. And very, very still. His head was matted with dried blood and there were slashes and cuts all over his body. He was shirtless; whip marks covering every inch that Ambrose could see. His eyes were closed, but around them were deep bruises.

Ambrose could not breathe.

Tomas leaned forward to swat the back of Ambrose's head, his voice angry. "You are always so fucking weak when it comes to this boy. Get yourself together. His chest is moving up and down, isn't it? So, he's obviously not dead. But he fucking should be."

Ambrose turned on his dad. "Did you do this?" He was shouting, screaming suddenly, not caring about the consequences. "If you did this, you know I will never forgive you!" He wanted to say he would kill him, but he had some small sense of self-perseverance in the back of his mind.

His father slapped him across the face this time. "I don't break my promises, brat. Want to know who did this? It's your own fault, son. You're own carelessness." He then dragged out the next word like it gave him pleasure. "Ch-e-co. Checo did this. But you were too stupid and blinded by your fondness for the man to notice any signs that he was a fucking plant. You get too fucking attached, you always have. It's always your downfall, isn't it?" he sighed. "You never ever learn."

He registered the words but hardly the meaning; he was too dazed as he moved forward, trying to go to Callum. His father grabbed him by the arm. "Uh no, no, no. I just wanted to show you this mess before we go to Checo. He's in the adjacent room." His father grabbed Ambrose by the chin and spat. "And you are going to kill him."

His head suddenly cleared up, slightly. "What happened?" he asked. "Why would Checo do this to Callum?" His voice broke on the name and he had to bite down on his tongue to prevent himself from sobbing. In front of his father, any sign of weakness was only asking for trouble. He kept his eyes on the man that raised him, forcing them away from Callum so he could use his head, so he could think. He wasn't dead, his father was right about that. He was alive. That's what mattered right now.

"Why do you think?" his father snapped. "Use your brain,

fool."

Why? The answer was easy, but Ambrose did not even want to think about it. To have to shoulder the blame for this, he could not live with himself. But Checo knew Ambrose through and through, every bit of him and, stupidly, Ambrose had shared parts of his past, parts that included Callum. Checo would have had to be pretty stupid to not get that Callum was someone important to Ambrose.

"No," he said, though it was weak. "No." His eyes wandered to Callum's body again, almost reluctantly, but his father tightened his grip as if he sensed what he was thinking.

"Yes," his father said, firmly, "yes."

After a beat, he added, "Checo did this to get to you, which would get to me. And it's put us in a big fucking mess now, hasn't it?"

"I'll kill him," Ambrose spat. "Take me to him and I'll fucking kill him."

"That's the spirit," his father said with a small smile. "That's my boy."

***

Checo was lying on the floor, though his arms were up above his head, tied in chains, and connected to a bar. Ambrose thought he would feel only anger when he saw him, but there was sadness too. Which made him angrier. He didn't deserve any sadness from him. Not after this. Three guards were posted in the room, Marco among them.

"We had been following a lead on Checo for some days now," Marco told Ambrose without being prompted. "We happened upon him last night, fortunately in the nick of time. Much longer and Callum would be d—"

"Don't say it," Ambrose snapped, his eyes never leaving Checo. "I get it."

"Yes, sir," Marco said with a slight nod.

Checo smiled at Ambrose as if he didn't have a care or fear in the world. His lip was split and one of his eyes was bruised, but aside from that, he seemed in okay condition. But Ambrose knew him and knew that the slight tremble in his fingers meant that he was terrified.

And that brought Ambrose joy.

"How do you want to do this, Son?" his father asked, shutting the door to the room. It was unnecessary. Everyone who worked for the Romanos understood violence, but it was still something they always did.

Once, a few years ago, Checo had told Ambrose his greatest fear was fire. He had been twelve when his family's house had burnt to the ground in the dead of night and they had all barely gotten away with their lives.

Ambrose grinned.

"Marco, send for my lighters," he said casually. "Oh, and some gasoline."

The sardonic smile fell from Checo's lips instantly. "You fucking pig," he spat. "Just like the rest of them!"

"Perhaps," Ambrose said, idly stuffing his hands in his pockets as Marco stepped out of the room, "but you are one to talk, aren't you?"

Checo laughed. "Because I hurt your precious Callum? He doesn't even fucking remember you. You probably disgusted him so much that he forgot everything about you."

Ambrose calmly pulled up a metal chair and took a seat, the back of the chair to his front, leaning forward. He made a motion with his hand and everyone in the room left. His father said, "We will be right out here when you are ready." There was a hint of pride in his words, like he was overjoyed Ambrose was finally embracing this life.

Alone, neither of them spoke for quite some time. They just looked at each other, both with disgust. Ambrose with a little added disappointment, reluctant fondness, and anger. Checo with hate.

"Did the Campanos have an offer you couldn't resist then?" Ambrose finally gritted out.

Checo barked out a laugh. "You really don't know me at all. I would rather hang myself than work with the Campanos!"

Ambrose didn't allow any surprise to show on his face. Checo had said it with such conviction that he believed him. So, "What then? Why? Was I not good to you?"

"You are so fucking self-absorbed. It's always about you, isn't it? It had nothing to do with you."

Ambrose cocked his head. "Oh sorry," he deadpanned, "Callum is in the other room, beaten half to death. I guess it was stupid to assume this could be about me."

He had a feeling of emotional whiplash. Just a few weeks ago, he had been laughing with Checo, having a drink with him. *Trusting* him. Just then, something dawned on him and his face paled. "The attack last year," he breathed, "Checo, did that... did you have something to do with that too?" He remembered now that Checo had the day off that night, his only day off of the month but he had come running over the moment he heard. Now it seemed... too coincidental. He should have realized sooner, just like his dad had said.

Checo smirked. "Using your brain finally, I see."

Ambrose wanted to cut his tongue out and then make him swallow it. But instead, soft words came out of his mouth. "I thought we were friends."

Checo laughed again. "Of course you did. Of course, you would be stuck on that. You are so easy, Ambrose. So transparent."

Weak. Sentimental. Emotional.

Words his father often threw at him.

"You are going to die tonight," Ambrose stated, almost sadly, "but how you go can be up to you. Just... tell me why? Which of the five families are you working for if not Campano?"

"Fuck the five families," Checo spat, "fuck the entire Mafia!"

"Then who?" Ambrose asked. Checo's words made him angry, but in a strange way he agreed with them. A funny feeling washed over him.

Checo shook his head. "The five families are the least of your problems."

"Delightful," Ambrose said, leaning forward more in his chair. "I'll have ninety-nine problems, but Checo won't be one."

"Just kill me," his ex-bodyguard stated, "do it in whatever sick, twisted way you have planned. I'm not telling you a thing."

"Your greatest fear is fire." He was casual as he said it, even as he felt disgusting for it. "Stupid of you to ever let that slip, especially if you were working against me."

"There you go with that me stuff again." Checo pulled uncomfortably on his chains before slumping forward. "Does the name Phoebe Wren ring any bells?"

"Wren? Relation to Isaac Wren?"

Checo nodded, his eyes lowered and sad. "That would be her father."

Ambrose did not know Isaac Wren personally, only that he had done some work for his father and later borrowed a hefty sum from his father, too. He hadn't heard the name in quite some time, so he figured their business was done.

"And?" He prompted, losing patience.

"*And.*" Checo mimicked. "And? And she's fucking dead. Ten years ago, she died carrying my child. Our child."

"Okay," Ambrose said slowly, having an idea of where this was going. "I'm sorry. I am."

"It was your father's order. Her dad couldn't pay up, so *she* died, Ambrose. Her. Not him. She didn't even have a speaking relationship with her shithead dad, and she had to die for his sins." Checo seemed to deflate more and more as he spoke.

Ambrose wasn't heartless. In fact, he felt pity for Checo, even anger on his behalf. He hated certain parts of this life more than anyone could know. But...

"So, since she had to pay for the sins of her father, Callum has to pay for the sins of mine? Do you realize how stupid and hypocritical you sound, Checo?"

"No," Checo said simply, "that wasn't our plan at all."

"Our plan? Who else?"

Checo let out a sharp laugh. "Can't even count the number of us. Like I said, the five families are the least of your problems now. The Resistance is strong, and stronger by the day, and every single person has the desire for revenge."

"Are we in Star Wars?" Ambrose asked in disbelief.

"If we are, you are the fucking bad guys and you will end up dead."

Ambrose stood, kicking the chair out of his way. He crouched, so that he was eye level with Checo. "We will all end up dead. It just so happens you get to go first and save me a place in Hell."

Checo said nothing.

"Come in," Ambrose called towards the closed door.

He felt something almost like pride when Checo did not even flinch, even after three men came in covered head to toe in protective gear, carrying a gallon of gasoline. One of them had a finely carved wood box, and he approached Ambrose with it. Ambrose flipped it open and eyed his Zippos, finally settling on the maroon one with his initials in gold lettering.

"I wish I didn't have to do this," he said to Checo as he took the gasoline from the man and sprinkled it in a small circle around his old friend, then poured the rest over his head, drenching Checo from top to bottom. "You don't fuck with what is mine and get to live."

Checo chuckled at that, bold in the face of death. "What's yours doesn't even remember your face."

Ambrose smiled as he snapped open his lighter, shut it, opened it again as if taunting him. "Last chance, Checo. Tell me everything I need to know about this *Resistance,* and I'll give you a quick death. Otherwise..." he waved his hand around the room, "well, otherwise this."

"Fuck you," Checo spat, "I'm dead either way. Don't fucking care how I go."

Ambrose felt his stomach sink. He wished Checo didn't have to be so almighty stubborn. He couldn't go back on his promise now either, not with his men in the room, not with his father watching from a safe distance by the door.

He sighed, heavily, popping open the lip of his zippo. "I'm sorry, Checo," he turned to walk out of the room, tossing the lighter from behind his back. The screams came almost instantly, but Ambrose did not turn around. He exited the room with the guards in their gear and they shut the door behind them.

The screams seemed to go on for an eternity. Ambrose could not even flinch, not when his father was watching him with such a look that expected failure.

"We will put the fire out before it has a chance to cause any harm to the foundation," one of the men said, addressing Ambrose's father, patting the fire extinguisher strapped to his chest. "You and Ambrose may go to a more comfortable setting. We will update you when it is done."

Tomas smiled. "Excellent. And tonight, I want a meeting with every guard on the estate. We are making this Resistance nonsense a top priority."

Ambrose followed his father down the hall, but stopped in front of the room where Callum had been. "We moved him to a guest room upstairs," his father said, almost kindly, "we need to discuss that problem too."

"Let's just get out of here," Ambrose said. The screams had stopped, silence blanketing the basement. It felt so final. And so much worse.

CHAPTER 11

AMBROSE

That night, Ambrose tossed and turned in his bed, sleep out of his grasp. He threw off his shirt, sticky with sweat, and ran his hands through his hair. After a while he got up, slipping into the house shoes at the foot of his bed.

He wandered over to his wall length window, facing the backyard of their estate, the sprawling well-kept lawns dotted with coy ponds and patches of little flower gardens. He crossed his arms over his chest and just stared.

Checo didn't deserve to die that way. Not even for what he did to Callum. He could have just cracked his neck or shot him in the head, something quick. It didn't have to be... so Tomas-like. So psychotic.

His breathing quickened, short and shallow breaths. He leaned his forehead against the pane of glass. "Fuck."

After a few moments, he walked over to his wardrobe, snatched a light robe, and headed to the first floor where the guest rooms were. It was very quiet. Only a few guards remained awake at their posts.

He nodded, greeting the man posted outside of Callum's room. Earlier, his father had briefed him on a few things. Their physician saw him and cleaned up his wounds, gave him stitches where they were needed and ran a few tests. Callum was fine, well, as fine as one could be after something like that, but he wasn't waking up. The physician told Tomas that it's up to Callum now. He'll wake up when he's ready.

Callum looked strangely peaceful now; he had been changed into sweatpants and a plain black tee. His face had several bruises and cuts, the visible parts of his arms were covered too with marks. Suddenly, Ambrose felt less ashamed for what he had done to Checo.

He sat on the edge of the bed.

"Callum," he whispered "I doubt you can hear me, but I can't sleep." The words caused a lump to form in his throat as it brought him back to the past. He leaned forward, leaning his elbows on his knees, and stared ahead at a spot in the wall as he continued, "You don't remember me. If you did, you would be so ashamed. Especially—especially after tonight."

He didn't look at Callum as he spoke, secretly hoping that he was showing some sign that he was listening. And as long as he didn't look, he wouldn't know any different. "I killed someone again. Checo. He came after you, but I think you would have liked him. If, well, you know, it didn't lead to all of this. He was my only friend, and I killed him. I had reasons, what he did to you, for betraying me. But I knew he hated fire and so I burned him alive. Callum." Ambrose bit back a sob. "I hate myself. I hate who I've become. And I know you would hate me, too. It's almost a blessing you don't remember me." A few moments passed. Ambrose had wetness gathering in his eyes. "I want you to remember me."

He gently moved Callum over a little in the bed. "Can I stay with you tonight?" he asked, slipping out of his house shoes. He lay on the bed, stiffly, next to Callum, and closed his eyes. He didn't touch him, didn't even face him, but his body relaxed and before he knew it, he was falling asleep.

He was awoken later the next day by a sharp knock on the door and the guard clearing his throat. "Sir, your father will be here shortly. With Sia."

Ambrose bounded out of the bed. Callum was still in the exact same position, still essentially lifeless. The last thing Ambrose needed was his father finding him in this room, sleeping next to him; Callum, and Ambrose's weakness for him had always been a pain point for his father.

He slipped back into his robe and left the room, thanking the guard on his way out. When he was back on his floor, he called for Antonio.

"Is... Sia taking Callum then?" he asked. He didn't even bother with feigning casualty. His hands were nervously balled into fists at his sides.

"No," Antonio said, and Ambrose felt his own shoulders sag in relief. He wasn't sure if he could ever sleep again if Callum left, especially after this. "Your father has arranged for Callum and Sia to remain here at the estate for as long as necessary."

"Oh. Sia too?"

Antonio nodded; voice clipped. "Apparently so."

"That's rich," Ambrose said bitterly. "I have a feeling if Sia weren't involved, and it was just Callum on the line, my dad wouldn't do this."

Antonio said nothing. After a while, he hedged, "I am sorry about Checo. I know it couldn't be easy."

Ambrose flinched. He had almost forgotten and now it was fresh in his mind; Checo screaming, the smell of burnt flesh, all the years with Checo by his side. Sadness, bitterness, and anger swirled inside him. "It's alright," he lied. "I was an idiot. Any progress on who he was working with?" Ambrose shook his head. "He had seven fucking years of information. What could he have been after that he didn't already know?"

The guard gave him a funny face. "Well, we had reason to believe he was looking for the Kansas estate."

Ambrose froze. It was so obvious. The one thing that no one knew, save for himself, his father, Marco and... Callum and Sia. Or at least Callum would have known if he hadn't forgotten the entire year.

"So that's why he went after Callum?" Ambrose warred between feeling guilty about killing Checo and elated. "He was trying to get the address."

"Perhaps," Antonio said. "Perhaps not. We can't know now. We just need to focus on this group of... whatever weird name they gave themselves, and end this."

"Why didn't they just fucking go after Sia?" Ambrose

muttered aloud to himself, bitter.

Antonio smirked. "They would have to be truly mad to fuck with your father that way."

The words stung a little. After last night, who would dare fuck with *him?* Who would dare come for Callum? They would be burnt alive, his face the last thing they saw as they tumbled down into Hell. Ambrose shook his head. That was exactly the kind of person he was scared to become, his father. Yet, now, he understood him just a little.

"Alright, just keep me updated. Any news on the Resistance I want to know of immediately."

"Yes, sir," Antonio said with a slight bow before leaving the room so he could change.

***

Ambrose wandered into the breakfast room, after changing into crisp jeans and a black t-shirt. He immediately regretted it when he came upon Sia seated at the table staring at the wall, looking every bit as lifeless as Callum. Untouched on the plate before her were eggs, sausage, and pancakes. She saw Ambrose before he could retreat. A complicated look was on her face, mirroring the complicated look on his own face.

How could you both love someone and hate someone so much? They were both wondering this about each other as they stared in awkward silence.

Finally, he said, "You—you look just like you did seven years ago, Sia." Despite everything, his voice came out soft, gentle. He had the urge to rush over to her and hug her, apologize, beg her to apologize, scream.

She laughed lightly. "You're ever the charmer."

He hesitated before taking a seat across from her. Instantly, a servant came in with a plate for him before bowing and leaving them again.

"It must have been a shock for you," she said, "to see him."

Ambrose moved his scrambled eggs around on the plate idly. "It was. More of a shock to see that he didn't remember me."

Sia gave him a sympathetic look, pursing too-thin lips. He had lied. She looked much different, much, much worse, like a bag of bones, her cheeks so sallow she was practically skeletal. "I guess they were right." She averted his eyes when she said the next part. "ZIP combined with Propranolol works wonders for the mind."

Ambrose let his fork drop to his plate with a startling *clang*.

"What did you just say?" his voice was dangerously low.

ZIP. He knew it was a drug that had yet to be approved by the FDA and that his father had his hands on a massive amount. It was a big win for him in the eyes of the Lastra family, taking the family a step into the lucrative and profitable drug side of things.

Sia looked concerned. "Did—did you not know?"

"Callum has Dissociative Amnesia," he said, even as he realized how stupid he had been for believing it.

She nodded, biting at her lower lip, fear in her eyes. "Yes. Yes,

that's right. Sorry, my brain is just... ugh all over the place. Yes."
She picked up her fork and stabbed mercilessly at a sausage.
"Yes."

"Stop," he snapped, reaching over and pulling the fork from
her hands. "Tell me now."

"ZIP and Propranolol," his father's voice came from the door
as he sauntered in, "when combined and taken daily, along
with the Dissociative Amnesia, keeps his memories locked
away. Sia has been putting it in his tea every morning."

His father took the seat next to Sia, a hand on her shoulder,
either threateningly or reassuringly. Ambrose couldn't tell.
From the look in her eyes, Sia couldn't tell either.

But Ambrose didn't care. He clenched his fists as he bit out.
"You fucking did this? You *forced* him to forget?"

His father waited as a servant placed a plate before him and
then casually picked up a napkin, slowly spreading it over his
lap, in no rush. "Yes. And you were not informed because of
emotional reactions like this."

Ambrose hated him. He had always warred with the
feelings he had for his father, respect, fear, dislike, admiration.
Especially after everything that happened that year. But today
it was hate. It would only ever be hate again. He was about to
speak, but his father cut him off. "It was for his own good and
yours. Don't be dramatic. Control those... emotions," he said
the last word with a disgusted wave of his hand, as if it was
his greatest shame that his son had them. Ambrose knew the
real reason. His greatest shame was that his son, his only heir,

preferred a certain sex over the other.

He bit on his tongue before snapping, "You can't just fucking do things like that! Not to Callum."

Sia cleared her throat. "Perhaps I should leave."

His father's grip on her shoulder tightened. "No. Stay." "What about her?" Ambrose asked, tilting his head towards Sia, going for a low blow, "Your little fuck buddy gets to keep her memories, but mine doesn't?"

Sia flinched. Before Ambrose could even blink, his father was up and over the table, his fist connecting with Ambrose's jaw. His whole body snapped back with the blow, his chair tipping over and spilling him out.

Ambrose stood, smiling, blood spilling from the crack in his lip. "Exactly," he said, bitterly. He turned around and walked out of the room, dusting off his jeans.

He headed straight for Callum's room. The physician was there, cleaning and re-bandaging some wounds on his chest. Ambrose stilled for a moment. Callum's body under all the wounds and scars was so thin. Had he struggled just as much over the past years, even with the memory loss?

"Are you still feeding him the ZIP?" Ambrose snapped at Dr. Lindon.

The doctor turned and cleared his throat. "Yes. In his tube every morning." "Well stop," Ambrose snapped again, even though he wasn't sure if it was selfishness that was ordering this. "That's an order. And if I find out you haven't, I'll burn you too."

Dr. Lindon said calmly, "But your father..."

"I'll take care of my father," Ambrose said, "you'll be fine."

With one last look at Callum, he left the room, angry, confused, and alone.

PART TWO
Where It All Began (Seven Years Ago)

CHAPTER 12

CALLUM

Callum had a rhythm down after a few weeks of school. He no longer had to check his schedule to remember what class came next, and he didn't have any of the anxiety of the unknown as we walked into the building every morning. Well, no more than ordinary.

Ambrose seemed to have a strange fascination with Callum; approaching him any chance he got, with a big disarming grin and endless chatter. One day at lunch, he even dragged Callum over and taught him how to play Hearts.

It was the following day when things started happening. Callum was on his way to the third period, passing the restrooms, when Liam popped up and grabbed him by the collar, dragging him into the men's room. It was full of chattering students, but the second Liam inclined his head to the door, they all scrammed immediately. It was reminiscent of when Ambrose seemed to spook the life out of the giant kid Shane.

Callum watched, interested, even as Liam kept a firm grip on his collar. He wasn't really panicking, not yet. Maybe because this was so out of character for Liam.

When the bathroom was emptied out of all other students, Liam released his hold on Callum only to grab the front of his shirt and push him up against the wall.

"What the hell, man?" Callum snapped, finally losing his patience.

"Listen to me and listen good," Liam started. "Ambrose seems to have taken a liking to you for God knows why and I am telling you right now that is never a good thing."

Callum tried to pull away, but Liam only pushed him harder, his back scraping the wall. "Ambrose doesn't do anything half-heartedly. He's obsessive and intense, but most importantly he's fucking dangerous. And another person in his life that isn't part of his crew is fucking dangerous *for* him. So if I were you, I would stay away. Find another friend, or better still, just stick with your family. It's your safest bet."

He released Callum, who angrily smoothed out his shirt. "You are incredibly strange," Callum said after a beat. It was the only thing he could think of to respond with.

Liam smirked at that, almost friendly, which gave Callum a sense of whiplash. Which one was his genuine face?

"I warned you. If you can handle a friendship that is all-consuming and potentially life-threatening, then who am I to stop you?"

"Uhm." Callum shifted. The first bell rang. This was, quite possibly, the most obnoxious conversation he had ever been part of. Finally, he rolled his eyes. "A bit dramatic. Can I go to class now? May I have your permission?"

Liam didn't say anything as he stepped aside. Gingerly, Callum walked past him.

"Fucking weirdo," he muttered when he was back in the crowded hall. His original opinion of Liam had been that he was nice, but after a quick reassessment, he decided on psycho.

He headed to his locker and spotted Ambrose leaning up against it, waiting for him. Before Ambrose had a chance to see him, he quickly turned around and decided to head to fourth period without his books. It wasn't like he didn't enjoy chatting with Ambrose, but after that fiasco, he was fine with pushing through the day without any more social interaction.

Fourth period was history. He was one of the last to arrive and wasn't given many options where to sit, so he found a spot in the back next to Dawson, the boy with the missing hand.

Callum had met him a few times. He was shy and quiet. He heard from Mick that before he lost his hand, according to Asther, he was a massive douchebag, but that was hard to picture now.

"Hey," Callum said as he took a seat.

"Hi Callum," Dawson returned with a little grin. He usually sat alone. In fact, Callum couldn't remember a time when he'd seen Dawson sitting with anyone. Maybe that had something to do with Ambrose and the missing hand.

***

When class was out, he waited until Dawson left and then followed him out.

"Hey," he said to him in the hall. He wasn't sure what prompted him to do it. Maybe he felt bad that he was always alone. He knew what that was like, and he didn't think it was something anyone should have to deal with. "I've never seen you in the cafeteria at lunch. Where do you go?"

"Oh." Dawson's eyes shifted from left to right as if he wasn't accustomed to being talked to when it wasn't necessary. "I actually go to this little diner down the street for lunch."

"Can I join you?" Callum asked, shouldering his bag. Dawson froze. "Only if it's cool!" Callum quickly added.

"Why are you doing this?" Dawson's voice came out strained and a little panicked, "Shouldn't you be having lunch with Ambrose?"

Annoyed, he responded, "He doesn't own me. What's with this school?"

"Well, he doesn't really like his friends to hang around other people," Dawson whispered nervously, scanning the bustling halls as if terrified Ambrose would show up at any moment.

Callum rolled his eyes. "Good lord, is he the Queen of Sheba? Come on. Now I really want to leave."

"Okay," Dawson said, but he couldn't be less enthused by it.

Callum mentally noted to give Ambrose a piece of his mind the next time he saw him. He had this poor kid scared out of his wits for the stupidest reason.

He rode with Dawson in his beat-up Tacoma truck to a diner, a quick ride from the school. Inside, it was keeping to a fifties theme, and they had to sit on stools at the bar. It was a tiny place; the bar and a few tables compromising the seating. The tables were taken by groups of elderly people enjoying hot coffees.

"I know what you're thinking," Dawson said, sliding Callum a laminated menu, "but this place has the best burgers and shakes."

"What was I thinking? I think it's great."

Dawson smiled shyly. "Oh."

They both had burgers—Dawson hadn't lied, they were delicious. They didn't talk much, but the silences weren't awkward, just quiet. Dawson was a lot like Callum. They were both shy and quiet, both a little used to loneliness. Callum wondered if Dawson's loneliness was a product of his missing hand and all the rumors surrounding it.

When they walked back into the school, it was right as the first bell was ringing. The halls were already crowded as students went to their next classes. Ambrose was leaning against Callum's locker again, looking like a panicked rabbit. When Dawson spotted him, he practically flew away from Callum and began walking in the opposite direction.

"Dawson, hey—" Callum called after him before an arm was loosely thrown over his shoulder.

"Let him go," Ambrose said with a big grin. His smiles were always a little strange, like they were trying to be real, but they couldn't quite manage it. "Long time no see, huh?"

Annoyed, Callum pushed his arm off. "What's your problem?" he asked sharply. The students that were close enough to hear seemed to all freeze collectively at Callum's words, which only annoyed him more.

Ambrose's face fell. "Callum, have I offended you?"

He looked genuinely hurt by Callum's tone of voice, which threw him off momentarily. If he thought about it, Ambrose actually hadn't done anything. Except...

In a lower voice, less snippy tone, Callum said, "Dawson didn't want me to go to lunch with him because he was afraid of pissing you off." He left out the part about Liam earlier in the bathroom. He was originally pretty annoyed about that, but that wasn't technically Ambrose's fault.

Ambrose knitted his brows together. "I'm not pissed. Why would I be?"

"Exactly."

Callum moved around him and started digging in his locker. Ambrose leaned against the adjacent one, stuffing a hand in the pocket of his faded jeans. "Sorry," he said, "if I ruined your conversation with him by being here. I feel bad now."

Callum stuffed the books he needed in his bag, returning the ones from the morning into his locker. "It's okay," he said. Any annoyance or anger deflating, he hadn't expected Ambrose to apologize. "It's whatever. I'll just talk to him later. Though, you should too. So he knows you don't actually care if he talks to me like he seems to think."

A complicated look crossed over Ambrose's face before he replaced it with one of his smiles. "Not a great idea."

The second bell rang. Callum had never been late to a class yet; his annoyance quickly returned. "Why not?"

Ambrose shrugged. "Rumors. It's better for Dawson's sake that we just don't cross paths."

"This school is so fucking weird," Callum said with a sigh.

Ambrose barked out a laugh. Unlike his smile, there was no doubt that it was genuine, and it seemed to surprise even him. "And you're just noticing that now. This school's always been strange."

And you seem to be at the center of it all, Callum thought.

Aloud, he said, "Well, I gotta get to class."

He started to walk away, but Ambrose grabbed his arm. "Give me your number," he said.

"Ask nicely."

Ambrose grinned, amused. "*Please* give me your number."

"Why should I?"

Ambrose shook his head, still grinning. "Because friends have each other's numbers."

"Are we friends then?" Callum asked, raising a brow.

Ambrose scoffed; a hand thrown over his heart. "You wound me! That is exactly what we are."

Callum rolled his eyes, even as he felt a strange feeling in his stomach. The word *friend* seemed to do it. He'd never really had a friend outside of his cousins. He wasn't sure that he would actually consider Ambrose a friend; more of a chatty nuisance, but it still felt kind of nice to hear Ambrose call him one.

"I'll give it to you later." He slipped out of Ambrose's grip and started jogging down the hall. He shouted back, "if you can find me!"

***

Ambrose was leaning against his locker again when Callum finished class. He grinned, and before Ambrose spotted him, he walked the other way. The same thing happened after the next class, too.

After last period, he skipped the locker entirely and went straight to the parking lot. Lucas and Mick were waiting by the car. So was Ambrose, leaning against the hood, greeting Callum with a delighted smile. "I found you," he said.

"You did," Callum agreed, and for some reason he found himself smiling.

That evening, Sia sat down with them for dinner. It was unusual for a weeknight; whoever her new client was kept her incredibly busy. She worked at his company all day and sometimes half the night.

Still, the boys had no idea who it was. Client confidentiality, she would say. They didn't want to know, she would add. Mick had a thousand theories, but they were all slightly more dramatic than the last.

She made a lasagne and whipped up a salad, and they all sat

around the small table in the kitchen. They had a dining room with a massive table that seated twelve, but they had yet to use it since they moved here.

"How has school been?" she asked them. "I feel terrible that I've been so busy. Between settling the move and working, I never get quality time with you anymore."

"School is fine," Lucas said, never one to over share.

"It's great," Mick started, before launching into great detail about his day-to-day life, the opposite of Lucas in every way. It caused Callum to smile.

"Do you have any new friends to tell me about?" Sia asked the three.

"Asther is my best friend!" Mick stated enthusiastically. Callum was a little surprised. He wondered if Liam had approached Mick too, but relaxed when he decided that Mick would have told them all first thing in the car. He loved to share everything, and that was surely something he would love to talk about. "Mom, he's so cool. He's always wearing skirts and painting his nails but, like, at the same time, he could crack someone's skull with his biceps. He doesn't talk a lot except to me." Mick grinned then, in a victorious way.

Sia smiled. "You should bring him over sometime so I can meet him. What about you Callum?"

"A few," Callum told her. He was more like Lucas in the sense that he didn't share much. His reasons were different, though. Where Lucas just didn't feel the need; Callum didn't want to burden his aunt, or anyone else, for that matter.

It was irrational, but he often found himself fearing that his aunt would regret taking him in unless he was perfectly well-mannered and always behaved. Realistically, he knew he was a part of their family. At least he was pretty sure he knew that. But his brain would remind him that as his own parents didn't want him, why should anyone else?

"Don't be so modest, Callum!" Mick supplied, filling in for his aunt what Callum wouldn't. "The most popular boy in the school is obsessed with him. Literally, every time I see Ambrose, he's either talking about Callum or asking about him."

Callum ducked his head, feeling awkward.

Sia calmly placed her fork down and calmly asked. "Ambrose who?"

Mick, again, "Something Italian. Like Bocelli."

"Romano," Callum supplied.

Her jaw visibly ticked. "Callum," she demanded in a voice he had hardly ever heard her employ, "do not associate with him. Understood?"

He felt uncomfortable under her gaze, her eyes piercing through him almost unkindly. His chest ached. "Do—do you know him?"

After a pause, she shook her head. "Of course not. I've heard rumors from other parents. Apparently, the Romano family in general are not to be trusted." She had her usual smile back on her face, her tone softer now. "Sorry, I'm just worried for you. Be careful. Try to find a new friend."

Out of all the people in the entire world, his aunt Sia was

the last person he would expect to put stock into rumors and to hold such a judgemental stance. He was silent. There wasn't really a way to respond. She was strangely silent, too. There seemed to be more to it than she was letting on, but how could he ask? He had already upset her, and that was exactly the opposite of his plan. Lucas cleared his throat, deflecting the conversation to him. Callum breathed a sigh of relief and shot his cousin a grateful look.

"I—I have a date tomorrow night. So I'll be missing dinner. Also, don't wait up."

He wouldn't directly look at anyone, his eyes fiercely piercing into his lasagne like it had wronged him.

Mick grinned. "OMG, who?"

Lucas rolled his eyes. "Don't speak how you text, Mick. And..." he cleared his throat, "I hope everyone at this table can respect my decision not to say who just yet. We want to keep it quiet for now."

Sia smiled and started asking other questions—what was she like? Was this person a she? Where would he take her? Callum had a strange feeling overcome him that he couldn't quite place. Lucas was not one to over share on the best of days. In fact, it was pretty hard to get anything out of him, but over the past years that had shifted for Callum. He would go to Callum before anyone because Callum would listen. Maybe the feeling was jealousy or hurt. Callum found that he desperately wanted to know who the girl was. But he knew he had to respect Lucas's wish.

"Lucas," he said, forcing a smile, "that's great!"

His cousin shot him an almost apologetic look, followed by a grateful smile. "Thanks, buddy."

As far as their little dinners went, this one was pretty strange.

CHAPTER 13

AMBROSE

"Ambrose Tomas Romano," his father demanded when Ambrose walked into their estate after school. He held in a sigh and fought the urge to roll his eyes. When his father called him by his full name, it was never a fun time. The fact that his father's personal bodyguard, Marco, was standing at attention behind where his father sat was just another concerning addition.

Ambrose sauntered as respectfully as he could over to where his father sat in their overly large, ostentatious living room. "Yes, sir?"

"I just got off the phone with my lawyer," his father snapped, which was the last thing Ambrose had expected to hear while also being the last thing he had wanted to hear. "She says you are making awful nice with her son."

"No," Ambrose said, "her nephew."

"Watch your attitude," his father demanded coolly. Ambrose was lucky, he had to remind himself. People like Callum didn't have fathers. Other people had fathers who beat them or abandoned them. While sometimes his father would have Marco hit him, he himself never laid a hand on Ambrose, he always gave Ambrose plenty of attention, and there really was no doubt in his mind that his father loved him. T He often had to remind himself that he was lucky.

"Sit."

Ambrose sat gingerly on the sofa chair across from his dad.

"I told you to stay clear of them," his father continued. He had; Ambrose recalled vividly. Sia was his father's new lawyer, a mastermind and genius in her field. She had agreed to be his personal lawyer and to take care of the excess of cases he got in return for a hefty salary and the promise that her children would always be safe and uninvolved. Had she ever watched a show or read a book? Her father could promise her the moon, but he was a pretty big figure *in the mother-fucking Mafia.* Trouble was bound to find them all sooner or later, even in Kansas.

The moment his father had told him to stay away from the new students and why, Ambrose had immediately decided to quietly do the opposite. His intention had been to introduce himself to the oldest; Lucas, and strike up a friendship, sort of as a fuck you to Sia for no reason at all, really. Just that she was dumb to get involved if she truly wanted to keep her children safe and he was bored. But then he had come upon Callum and all his intentions had changed.

"Don't ruin this for me, Ambrose. She is an excellent lawyer. Quite possibly the best. I can't lose her."

"It was an accident," Ambrose said, because that wasn't a lie.

"I ran into Callum, and he charmed me with his idiocy."

"Well," his father said.

"Well, what?"

"Marco and I have been talking," he said, inclining his head to Marco, who nodded in agreement, "and we believe it's time to take you to Boston. You're eighteen next month, so you knew it was coming. It's just for a week. But it will give you time to get your head on straight and show you exactly why you shouldn't have friends outside of our partners."

Ambrose immediately felt the panic rising and swelling inside him. He *had* known this day was fast approaching. As relatives of the Lastra branch, every member had to present in Boston when they became of age, a sort of official acceptance into the Mafia. They would meet the entire family, there would be celebrations, and Ambrose, the worst part of it all, would be expected to kill to be initiated. It was like a twisted, morbid, depressing Quinceanera.

"Let's just wait until next month, please," he said with a smile. "I'll stay away from Callum."

Marco made a disapproving sound, and his father shook his head. "No. You are getting too comfortable here in Kansas. I'm beginning to think you are forgetting who you are."

"Wasn't that the point?" Ambrose asked, keeping his smile, forcing his body to relax, refusing to show his father any weakness. "For me to have some semblance of a normal high school experience? To be safe until I graduated. That was the deal you made with my mother, wasn't it, whoever she was?"

Marco coughed and then his father shouted, "You know not to bring up that woman! Yes, yes, that was the deal, but you are almost graduated, aren't you? You'll come back after a week and finish. You just need to be reminded, Ambrose. You don't get to choose your life, not when you were born into this one."

Whoever his mother was, wherever she was, Ambrose hated her. Did she know what she had abandoned him for?

"Yes, sir," was all he said, even though he was feeling dejected and hurt. He had no choice though, that was something he had always known. Maybe his father had a point. Ambrose had felt a foolish bit of hope in the form of an innocent, doe-eyed new kid, and that was dangerous in his world.

It would be better this way.

Right?

***

Their estate was three stories. Ambrose and his father had their rooms on the second floor, and the servants and guards on the third. Ambrose had changed into sweatpants with no shirt and slipped into his bed. He was staring at the screen of his phone, an unsent text to Callum staring back at him.

Ambrose: *Hey, skinny jeans.*

He was warring with himself on whether to send it. His father had given the order for a second time and would not be so kind if Ambrose broke it again. He thought back to when he had spotted Callum, returning from lunch with Dawson.

Freaking Dawson. Ambrose hated him so much. First, he bullied him, then he tried to take his friend. Maybe he should tell his dad and relieve Dawson of his other hand.

Immediately, he felt guilty for even thinking that. He didn't have to feel guilty. In fact, his father would be disappointed if he knew that Ambrose was feeling guilty over a thought like that. This life he was born into thrived on violence and dominance; it needed it. Ambrose didn't fit in it all, at least not yet. He was too carefree, too spirited. All he wanted was to have friends and a good time. He was also a little soft and his father would say far too emotional. How was he ever going to kill someone? Besides, Dawson wasn't so bad these days. Ambrose still felt really guilty about the hand. He didn't hate Dawson, not really. He hated what Dawson represented; what Dawson reminded him of.

He sent the text. It took a few minutes before he regretted it. But then ten minutes later he got a response, and he stopped regretting it.

Callum: *Who is this?*

Ambrose chuckled to himself, because Callum probably meant it. He had literally never seen Callum pull out his phone and sort of doubted he was getting any large number of texts on a given day. Callum was a little anti-social. A little was a generous understatement.

Ambrose: *It's Ambrose. Who else have you been giving your number to? ;)*

Ambrose was already jealous at the thought of Callum giving

his number to other people. He was a possessive friend; Liam would say obsessively so. It wasn't normal behavior, according to the therapist his father sent him to for a while, in one of his strange bouts of normal-dad concern. Ambrose didn't really understand why it wasn't, though. If you had something, why did you have to be okay with sharing it?

Callum: *I gave Dawson my number.*

Ambrose smiled tightly. He tossed his phone onto his bedside table and sunk into his blankets, falling into a sulky sleep. Never mind, he really did hate Dawson.

***

His father hadn't been joking. The next morning, Lily came in and packed Ambrose's bags. His father was waiting for him out front by the Limo. Resigned, Ambrose got in the back with him and Marco. There were two other guards present as well.

Their driver, Pete, took them to the private airstrip, and they boarded his father's jet. It was off to Boston and what was not likely to be a remotely good time.

Chapter 14

Callum

Callum felt anxious all Saturday afternoon. When they sat down with Sia for dinner, the absence of Lucas made him feel awkward.

"Man, Lucas's dating," Mick said cheerily, "it really is something. I thought he was aro."

Sia furrowed her brows. "You thought your brother was Aromantic? Lucas? He's always had quiet crushes," she grinned. "He's just not loud like you."

Mick had a new crush practically every day. Currently it was a girl in tenth year, Kitty. Sia and Callum knew everything there was to know about her at this point, down to what her hair smelled like.

"True," Mick conceded, then winked at Callum, "guess you get to be the ace of the family."

His aunt reprimanded Mick gently. "Don't assume to know your cousin's sexuality," she said, then cleared her throat. "Unless, of course, you have expressed this, Callum?"

There was something absolutely mortifying about all this, but Callum was hung up on the fact that Mick called him family. No matter how many times they used that word when referring to him, he would still feel absolutely honored and warm.

He stared at his dinner plate. "No, I'm not aromantic. I mean, I don't think I am," he paused, thoughtful. Actually, he never thought much about it, but now that he was, he really couldn't remember a time that he felt attracted to someone in that way. He had never had a crush on someone. When he was little he wasn't given that luxury; the truth was that he had never known another child his age.

"Hmm," he finally said, "I guess I could be?"

"Are you asking us?" Mick questioned, slightly appalled. "Cuz we really can't tell you, buddy."

"No," he admitted. "I guess I don't really care much either way. I just am whatever I am."

Sia nodded, as if that made perfect sense. Mick was a little aghast. "Would you want to kiss someone?"

"I don't know," Callum stated, honestly. "Haven't ever wanted to yet."

"You're almost eighteen," Mick stated, awed.

"Mick," Sia reprimanded again, "he is aware of his age. Don't pry. Can't you see you are making him uncomfortable?"

"Oh, no, he isn't!" Callum insisted. "Mick could never make me uncomfortable."

Mick grinned, delighted. "That is precisely why you are my favorite."

After dinner, Callum did the dishes while Mick pretended

to help. Then Mick retired to his room to call Asther. Callum wondered what on earth they talked about; the few times he had been around Asther, the guy had said maybe a word. Then again, Mick did like to talk, so perhaps they were the perfect set of friends.

Callum retired to his own room. He had always had his own room growing up; his parents had not been poor, but it felt different now. Back then, his own room only meant loneliness. Here, it meant he might belong, like he was here to stay.

He wandered over to his little desk and pulled his cell phone out of the top drawer. He rarely carried it on his person when he was at home. After he had told Ambrose that he had given Dawson his number—a total lie, he wasn't even sure what prompted him to say it, except that he knew it would irritate Ambrose—he had yet to respond.

He was so childish.

There was still no response. Callum rolled his eyes and stuffed his phone back into the drawer. He didn't care. Why should he care?

He positioned himself cosily on his single bed and picked up where he last left off in his book. He didn't really register the words; he was just reading to stay awake. Awake until Lucas came home.

It was well past midnight when Callum heard Lucas unlock the house door with his key and walk up to his room across from Callum's, lightly shutting his door. Callum shut his book, placed it on his nightstand, and finally lay down for some sleep.

***

On Monday, no one was leaning against his locker. Not that he was looking or anything. In fact, by third period, he had found out that Ambrose was gone and would be for a while.

"His dad is super rich," Mick explained to him. They were walking to fifth period, which they shared. "Asther told me a little about it. Like ricccccch rich, you get?"

"I guess. What does that have to do with him being absent?"

Callum figured that Ambrose was rich. One time he had come to school in a Celine t-shirt. Mick had informed Callum that those were hundreds of dollars apiece, at least. His jeans were always really nice, too. His hair looked expensive.

Mick shrugged. "I think Asther knows but won't say. He gets really... odd when he is avoiding a topic. It's quite funny."

"Asther is really close with Ambrose, isn't he?" Callum asked, as they entered their classroom, walking to the back table where they usually sat together.

Mick plopped his bag down and took his seat. "It appears that way, though Asther is weird about stuff, so who actually knows? They have known each other for a long time, apparently."

"I see," Callum stated, setting his own bag down much gentler and taking his seat.

"Why?" Mick teased. "Scoping out the friend competition?"

"Is this grade school or high school?"

"Kids all act the same," Mick informed Callum, in a faux educational tone, "whether they are in first grade or twelfth."

"Whatever you say," Callum agreed diplomatically.

Their teacher for fifth period—Classic Literature—was a quaint older lady, Ms. Triple. She was sweet, but the class was terribly boring; Callum didn't really care about the classics. He used his book— *The Scarlet Letter*—as a shield and ducked his head to take a nap.

On his way to the car after classes, he ran into Rose.

"Hey Callum," she called, catching up to him. "Ambrose asked me to check up on you."

Callum felt indignant. "I'm not twelve."

She grinned. "He's just like that. Always has been. Try being his girlfriend of four years. It can be pretty exhausting."

"I'm sure it would be, if he had one," Callum agreed.

Rose made a funny face. "I *am* his girlfriend. Of four years."

Callum felt strange. "Oh, I'm sorry. Must have slipped my mind."

The truth was, Ambrose had never mentioned that. Looking back, Callum could see it. Ambrose was the most popular guy in the school, according to Mick, and Rose was your classic beautifully tanned blonde and wasn't that usually how it worked in high school? Now that he thought about it, Ambrose smiled at Rose a lot, and not his usual strange smile that looked forced and a little manic. It was always genuine.

Rose seemed hurt by this. "That's just like him. Anyway, how was school? Ambrose won't be back for a bit."

Callum shifted his weight from one leg to the other. What was with these people? It wasn't like he couldn't function without Ambrose. He barely knew the guy. Liam was right; they were all obsessive and just a little crazy. Of course, Liam hadn't said the second part. Callum filled that in.

"School is the same. Where is Ambrose?"

"Boston," she stated, twisting a strand of her long hair around her finger. Was she attractive? Callum was trying to notice these sorts of things, especially after his conversation with Mick at the dinner table. Still, he couldn't decide. She was just... Rose. "Visiting family."

"Oh, did something happen?"

Rose raised a brow. "No? What would have happened?"

"Umm, well usually when people miss a bunch of school to visit family, it means there was like a death or something."

She cocked her head, thoughtful. "Makes sense. I guess there could be a death."

Shouldn't she know this as his girlfriend? Isn't that what being in a relationship was?

Then she seemed to have a pitying look on her face. "Look, Ambrose has a rich, important family. They do a lot of strange things. You are better off not knowing details."

"Whatever," he responded.

Was he a prince? At this point, that's how everyone acted. Secret this, secret that, blah blah blah. He was just a guy.

"I'll catch you later," Callum said, leaving her to join Lucas and Mick at the car.

"She's hot," Mick declared, when Callum was in earshot.

"Is she? She's Ambrose's girlfriend, apparently."

Mick laughed. "Everyone knows that. Doesn't mean she isn't hot."

Lucas shifted uncomfortably. He had a strange, almost pained look on his face. "Anyway, let's go," he said, sliding into the driver's seat, before adding, "Mick, don't objectify women."

Mick rolled his eyes, getting in the back.

"What makes her attractive?" Callum asked, curiously, after he buckled. Lucas sighed as he pulled out of his parking space, but Mick took the question very seriously.

"She has a nice face, nice jawline, nice plump lips, nice waist, nice hips. She is overall nice to look at. Right Lucas? Help me out here."

"I guess so," Lucas responded stiffly. "Objectively she could be considered attractive."

"Wow," Mick whistled. "You go on one date and you're so whipped you can't even call another woman hot?! Who is she, Lucas? We have to know!"

Lucas didn't tell them. His hands gripped the steering wheel tightly and there was an odd little tick in his jaw.

That night, he got an unexpected text.

Ambrose: *I miss Kansas.*

Callum didn't know much about Boston, but he assumed it was probably a little more exciting than the sunflower state. He wondered if maybe there was a funeral after all, and Ambrose was having a hard time with it. So instead of his original intended snarky response, he responded kindlier.

Callum: *It's okay. Kansas isn't going anywhere.*

CHAPTER 15

AMBROSE

Ambrose grinned slightly at his phone. His eyes were cloudy with unshed tears and there was still blood on his fingers. He felt like this week had ripped his heart out and stomped on it before shoving it back in. The least it could have done was leave his heart out so he wouldn't have to feel like this. He wondered if he could ever come back from the things he had done, the things he was made to do here in Boston.

But that stupid little text made him smile.

He didn't get to text Callum again for the rest of his days in Boston. The initiation was taking up all his time and at one point, his father took his cell phone from him.

"Focus. Pay attention. This is life or death."

This is life or death.

He had heard those words at least ten thousand times, since he was old enough to understand them and probably even before that.

That night, his father accompanied him to a party. It was at the Lastra estate; a mansion so massive it made Ambrose's estate back in Kansas feel like a shack.

"You should have sex tonight," his father said as they climbed the many, many stairs that led to the mansion. "I know you've been dating Rose, but I also am not blind. You avoid touching her like she's made of glass. It's an important relationship to stay on good terms with her father, but you don't have to remain loyal. What she doesn't know won't harm her."

Ambrose wanted to lean back and let himself fall down the stairs to his delightful doom. "Dad, why would I show public displays of affection with Rose in front of you? My father? Are you encouraging me to cheat on her right now?" His voice was tinged with disbelief. He knew his father lacked morals, he was in a moral-less line of work, but this was a lot even for him. "Never mind, actually, I would prefer not to discuss sex with my dad."

Especially because of his secret. The one his father could never know.

"I'm just saying," his father continued, pausing on the last step that led them onto the porch, "you are almost an adult. It's good to get a release..."

"Dad," Ambrose said, through gritted teeth before walking away, through the big doors, "let it go."

He entered a great room that looked like a ballroom, already bustling with Mafia in their Sunday best—they had literally gone to Mass all together that morning. The hypocrisy was laughable.

There was live music and tables stacked with food. This was the last place Ambrose wanted to be. Especially after last night. But he shook those thoughts away as quickly as they came. He was pretending that last night never happened; convincing himself it was all just a dream.

He hadn't pointed the gun.

He hadn't pulled the trigger.

He hadn't watched as detached as he could feign as the old, probably innocent, man fell to the floor, his brains splattered against the wall.

That was all just a dream.

"Hey, Brose," an arm came around his shoulders. He smiled tightly.

"Hey, Sean."

Sean wasn't a member of the Lastra family or even a relative; Ambrose wasn't quite sure what his story was, but he seemed to be held in high regard by Mr. Lastra himself. He was Ambrose's own age and always gave Ambrose a pang of homesickness. He had hair a lot like Callum's; rich brown and curly, a little overgrown. But then he would open his mouth and he was nothing like Callum.

"What's up?" His Boston accent was heavy. "Why the glum face?"

"My dad just had a sex talk with me," Ambrose said, with a forced laugh, languidly putting a hand into his pocket. He was so good at being a pleasure to be around. He was so good at pretending.

"Ooff," Sean said, steering Ambrose away from the main room, through a door that led to another. It was populated with people more his age, late teens, and early twenties, lounging on couches, drinking and most definitely snorting cocaine.

"Take your pick," Sean whispered in his ear, pointing to a couch where two women were lounging, showing plenty of skin. Both had hair dark at the roots but blonde going down. "Wouldn't want to disappoint the ole man."

Ambrose removed himself from Sean's grip and grinned. "Not my type."

"Oh, yeah?" Sean looked taken aback. "Nina and Tria are everyone's type."

"Oh, yeah?" Ambrose echoed. "I prefer brown hair. Rich and curly."

Sean grinned from ear to ear.

Ambrose realized his misstep and walked it back. "Big boobs," he added quickly, "those too."

Sean slipped a whiskey glass that he'd snatched off a passing tray into Ambrose's hand. "Well, Ambrose. You're a man now. This land is your land. Take whatever you want." As he spoke, his smile was terrifying. Ambrose hated it here.

CHAPTER 16

CALLUM

"I have a date again tonight," Lucas informed them on Sunday afternoon.

"On a school night?" Sia asked, her brows furrowed. They weren't furrowed at her son, but something on her cell phone. She seemed to be extra busy with work all week and was a little stressed. Mick had tried prying from her who her employer was, but she wouldn't give an inch.

Lucas still wouldn't say who the girlfriend was. It looked like this family was full of secrets. Callum wished he had a secret of his own. At least there was Mick, an open book always. He couldn't keep a secret to save his life.

"I won't stay out too late," Lucas promised. "It's the last time she can see me for... a while."

"Can Asther come over?" Mick asked.

"Of course," his mom replied.

Mick rushed off to call him. Callum wished he had someone to call. It wasn't like he had ever cared about things like this before. He had just been happy that his aunt seemed to want him and in having the company of his cousins. But they were all growing up. Callum never wanted to be a burden, so he excused himself and holed up in his room.

Ambrose hadn't texted again for days. Callum was bored. He finished the book he was on and even some school reading and didn't have much left to do until school tomorrow.

Would Ambrose even come back?

Whatever, who cared? Ambrose was annoying with his all-consuming attention one moment and then his total disappearance the next.

Callum reached into his dresser drawer, checked his phone again, rolled his eyes and put it back.

Mick poked his head in, "Hey, Asther is here, wanna come hang out?"

"Oh. Is that okay?"

Mick made a strange face. "Duh? We want you too."

Callum checked his phone one more time before following Mick down the hall to his room. Asther was lounging on the bed in very skinny pants, black and ripped.

"Hi," he said.

"Hi Asther."

Callum felt awkward, but Mick plopped on the bed next to Asther and signaled for Callum to join.

Asther smiled at Mick and moved a little closer. Then he turned to Callum and said bluntly, "Bet you miss Ambrose."

"Ahh, not really," he replied with a little laugh. "Everyone acts like we are connected at the hip, but I barely know the guy."

Asther smirked. "I've known him for years. There's something about him that's magnetic."

These were the most words Callum had ever heard Asther speak.

"Totally," Mick agreed, bumping his shoulder with Asther in solidarity, "he's like a celebrity. He's rich enough too."

"I'm rich too," Asther deadpanned.

"Wait, are you really?" Mick asked.

"I've told you this. Yes, really. My dad's a stockholder for a lot of banks, but really he practically owns them entirely. I've told you this."

"I thought you were being funny," Mick admitted.

Asther smiled again. His smiles were small but bright. "What's funny about that?"

Callum was inclined to agree. Mick could find anything funny if he thought it was a prank. He was a little prankster himself, but ninety-nine percent of the time they weren't funny at all. Callum surely didn't have the heart to point it out, and neither did Lucas nor Sia. I guess they were funny in the sense that Mick thought they were funny.

"That's why you always wear those nice Stompers. Are they real?"

"Yeah," Asther said, and casually added, "I can buy you a pair. I can buy you whatever you want."

Shamelessly, Mick perked up. "Really?"

"Mick, your mom has a lot of money," Callum pointed out. "I'm sure you don't have to rely on Asther for the things you want."

Asther shrugged and seemed to inch even closer to Mick. They were basically on top of each other. "I like it."

Callum was working out in his brain how to casually bring Ambrose back into the conversation. Then he realized what he was doing and rolled his eyes at himself. He wasn't desperate to be liked by the school's popular boy and he needed to stop.

He heard Mick say, "Help me figure out how to ask out Kitty."

Asther clipped, "Kit Dree? From tenth year?" he inched slightly and subtly away from Mick, but Callum noticed. He was beginning to understand something.

"Yeah," Mick's face fell. "Why? You don't like her?"

"Oh," Asther toyed with one of the rips in his pants. "I guess she's okay. Doesn't seem like a good fit for you."

"Why?" Mick asked, genuinely curious. He closed the tiny gap Asther had made between them.

"She just doesn't seem like your type," he responded with a shrug.

"What do you think, Call?" his little cousin asked, dragging him into this.

Callum couldn't help but smile. "I just assumed everyone was your type."

Mick scoffed. "Whatever. You two are no help. Let's play a game."

Callum followed them out of Mick's room to the living room, where they kept their game shelf. He watched Asther watching Mick, like he hung the moon.

***

They were playing Monopoly because Mick was strangely obsessed with the game. He also cheated a lot, but Lucas or Sia or Callum never acted like they knew. Callum was realizing they kind of spoiled Mick. It was just easy to do.

Callum noticed that Mick wasn't cheating today, though.

"Is it hard for Rose?" Callum asked when there was a lull in the conversation.

"Nothing is hard for Rose," Asther stated, almost bitterly. "But what are you talking about specifically?"

"Ambrose being gone. They've dated for so long."

"Oh." Asther chewed on his lip. He looked at Mick and Mick nodded before Asther said, "Just between us, she cheats on Ambrose all the time."

"What? Why would she do that?"

There was a pause again before Asther said, "It's complicated. Ambrose knows."

"He knows?" Callum asked, unable to hide the disbelief in his voice. He rolled doubles for the third time and groaned as he put his piece in jail.

"Tough break," Asther told him about the jail. About Ambrose, he said, "Yeah. Like I said, it's complicated. And not really my story to tell."

Asther looked right at Callum then before adding, "But trust me, he'll tell *you*. Sooner or later."

Callum ducked his head. "Why would he tell me?"

"Because he wants to be your friend. And he's obsessive and possessive and all in when it comes to his friends."

Callum snorted. "Liam said something very similar when he was pushing me up against the bathroom wall and spitting in my face."

Mick gasped, but Asther's face paled.

"You can't tell Ambrose," he said, so firmly that even Mick looked a little uneasy. "Liam is a fucking idiot, but he means well. For real. I'll talk to him about that, but please don't tell Ambrose."

"Contrary to what the whole school seems to think," Callum said, frustrated. "Ambrose and I aren't close. We aren't attached at the hip. We don't tell each other everything."

"You will," Asther said with conviction.

They finished monopoly with less talk about Ambrose. Mick won as usual, even without the cheating.

Lucas got home before Asther left and was stiff around him. Callum was pretty sure that was why Asther left finally; he probably never would have left otherwise. Not the way he looked at Mick.

Did Mick realize?

Callum decided it wasn't his place to pry and slipped off to bed, leaving Mick to scold Lucas for the way he treated Asther. Lucas was like that. He always had been and he probably always would. He made people uneasy simply because if he didn't feel like trying, he wouldn't. Callum loved him with his whole heart, but Callum knew him and understood him. He wasn't malicious. He was just Lucas. Callum hoped that whoever the girl was, she would give Lucas a proper chance.

CHAPTER 17

AMBROSE

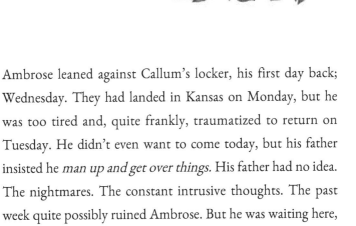

Ambrose leaned against Callum's locker, his first day back; Wednesday. They had landed in Kansas on Monday, but he was too tired and, quite frankly, traumatized to return on Tuesday. He didn't even want to come today, but his father insisted he *man up and get over things.* His father had no idea. The nightmares. The constant intrusive thoughts. The past week quite possibly ruined Ambrose. But he was waiting here, at Callum's locker, with the tiniest bit of hope. There was some comfort in the bustling and noise of the students around him, rushing to get ready for first period.

He spotted Callum walking toward him, in his usual ultra-tight jeans, his backpack hung haphazardly over his shoulder. When he saw Ambrose leaning against his locker, he grinned. Ambrose jolted. He had seen Callum smile before, but it was never like this, so genuine and directed right at him. That was probably why, when Callum got close enough, Ambrose threw his arms around him. He startled Callum. It would be too dramatic for Ambrose to say that he missed him; he had enough sense to know that, but he wanted to. He wanted to just stay like this.

When he pulled away, Callum rubbed at the back of his neck awkwardly. "You really missed Kansas."

"You have no idea," Ambrose grinned.

Callum didn't ask anything about Ambrose's absence, and he didn't know whether to be relieved or disappointed. But Callum did say, "I bet it was hard to be away from Rose."

Ambrose schooled his features into neutrality. "Oh, yeah. It's always hard to be away from them all, Liam, Asther, Rose. It's great to be back." Callum made a face but said nothing. "Which, we are going to the diner down the street after school, by the way! You are coming too. They make mean milkshakes. The best."

"Yeah, so Dawson says," Callum replied, a tiny smirk on his lips.

"Whatever," Ambrose said good-naturedly. At least, that's how he intended to sound. "Come to my Jeep after school."

"What if I don't want to?" he asked, but he was grinning. "You are quite bossy, you know?"

Ambrose nodded. "So I'm told," and he started walking away, throwing back, "See you then. You want to come."

CHAPTER 18

CALLUM

At lunch, Callum sat with Asther and Mick. He didn't see Ambrose at all in the cafeteria, but Rose and Liam joined them, to Callum's chagrin. Lucas sauntered over too, a little late.

"Detained," he said by way of explanation when Mick asked.

"Detention?" Callum asked in disbelief. Lucas had always been a lot like Callum in the sense that they were pretty straight edge and hated breaking rules.

Lucas sat next to Callum. He nodded at Rose and Liam. "No, detained to discuss my art project."

Callum felt oddly relieved. Some things were still the same. Liam annoyed Callum a lot lately. Ever since he cornered him in the bathroom, he acted as if nothing had ever happened. He would even smile and wave at Callum if they crossed paths in the hall. Did he suffer from short-term memory loss, or was he just an ass? The latter seemed more likely.

He addressed Callum now. "Are you coming with us after school? It's tradition whenever Ambrose gets back from one of the family trips."

"Oh. Does he go often?" Callum asked.

"Unfortunately," Rose said with a small sigh. Lucas dropped his fork, bumping Callum's arm in the process. Callum shot him a strange look.

Asther and Mick were whispering to each other. Asther looked over at Lucas and giggled. It was literally a giggle, and Callum almost dropped his own fork. Giggling and Asther were two things he would never imagine to ever coincide.

"Well," Rose hedged, "are you coming, then?"

"Oh. Yeah, I guess. If that's alright Lucas?"

Lucas rolled his eyes. "You are practically eighteen. You don't need anyone's permission."

Rose smiled at Callum. Maybe he was in his head, but it felt more threatening than sweet. "Well, I'm not even hungry," she said, standing and gathering her tray. "I guess I'll see you then."

"Don't mind her," Liam said with a smile that was a lot less threatening and a lot more confusing. "She gets greedy with Ambrose's attention when he's been gone for a while. She'll sulk for a bit and then all will be well."

"How delightful," Lucas clipped. "I'm sure it will be a great time, Callum." His tone oozed sarcasm. He then took his own tray and, before storming off, said, "I've completely lost my appetite."

"What the fuck?" Mick supplied cheerfully.

Liam chuckled, tipping his orange juice in Mick's direction, "I am inclined to agree, buddy."

Callum stared at his own tray. Was Lucas mad that Callum hadn't asked him to tag along? That Callum wasn't hanging out with him as much? That went two ways. Besides, it was never like Lucas to give two thoughts to things like that. He was acting really strange. Not that anyone else at the table was acting any less strange.

***

After classes, Callum headed to the Jeep. At first glance it looked like he would be the first to get there, but as he approached, he heard voices coming from behind it.

"Why do we have to have Callum come? I thought your dad was particular about keeping your friends in the business."

It was Rose's voice.

Ambrose replied, gently, but with a definite undertone of no-nonsense. "Who cares what my dad says? I like Callum. I can be friends with people I like."

"Ouch," Rose deadpanned.

Ambrose sighed. "You know what I mean. Of course, I like you. Of course, I like Asther and Liam. I'll always love you guys. It just feels nice to choose something for myself. Besides, Callum isn't entirely separate from the business."

"What do you mean?" Rose snapped.

Callum, though also curious as to what he meant, felt this was all too personal and turned around. He only circled back when Asther and Liam approached. Mick was with Asther.

"Are you coming too?" Callum asked his cousin, as Rose and Ambrose approached from behind the Jeep. Rose smiled directly at Callum. He wanted to roll his eyes. Or tell her he heard everything. Instead, he just ignored her.

"Yup," Mick smiled, and then added, in a mock tone: "Where Asther goes, I shall follow."

Asther had the tiniest hint of pink show up on his cheeks.

"Callum, that means you are upfront with me and Rose," Ambrose said with a delighted grin as he hopped into the driver's seat. Liam, Asther, and Mick crowded in the backseat; Rose sidled up close to Ambrose.

Callum got the absolute pleasure of being jammed in next to Rose. To his horror, none of them wore seatbelts. He buckled his and shot Mick a pointed look to do the same. Thank God the ride was short.

They took up the whole bar portion of the diner and ordered shakes. Callum didn't care for ice cream, but the vanilla shake wasn't awful. Rose kept touching Ambrose like she had been deprived for too long and Callum couldn't help but recall what Asther said about her cheating a lot and Ambrose being aware. Something twisted in his chest. When they were finished, they headed back to the Jeep.

"Be right there," Ambrose called to them, "you know the drill."

Liam grinned from ear to ear. "See you in a minute."

Ambrose hung back. At the Jeep, when Callum was pleasantly seated next to Rose and her delightful personality, he asked, "What's he doing?"

She said, "You'll see."

Ambrose came sauntering out of the diner minutes later and got back into the driver's seat.

"On to the fun part!" he declared. He pulled a packet out of the pocket of his pants and tossed it back. Liam caught it with a grin. Callum had seen that suspicious white powder before. His chest sank.

"I think Mick and I should get back," he declared.

"Nah," Mick said, oblivious to it all. "Mom said to be back by midnight."

"Oh. Ok."

Ambrose leaned over Rose so he could grin at Callum. "Don't worry," he said. Callum smiled tightly. What was there to worry about, in a Jeep full of high schoolers who didn't wear seatbelts and snorted cocaine bought from a milkshake diner?

He buckled.

Ambrose drove them down residential streets until they came to a bend in the road that led them off into dirt roads. They drove the dirt road for several minutes before Ambrose stopped the Jeep, pulling off the road slightly and parking in a field. It was just a huge field of grass that spread out for as far as you could see. It was fenced, and Callum spotted a few cows grazing in the distance.

Liam immediately hopped out and proceeded to climb onto the roof of the Jeep. Asther followed. "Come on up, Mick."

Callum leaned back and grabbed Mick by the arm before he crawled out. "Don't do the coke," he commanded.

Mick looked shocked. "Why would I do coke?"

When he was out of the Jeep, Ambrose leaned over Rose again. "Don't worry. I already told Asther not to let him touch the stuff."

"Oh. Thanks."

Ambrose grinned. "I don't do it either much, but these guys love it."

"Just occasionally," Rose added, pushing Ambrose back so that he wasn't leaning over her, "you make us sound like addicts."

Ambrose smiled at her. She leaned into the smile and her lips met his. Callum wanted to die. How could he leave without making it more awkward? Ambrose wrapped an arm around Rose as if to deepen the kiss, but his hand landed on Callum's knees. Shocked, Callum met his eyes. They were wide open, even as Rose's tongue practically devoured his. He winked at Callum. Slowly, his hand went a little higher. He kept his eyes open and on Callum the whole time. Callum felt an unfamiliar sensation, like a tight pooling in his lower stomach. He couldn't pull his eyes away from Ambrose. He wanted to cry or laugh; he wasn't sure which. Rose pulled away and slowly, gently, Ambrose pulled his hand away from Callum, putting a lock of Rose's hair behind her ear.

"Now that that is out of the way," he said with a grin, "go have some coke. Before they snort it all."

She climbed over Ambrose to get to the window and then hopped onto the roof of the Jeep to join the others. Ambrose rolled up the windows. He moved a little closer to Callum.

"Sorry about her PDA. It's a marking her territory sort of thing. I hope you weren't uncomfortable."

Well, what was going on with your hand? Callum wanted to ask. But Ambrose hadn't brought it up, so he stubbornly didn't either.

"Oh, yeah," was all he said, with a chuckle that sounded stupidly nervous. That unfamiliar sensation in his stomach had just subsided, but Ambrose moved even closer, and it was back again.

"She and I have a complicated little thing," he offered.

"I didn't ask," Callum retorted. His palms were feeling oddly sweaty.

"Okay, then." Ambrose grinned, reaching over to the glove box. He pulled out a pack of cigarettes. This day couldn't get any worse.

He offered the pack to Callum after slipping one between his lips.

"No," Callum said curtly. Now his palms were sweating for an entirely different reason.

"Suit yourself," Ambrose said with a grin, pulling a zippo from his pockets and lighting his cigarette.

Callum thought of all the good things that had happened in his life. His aunt found him. Lucas, Mick. A home, his own room. Still, after Ambrose had taken a few puffs, the smell of smoke was too overpowering to ignore.

"Woah man," he heard Ambrose say, but it sounded so distant, "what's going on?"

Callum realized then that his breath was coming out in quick, loud huffs. "The smoke," he said, looking down at his shoes.

Ambrose rolled down his window slightly, flicked his cigarette out and rolled the window back up. He smiled at Callum.

"Sorry," Callum said, frustrated with himself. It was such a stupid thing, but he had never been able to shake it. Sia quit smoking cold turkey over it, whereas Callum's dad had been a chain smoker. When he was close enough to someone smoking, the smell triggered all these things inside of him. Loneliness, abandonment, the feeling of being a burden. Ironic, since that was exactly what he was being now. It just brought him back to the days with his father, the smell would forever remind him of the man and the detrimental affect he had on Callum's childhood.

"Pfft, don't say sorry," Ambrose insisted. "It's just a cigarette. Are you okay?"

"Oh yeah," Callum lied, refusing to be any more annoying than he had already been. "Yeah."

Ambrose pinched his brows together slightly. "Asthma?"

"No," he admitted, staring at his shoes, burning a hole right through them.

"Okay. Whatever it is, it's fine. I won't smoke around you."

Callum wanted to disappear. He only nodded slightly. "So you were saying, you and Rose have a complicated thing?"

"I thought you didn't ask?" Ambrose responded with a little

grin. He angled his body slightly, so he was facing Callum fully. "Yeah. It's complicated."

"Are you in love?" he asked bluntly.

Ambrose got a strange look on his face but before he could answer, the others started jumping off the roof. Liam knocked on Ambrose's window. "Come on! Let's chase some cows!"

As Callum followed Ambrose out of the Jeep, he felt a weird sense of disappointment at not getting a response. He wasn't sure why, but he felt like the answer was important. That if two people who had been together for so many years didn't love each other, there wasn't a lot of hope for anyone. Also, he sincerely hoped they weren't actually going to chase cows.

CHAPTER 19

CALLUM

"I have to tell you something," Mick said sombrely, as Callum and he entered their house. "It's about Ambrose."

"Okay," Callum led Mick into his room. Mick got comfortable on the bed. Occasionally, Mick would just fall asleep in Callum's room if they were talking late at night, and it would turn into a sleepover of sorts. Mick snored, though.

"What's up?" Callum asked, sitting on the edge of his bed.

"Asther told me something," Mick blurted, through pained expressions, "after he did some coke. He said not to tell anyone, but I need to tell you."

Callum's face fell. "Coke is not something Asther should be doing. It's dangerous."

"Callum! That's not even the point right now."

He cleared his throat. "Fine. Sorry. But if Asther told you in confidence, maybe you shouldn't tell me. You two seem really close."

Mick nodded seriously. "Yeah. he's my best friend."

"Okay," Callum said, standing, "that settles it. You must keep his secret."

Mick leaned over and snatched Callum by the wrist, pulling him back down. "No. Listen. He knows I can't keep a secret. He literally knows everything about me! So I'm pretty sure he told me so that I would tell you."

"That makes no sense." "Ambrose's dad," Mick ploughed ahead anyway, "he's an important man. That's why Ambrose misses school a lot. But guess what organization he is important in?"

Mick spoke fast, with equal parts excitement and horror.

Callum *was* curious. People acted like Ambrose hung the moon because he had unlimited amounts of money. Yet no one knew what exactly his father did. There were rumors of course.

"He's in a gang, Ambrose," Mick stated. "He's like a member of the top family of some big gang!"

Callum barked out a laugh. Mick didn't laugh. "Oh, you're serious?" Callum said with a grin. "Asther was definitely pulling your leg. You are too easy, Mick."

Mick shook his head vehemently. "No, Callum, think about it! You know Dawson? Asther said that he had bullied Ambrose bad back in ninth grade. Ambrose's dad had his men cut off Dawson's hand! Asther told me everything. Dawson was only able to go back to school after spending a week in some asylum where the gang was feeding him some memory loss drug." Callum didn't say anything. "Asther said it wasn't what Ambrose wanted, and he secretly gave Dawson's family a million dollars. Callum, do you get it? One. Million. Dollars."

"Apparently, coke turns Asther into an imaginative little thing."

Mick groaned. "He isn't lying. He definitely isn't teasing. Asther doesn't tease. And Asther's dad works for Ambrose's dad."

"So Asther's family is part of this gang, too?" Callum put 'gang' in air quotes.

"Kind of. They work for the gang. Same with Liam's family and Rose's. Apparently, Liam gets crazy when Ambrose tries to be friends with other people because he secretly has this big consequence and he worries it's too dangerous. That's why he cornered you. He wanted to scare you away. For your own sake. Asther told me all of this."

"What the fuck?"

Both Callum and Mick jumped out of their skin at the sound of Lucas cursing at them from the door. He came in, shutting Callum's door behind him. "Mom works for Ambrose's dad," he said, his face twisting. He came over to the boys, an urgency in his steps, and said, "My... uh, my girlfriend told me."

Callum had originally been writing off everything Mick was saying, but now that Lucas had come in and had this look of concern on his face, it was much harder to do. Suddenly, Callum remembered all sorts of things. How, back in Oregon, when their aunt sat them down to tell them she got a new job, she had shifted away from all questions about her employer. But she had looked pained. The way Sia had acted when she heard Ambrose hung around Callum, like it was some terrible thing. Could Sia really have moved them all to Kansas for a job with a gang? That would explain her ridiculous salary.

"Why would Aunt Sia ever take a job with a..." Callum lowered his voice, whispering the last word, "gang?"

Lucas lowered his eyes.

Mick and Callum caught on. "What do you know?" Mick asked him, a little betrayal in his voice. "Do you know something about this?"

The oldest sighed. "Look, Mom didn't tell any of us, but I overheard a conversation she had on the phone. With... Dad."

"Dad?!" Mick bounded off the bed. Every emotion was plain on his face; anger, excitement, hurt, and confusion. Their dad had run off well before Callum had been in the picture and they never knew where.

Lucas quickly explained, "She doesn't know I know. From what I gathered from just hearing Mom's side is that dad blew all of our money, and we were about to be bankrupt. She sounded really upset. After that, I noticed for several weeks we were having a lot of rice and mom put her Tesla up for sale. Then, suddenly, she got this new job that paid really well and here we are in Kansas."

Mick was still restless. "Why didn't you say anything?"

"You know Mom. She's proud and unmovable. She thinks she must hide every bad thing from us and give us a perfect little life. She probably felt she had no other choice but to take the job."

"But," Callum insisted, "maybe he isn't in a gang. There are rich people with perfectly decent jobs."

Lucas pursed his lips. "I..."

Callum was sure he had something to say, but then he just shook his head and sighed.

"Should we talk to Mom?" Mick asked.

"No!" Callum and Lucas said simultaneously.

Callum was sure that there was a perfectly reasonable, non-gang related explanation to this all. But, even if there wasn't, approaching his aunt would be the last thing they should do. Lucas was right. She was proud.

"You could talk to Ambrose," Lucas hedged.

Callum barked out a laugh. "Oh sure. Hey buddy, how was your weekend? Is your dad by any chance in a gang?"

"I can find out more from my girlfriend," Lucas said, in a tone that left no room for any questions about said girlfriend.

"And I can find out more from Asther," Mick stated. "Next time he does some coke. He's chatty on coke," he grinned, "it's funny."

Lucas shook his head. "Don't you be doing coke."

"Obviously," Mick scoffed.

Callum groaned. "I'm tired."

And upset.

A niggling in his brain insisted that his extra mouth to feed could have been the push over the edge for Sia, the final straw that led her to taking a job that could potentially be dangerous.

"For the most part," Lucas cleared his throat and stood tall and important, "nothing changes. Mom doesn't want us to know who her employer is. There must be a good reason. We just ride this out for now."

Callum agreed. Let nothing change. He hated change. He wanted to panic right now, he wanted to throw up. For some reason he had the urge to take out his phone and text Ambrose. Instead, he changed out of his clothes into sweatpants and went to sleep, full of anxiety in a way that he hadn't been in years.

CHAPTER 20

AMBROSE

"Didn't your dad forbid you to hang around Callum?"

Ambrose's patience with Liam was wearing thin. They were driving to school together—Liam's car was in the shop—and his friend took it as a golden opportunity to do some nagging.

"My dad doesn't *forbid* me anything. I'm an adult. He strongly suggests."

"Technically, you aren't an adult for another week," Liam pointed out delightfully. He pulled a cigarette from his pack and was about to light it.

"No smoking in the Jeep anymore," Ambrose declared before replying. "Do you not like Callum or something?"

He almost laughed at his own question. Not like Callum? There was literally no reason not to.

"I like him fine," Liam confirmed, "which is why I think you are being a bit of a dick."

"Elaborate," Ambrose demanded, his grip tight on the steering wheel. But he knew. Liam was right, of course.

"Two reasons. The less important one; it's dangerous. The more important one; his aunt has an agreement with your dad!

Your dad is scary, dude. I know he lets you get away with everything, but if you lose him his best lawyer, I doubt he'll be so understanding."

"I know," Ambrose admitted quietly.

Liam gasped dramatically, and Ambrose only rolled his eyes.

"Look. I'll be careful. I'll just be his school buddy. We literally can't avoid each other at school. Sia and Dad can deal with it. They should have thought this through before putting us in the same fucking school."

As Ambrose pulled into the school, Liam wondered, "What is it about Callum?"

What was it about Callum? Ambrose found himself often thinking back to the moment in the Jeep when Rose had kissed him. Kissing Rose was a chore, not a pleasure. But it wasn't half bad when he was looking at Callum.

"He's hot," Ambrose stated. He would rather play it off as a little crush.

Liam shook his head. "Okay. But..."

"I know," Ambrose snapped. He parked and shut off the Jeep. "I know my dad can never know I'm gay. I get it. That doesn't mean I'm not gay."

"Hey, hey. I get it. I'm just saying be careful."

Ambrose hung back in the Jeep for a while after Liam left. He rested his head back on the and sighed. He wanted to scream. When he was twelve, he had been learning about himself, understanding this part of him. He was thinking of how he could broach the subject with his father—at that time he told his father everything. It was only a few days later that his older cousin, Nando, was found sleeping with a man. To this day, Ambrose didn't know what actually became of Nando, what they did to him. He just remembered the ripple of shock and horror, and most painfully, disgust, that had run through the family. His week in Boston taught him it was the whole branch. They did not look kindly on homosexuality in their ranks.

He never told his dad, of course. Especially not after the words his father spoke to him regarding his cousin. "Nando has disgraced our family. You will never see him again, my son. Don't waste any tears on him. He was a pig, not a man. He deserved much worse. He deserved death."

He deserved death.

Ambrose punched the steering wheel. Then he punched it again. After, he put on a smile on his face, shouldered his book bag and got out of the Jeep.

The next week, Ambrose skipped school again. He was eighteen now. He knew this day would come, obviously, but knowing it was coming and living it were two different things. Eighteen meant his life was over. Eighteen meant he belonged to the Mafia, he belonged to the Lastra.

Eighteen meant fucking hell.

CHAPTER 21

CALLUM

"Asther wants me to go to Ambrose's birthday gala with him on Saturday," Mick declared one evening when the three of them were eating dinner. Sia was out. She had been out the last week working overtime. Callum tried not to think about her work.

"What?" he said now. He hadn't heard from or seen Ambrose in a week again. "Was it his birthday?"

"Yeah! He didn't tell you?"

Callum looked at his plate. "It never came up."

Because nothing had come up. Callum texted once during the week. He never texted people first, because he just never thought of it, but he texted Ambrose to check in. He never got a response. It didn't bother him then. Ambrose had been patchy with his texting in the first place. But now it bothered him.

"Well, I don't want to go unless you both come with me."

"Sure," Lucas said, immediately. Callum almost fell out of his chair. Lucas hated events. And hadn't Mick used the word *gala?*

"Should I?" Callum hedged. "I wasn't invited."

"Pfft, Ambrose is obsessed with you. He wants you there."

Callum couldn't even count on his hands how many times he had been told that Ambrose was obsessed with him. Was obsession ghosting people for weeks? And why was Callum so bothered by this, anyway? Now he was annoyed at Ambrose again, for popping into his life and making him think he had a friend. He was so... annoying.

"I'll go," he decided.

And give Ambrose a piece of his mind.

***

Mick informed Lucas and Callum that it was a black-tie affair when they were getting ready Saturday afternoon. Sia hadn't come home in days, only sending a few texts here and there to check in.

"Seriously?" Callum asked, putting the jeans he had chosen back in their drawer. "His birthday is a black-tie affair?"

Mick grinned and mouthed, *gang,* and Callum rolled his eyes. He opened his closet, and from the very back, he pulled out his only suit. He chose to pair the black suit with a grey button down. Mick insisted he added a tie and offered him one of his own. Callum felt absolutely idiotic.

Mick inclined his head toward a little package resting on Callum's bed as they waited for Lucas to be ready. "What's that?"

Callum snatched the box and slid it into his suit pocket. "Just something for Ambrose." "Oh, I didn't get him anything! Say it's from all of us! What is it?"

"Yeah, sure," Callum lied, and thankfully Lucas entered before Callum had to think of how not to respond to the question.

Lucas had done his hair slicked back, his forehead on display. He was wearing a crisp grey three-piece suit with a purple tie. He looked like he had, for the first time in his life, put excruciating care and effort into his appearance. Callum wondered if his girlfriend was going to be at this *gala.*

When they were in Lucas' car, Mick punched the address into the GPS. It was a fifteen-minute drive there, and the event started at seven.

"We are going to be late," Mick piped up from the back seat, his knees bouncing. "I hate being late."

Callum had a strange feeling, like nervousness, in his stomach. He hated it. But from Mick's bouncing knees, and Lucas drumming his thumbs endlessly on the steering wheel the whole drive, he knew he wasn't the only one. He wondered if Mick returned Asther's feelings and just didn't realize it. He wondered what girl was able to get Lucas's attention.

They were quite far away from the residential streets when the GPS had them turn onto a street. The street turned out to be a driveway, miles long, that led them to a grand estate with a massive, Italian-style estate home. It had a circle drive with a grand fountain in the center, spitting water. There were men in suits, with bands on their arms directing traffic. And there was a *lot* of traffic.

Callum swallowed. "Is this Ambrose's home?"

"Yeah," Mick said as Lucas whistled. "I'm surprised Ambrose has never taken you here. If I were him, I would love to show off this place to my friends!"

One of the banded men tapped on Lucas' window and when he rolled it down, the man asked, "Pass?" in a thick Italian accent.

Mick leaned forward, pulling a paper from his pocket, and showing it to the man. He nodded and then directed Lucas to the line of cars parked at the side, in the grass.

"We had to have a pass?" Callum squeaked. "Maybe I shouldn't have come."

"Pfft, Asther said the pass was fine for anyone in the car. It's a party, Callum, don't sweat it."

"It's a gala," Callum coerced.

Lucas chuckled a little.

"I guess we just follow the other people who are walking in," Mick said, bounding out of the car. Callum didn't appreciate that he only guessed. He felt like a fish out of water here. His suit was making him sweat, even though it was October.

They ended up in a line of people slowly entering the estate. Callum noted that most of them were older, business looking people, very few of their own age.

Inside, there was a large room cleared out of all the

furniture where people were mingling. Asther spotted them and immediately sauntered over. He dressed in a blazer, suit pants, over which was a maroon skirt with chains.

"You made it," he said with a grin.

Rose approached from another direction, where she had been chatting with a group of women. Her dress was bright red and skin-tight, accentuating her Monroe type body. She looked incredibly displeased. Callum swallowed.

"Asther," she hissed when she approached them, "this doesn't seem wise."

Asther rolled his eyes, grabbed Mick's hand and, completely ignoring Rose, said, "Come on. They have the best finger foods."

Mick willingly left. Rose glared at Callum and Lucas.

"Should we go?" Callum asked after a few moments of unbearable silence. Lucas, being Lucas, was glaring right back at her, neither making the move to speak first.

"Well, not now," said Rose, and she softened her voice. "Sorry, it's just that these things are more for show. They are more for Ambrose's dad. He's... a businessman through and through."

Callum scanned the crowd, looking for Ambrose. He saw a man that looked strikingly similar at the far end of the room, drinking whiskey neat and chatting with some other men, all in expensive suits.

"Is that his dad?" Callum asked

Rose nodded. "Best if you steer clear of him. Lucas, may I

have a word?"

Lucas shrugged and followed Rose, his hands stuffed languidly in his pockets, his posture relaxed. Though Callum noted, as he walked away and left him here alone to fend for himself, his shoulders were tense. No one else would have noticed. Callum stared awkwardly around the room.

"You came," a voice said from behind him and he startled a little, turning around.

Ambrose stood there, looking at Callum, his eyebrows pinched together in what appeared to be anger. Liam was with him, but walked away with a slight nod to Callum. Callum immediately regretted coming. Ambrose wore a red suit that matched Rose's dress, paired with a black tie, his hair combed back. He looked rich. He looked angry.

"Oh, yeah, sorry? Asther told Mick to come, and Mick dragged me along."

That caused him to smile, small. It lacked its usual touch of psycho, replaced with a tremor, perhaps nervousness. "You have to be dragged to my party, eh?"

Callum shrugged. "I wasn't sure you would want me here."

Ambrose inclined his head. "Of course I want you here."

Could have fooled me, Callum thought, itched to say, *I haven't heard from you in a week.*

Aloud, he only said, "Well, happy birthday."

Callum noticed a woman walking towards Ambrose's dad. His dad put an arm around her waist and drew her close.

It was Sia.

The floor was tilting from underneath him.

Ambrose saw where his attention had turned and frowned. "Come with me. Let's not let them see us."

Callum followed Ambrose as he led him down a hall to a small room at the end. It was a library of sorts and it was empty; Ambrose had to type in a code on a lock in order for them to enter. He shut the door.

"Why is my aunt here?" Callum demanded.

Ambrose smiled. It was his usual smile. It was fake. "I think you know."

Callum shook his head. "You aren't in a gang."

Ambrose chuckled. He leaned his back against the door, crossing his arms over his chest, "Not technically. I'm in the Mafia."

Callum's face fell. "Don't joke."

"I'm not joking," Ambrose said seriously, before smiling. "You look nice in a suit."

Callum shifted his weight from one leg to the other. He worried his lower lip. What would ever possess Sia to work for the Mafia?!

"I don't understand," he admitted, quietly, overwhelmed.

"Let me explain," there was an edge to Ambrose's tone now, almost defensive, "my dad is a first cousin to Ronaldo Lastra, head honcho of the Lastra family, a branch of the US/Italian Mafia. They own him, and therefore, they own me. I didn't invite you here because you don't belong here." Callum flinched. "I am a fucked-up person, with a fucked-up life,"

Ambrose went on. "Originally, I sought you out to piss my dad off, since Sia's only condition was that you boys were not to be involved. I thought it was hypocritical and ironic. But then I *wanted* to be your friend. I thought I could just be your friend despite it all."

"You can," Callum insisted, against his own better judgement. But he thought he knew where this was going and suddenly he realized he wanted to be Ambrose's friend, too. For the first time in his life, he desperately wanted to be someone's friend. Right now, he didn't even care about learning more about Sia's involvement. He just wanted to fix this. "We are friends."

Ambrose looked dejected for the briefest of moments before saying, "No. We aren't, Callum. There are too many things that I have done that would make you despise me. You stick your nose up at a line of coke. What about murder? What about taking advantage of the poor and weak?"

Callum shook his head. "That isn't you. I know it isn't you."

Ambrose laughed, a dark and wicked sound. "It is exactly me."

There was a beeping sound, someone punching in the code at the door. Ambrose's face changed instantly from this strange, cruel expression that didn't belong on his face to panic. His father walked in.

"What is going on, Ambrose Tomas Romano?" his tone was terrifying, his gaze icy. "Why is Sia's nephew here?"

Ambrose shrugged. "He showed up without my knowledge.

He was just leaving."

He shot Callum a pointed look as he said it and Callum's stomach twisted. Unwanted, unwelcome. It shouldn't hurt because it was just a part of his life, always had been.

"Yes," he said, not looking Ambrose's father in the eyes. He pulled the box out from his pocket and set it on the shelf closest to him. "Happy birthday." He walked towards the door, but Ambrose's father grabbed him by the elbow. Ambrose jolted forward but his father held out a hand and he stopped, a pained look on his face.

"Don't let your aunt see that you are here," the man demanded, his grip tightening, hurting, "or you'll regret it."

Callum swallowed. He needed to find Mick and Lucas. He hoped that they were okay. They had to be okay.

As if reading his mind, the man added, "Your cousins are outside waiting for you. I will never see you three on this property again. Understood?"

Callum couldn't find any words, so he nodded vigorously. The man let him go. Callum slipped out as fast as he could.

Lucas and Mick were waiting at the car, as the man had said. Lucas was pale in the face, angrily gnawing at his lower lip. Mick was crying.

Callum got into the passenger seat. "Mick, are you okay?" he asked, leaning back and looking his little cousin over. "Are you hurt?"

"Yes," Mick said through sobs. "My feelings are."

Lucas rolled his eyes, started the car, and began the

manoeuvre of getting it out around all the other cars.

"Ambrose's dad is so mean," Mick said. "He–he punched Asther! Right in the jaw!"

Callum didn't care about Asther right now. He leaned forward, his head on his knees, as Lucas sped out of the driveaway, and continued speeding as he went in the direction of their home.

"Mom," Mick sobbed, "Mom. Is she going to be okay? How did she get into this mess?"

Lucas sighed, but his reply was demanding and firm. "Mr. Romano made sure she didn't see us, and he made it very clear that we do not speak to her about tonight. He assured me she is safe," Lucas hissed. "I mean, they are definitely fucking, so I believe she is safe for now."

Callum flinched. "Don't be so crass."

Lucas laughed. He was upset. Callum had never seen him so upset. "I fucking hate it here," he said, "and I hate Mom."

Mick gasped. Callum felt inclined to do the same. "You don't mean that," Mick snapped. "Take it back." "No," Lucas said, his grip tight on the steering wheel. Callum wished he would slow down. What would they even say if they got pulled over? *Hey sorry, we found out the party we were at was a Mafia thing, just back there by the way, and oh yeah, our mom works for them.* "I hate her so much. You didn't see. She was all over Ambrose's dad. They were feeling each other up like their lives depended on it. She's putting us all in danger to work for some mafia man all because she's fucking him. I hate her."

Mick was crying harder. Everything was falling apart. Callum was panicking inside, and outside a little, as his breaths came short and fast. "Lucas, that's unfair," Callum said, although a tiny part of him agreed. "We don't know what led her to take the job, but you did say we were broke back in Oregon. We can't... we can't assume the worst."

Lucas sighed. "Mick, stop crying. It's okay."

"How can you say that?" Mick asked. He was curled up on the back seat. Callum couldn't even bring himself to tell him to buckle up. Lucas had finally slowed down. "What if Mom gets killed?"

Lucas shook his head. "She won't get killed. It's not like they are the *Mafia* Mafia, like from back in the day. Right, Callum?"

From the tone Lucas used, he was practically begging Callum to reassure him. Callum groaned. His stomach hurt. He needed Lucas to reassure *him.*

"I don't know anything about the mafia," he admitted, "but... I bet you're right."

What about murder? Ambrose had said.

"I bet they just launder money or something."

What about taking advantage of the weak and the poor?

"We'll be fine," Callum lied.

Lucas seemed to relax slightly. Mick stopped sobbing so loudly.

When they got home, they all wordlessly headed to Lucas's room. Callum brought a blanket over from his room and took up on the floor by the bed. Mick crawled into bed with Lucas.

They didn't even change out of their suits.

"We have each other," Lucas whispered. "We'll be okay."

***

It felt wrong to go to school on Monday, but they went anyway. Lucas had pulled Callum aside and insisted that they keep a sense of normalcy for Mick. Really, the two of them were too proud or ashamed to admit it was for themselves, too. If they could just pretend everything was normal, then perhaps everything could be. Callum kept recalling Lucas saying *I hate mom.* His throat felt parched and his stomach hurt.

No one was waiting for him at his locker. He did spot Asther at lunch with Ambrose and both were sporting some serious black eyes. Something twisted in Callum, but he refused to let himself care. Ambrose had made it clear that being friends was not an option. Callum wasn't even sure if he *wanted* to be friends with him after all. It was true, Callum played everything by the rules. He was terrified to do things any other way. Striking up a friendship with a member of the literal Mafia was exactly the sort of thing Callum didn't do. However Ambrose got the black eye, he didn't care. He didn't.

He sat with Lucas and Mick at lunch. He noticed Dawson walk into the cafeteria and waved him over, surprised he wasn't going to the diner. He didn't particularly enjoy Dawson's company. But he was feeling spiteful. Mick was, surprisingly, quite cheerful. He chatted amicably with Dawson. Lucas was his typical silent self, with an added dose of brooding.

Callum let his eyes drift casually to Ambrose's table. Ambrose's own eyes quickly drifted away, his jaw tense, as he returned to his conversation with Liam. He scooted closer to Rose, let his eyes drift back to Callum pointedly one more time, and then smiled down at Rose.

Callum rolled his eyes.

Lucas, beside him, was fuming. "Ambrose is being a dick."

"How?" Mostly, how did Lucas pick up on those subtle little things?

"Taunting you," Lucas said through clenched teeth. It had to be more than that, though. Lucas seemed to be taking it very personally.

He laughed lightly, a sensation settling in his stomach, something heavy. "It doesn't matter."

He turned to Dawson, striking up a conversation, ignoring the prickling feeling of being watched. Ambrose was the one who decided this.

"How *did* you lose your hand?" Lucas interjected himself into their conversation, in what might go down as the world's rudest way of doing so.

Dawson shook his head. "I mean, you've heard rumors."

Callum froze, and Lucas nodded. "Yes, but are they true?"

He sighed. "Look, I have no idea. It was pretty sketchy. I was a fucking dick to Ambrose, that's true, and then the next thing I know is that I don't have my hand. I don't have any memory of how it happened or the days that I spent in the hospital. My parents have no idea what happened. There was an investigation that went nowhere. Then, randomly, one million dollars show up in my parent's account. This town is weird, man. There is talk of a Mafia family, but we all just go on, pretending like there isn't."

Mick's jaw dropped. "Woah. So you're rich, rich?"

Dawson actually grinned. "I don't mind not having a hand for that amount of money, I guess. And I don't remember much so I don't even remember any pain," he shot the three of them a conspiratorial look. "And I get lots of sympathy dates and favors. Honestly, I'm better off than before."

Sounds a little douchey, Callum mused to himself. But Mick seemed fascinated. Callum couldn't understand why Mick was in such a good mood, arguably the best mood he'd been in in a while, when everything that had just happened... happened. It was so typically Mick, in a way.

Lucas pressed on. "Don't you want to find out, though?"

"No," Dawson returned, firmly. "I think it's too dangerous for me to care."

Lucas shot another bitter look towards Ambrose's table and dropped the conversation.

CHAPTER 22

AMBROSE

Ambrose was at Callum's locker early the next day. As the students started pouring in, he lost his nerve and quickly walked away. What was he thinking? This was for the best. He saw Liam headed in his direction.

"Your dad told me to keep an eye on you," Liam stated. He sounded about as pleased about it as one would imagine.

Ambrose flinched, but grinned. "Sorry, man. He's been intense since I turned eighteen."

Liam shrugged, barrelling through the students without a care. "He's right, you know. It's too messy to be his friend. For the both of you."

Ambrose nodded. Rose joined them at their table for the first period. Ambrose didn't even want to look at her right now. She was cheating on him; he always knew the signs. It shouldn't bother him since... the whole gay thing. Actually, it was pretty unfair for it to bother him at all. There was nothing in this for her. But she had to be so sneaky about it.

Rose knew he was gay. Ambrose had never told her, she just sort of figured it out and Liam confirmed it for her and later told him all about it. But Ambrose and Rose played a stupid little game and pretended. She pretended she didn't know he was gay, and he pretended that he didn't know that she knew.

It was survival on his part.

It was desperation on hers.

They both had fathers that dictated their lives and they both, stupidly, went along with it.

They were stuck in this stupid little act.

Ambrose put his hand in his pocket and thumbed the zippo. It all felt so unfair. But he would put a smile on his face; the same smile nanny after nanny told him was disturbing, and he would just go on. This was his life. He had to get used to it.

CHAPTER 23

CALLUM

Lucas was pacing in front of his car when Callum arrived after his last class.

"What's the matter?" he asked, noting the panic in his cousin's eyes.

"It's Mick," Lucas said, and Callum felt the beginnings of his own panic. "Apparently, he missed all of his classes today. He wasn't in third period, which we share, so I asked around and he was out. Callum, out all day."

Callum had his phone out in moments and, he wasn't sure why, he immediately texted Ambrose.

Callum: *Have you seen Mick at all?*

Maybe Ambrose could feel the desperation through the text because he actually replied.

Ambrose: *No. is everything okay?*

"Shit," Callum said out loud.

His mind immediately went to the Mafia. To Ambrose's dad. To how angry he had looked when they were at the party. From the looks of it, Lucas' train of thought was in the same direction.

"Oh my god," Lucas said. "He won't answer any of my calls. Now it's going to voicemail. Callum, should I call Mom?"

"Don't do that."

Both boys jumped at the voice and turned to see Ambrose approaching them. Callum felt the tension in his body lessen ever so slightly.

"Why not?" Lucas snapped.

Ambrose smiled. "Because Asther is gone too."

Callum put a hand on his cousin's shoulder, preventing Lucas from doing anything rash. His temper would get him into trouble someday.

"Ambrose, do you think they are together?"

Ambrose nodded. "Yeah. I have tracking on Asther. My car or yours?"

"Mine," Lucas snapped. "And I'm going to fucking kill them both."

Ambrose got into the back seat of the Toyota, and Callum took the passenger seat. Ambrose was calm, but Callum thought he detected a hint of annoyance pulling at his features. "They are kids," Ambrose stated, buckling his seat belt. He shot Callum a tiny smile. "Don't tell me you've never skipped class, Lucas."

Lucas huffed, starting the car. "Not at a time like this."

This seemed to amuse Ambrose, and he grinned, manic. "Oh. And what is a time like this?"

Callum picked at a thread in his jeans. Lucas barked out a cruel laugh. "A time when we find out your dad's a fuck who's simultaneously fucking our mom and our lives."

"Don't be crass," Callum stated with a wince.

Ambrose only laughed, directing Lucas as he pulled out of the school. "Lucas, isn't that something? Aren't you one to talk?"

Lucas blanched, his hands tightening on the steering wheel. Callum's eyes darted from one to the other, confused.

"I'm sure I have no idea what you mean," Lucas said through clenched teeth.

Ambrose sniffed once, twice. Then he leaned forward and pointedly sniffed Lucas's neck. Callum sunk into his seat, a strange feeling pooling in his stomach.

"What the fuck are you doing?" Lucas asked, taking a hand off the wheel to swat at Ambrose.

Ambrose laughed. It was a truly hideous sound. Callum wanted to hear it again.

"Nothing. Sorry, man. Just like your cologne. It smells really familiar." Ambrose instructed him to turn left. His hand landed on Lucas's shoulder, long, slender fingers squeezing tight. Then he sat back and chuckled softly. It all felt rather threatening. Callum felt defensive.

"What's going on?" he asked, turning in his seat to face Ambrose. "What's your problem with Lucas?"

"Drop it, Cal," Lucas stated. "Let's just focus on the problem at hand."

"Yes, yes," agreed Ambrose, delighted. "One problem at a time."

Ambrose directed them to a divey little place on the far side of town. It was part restaurant, part bar.

"Why would Asther come here?" Callum asked, as they piled out of the car. "I mean, why would Mick come here?!"

Ambrose looked at Callum, stuffing a hand in his pocket. He was playing with something. He cocked his head, as if trying to figure Callum out. "I think the answer might shock you."

He seemed strangely delighted by the prospect which prickled at Callum. Ambrose led the way in. He knew exactly where he was going. He had obviously been here many times before. He led them through the back, past the kitchens, where no-one so much as batted an eye, and into a private room.

Callum *was* shocked. He was sure that shock was written all over his face.

It was like a little living room, but there were two guards at the far end of the room. They dipped their chins in acknowledgement to Ambrose. On the couch, in the center of the room, Asther was shirtless and on top of Mick. Who, Callum noted, was also without a shirt and whose hands were traveling up and down Asther's chest and back with practiced ease as they made out. They were both startled when they realized they had an audience and scrambled for their shirts.

"Oh my gosh," Mick groaned. "I didn't realize the time!"

Callum placed a hand on Lucas's shoulder again. He felt so strange. He had seen the way Asther looked at Mick, but up until now, Mick had been entirely heterosexual. Like obnoxiously so.

"What the fuck?" Lucas snapped.

"I'm inclined to agree," Ambrose added, though without the anger. He seemed more delighted, a grin on his face. Mick kept his eyes on the ground, a shy smile on his lips.

Asther threw a protective arm around his shoulder. "We're dating," he declared. Callum was sure that Mick actually blushed. Suddenly, the anger he was beginning to feel dissipated. Sure, Mick should have let them know, and he was slightly offended that Mick didn't tell them, but now he got it. Mick was experiencing something different, something big. He'd had a million and one crushes on different girls throughout the years, but the longest they would last was a month at the very most.

Callum's eyes found Ambrose and he half-grinned. Ambrose smiled back.

Lucas, unlike the rest, was far from happy. "Mick, are you kidding?! You're no better than Mom then, fucking around with Mafia trash!"

Mick actually flinched. Callum was angry again. But before he could reprimand his older cousin, Ambrose stepped forward with a dark laugh. "Mafia trash, Lucas? Rich, coming from the man fucking my girlfriend. She's just as *Mafia* as Asther."

Lucas froze and had the decency to pale.

Callum shook his head. "No, Ambrose, you must be mistaken. Lucas has a girlfriend," but as he said the words, realization dawned. He shot Lucas a horrified look. "Lucas?! Tell me it's not true. Is *Rose* your girlfriend?"

"Why does it matter?" Lucas demanded, crossing his arms defensively over his chest. "Ambrose is g—"

Asther had a knife out in moments and before Lucas could finish his sentence, he had him in a headlock, the knife at his throat. "I would shut the fuck up if I were you," he stated coolly.

Everyone froze. There was an especially terrified look on Ambrose's face as his eyes flashed to the guards and back again. Mick was burying his face in his hands, hunched over.

"Mick," Asther said softly, letting Lucas go with a rough shove. He pocketed his knife again. "I would never actually hurt him." He crouched down next to Mick, rubbing circles on his back, gently.

"Oh my God... oh my God," Mick sobbed, rocking back and forth. "I'm so sorry."

Lucas was in shock. "You are apologizing to him?"

Mick looked up at his brother, and Callum felt terrified. Mick looked angry. That alone was terrifying, since the emotion was practically foreign to him. And the last person on earth he would be angry at was Lucas.

"Lucas," he seethed, through clenched teeth, "you can't say these terrible things about mom and me when you are literally the shittiest person in this room."

Callum was transported back to his old living room, his dad reading a paper, a cigarette between his lips, a dead look in his eyes. His mom, in the other room, on her phone. An emptiness. He tried to talk to his dad, say something, anything.

"Callum, for fuck's sake, leave me alone for once," his dad snapped.

Callum started shaking now as he remembered. He tuned out the argument happening between his cousins as the room started spinning. Leave me alone for once? Callum was nothing but quiet, non-existent.

At least Lucas and Mick were screaming at each other. They were fighting. That meant they were hurt, which meant they cared. Right?

When Callum came back to the room, he realized he was crouched on the floor, his breathing heavy. The room was silent, and Ambrose was sitting in front of him, his eyebrows pinched together. "Hey, where d'ya go?" he asked softly.

"I'm sorry," Lucas and Mick said, simultaneously and Mick added, "Callum, I'm sorry, we were being thoughtless. Come on. Everything's fine. Let's go home." Lucas nodded vehemently.

Ambrose reached out a hand, squeezing Callum's shoulder. "What do you need?"

"Nothing," Callum said, standing quickly, "It's nothing. We need to get home."

"Yeah, let's get home," Lucas agreed.

He started shepherding the two towards the door, but Callum stopped, turned back around to Ambrose. "Don't you need a ride?"

Ambrose had a strange expression on his face, but he smiled, inclining his head toward Asther. "I'll go with this one." Mick rushed over to Asther and wrapped him in a quick hug before coming back. Lucas clenched his jaw but said nothing.

"See you guys at school," he clipped.

Callum didn't look at Ambrose again as they headed out, past the kitchen, through the tables, and back to Lucas's car. He felt hot shame creeping in, showing itself in bright red at the back of his neck.

"No more skipping school," Lucas scolded in the car, but it was gentle. Callum knew they were both being gentle and walking on eggshells because of him. He was causing this.

"I won't," Mick promised. "Look, I'm really sorry, you two. We obviously can't really see each other unless it's at school. Mom would never let him come over again now that I am sure she is aware of who he is. We just got carried away."

Lucas nodded.

Callum wanted to ask him about Rose, about what he was going to say that caused Asther to put a knife to his throat, about so many things. But he could barely open his mouth and he knew that the words would never come out. He was already a burden. There was already so much discomfort between them all, everything was already falling apart. He was not about to help it along.

That night, Sia didn't come home. Callum was feeling anxious enough that he texted Ambrose.

Callum: *Is Sia okay?*

It was well into the night, so he didn't expect a reply, and not so quickly either, but moments later, his cell dinged.

Ambrose: *Yeah. She's with Dad. Are you okay?*

Callum stared at the second text. Ambrose had made it clear they weren't to be friends. His words still stung from the night of the party.

But strangely, Callum missed him. Did he even know him enough to miss him?

Callum: *I'm okay.*

Ambrose: *Mick and Asther, huh? Never would have thought.*

Callum: *I thought Mick was straight.*

Ambrose: *You have the worst gaydar.*

Callum thought about it, searching for any signs he might have missed, for any clue that Mick liked guys. It was true; he wasn't astute when it came to people and their emotions, not in the way that most other people were.

Callum: *Apparently so.*

Ambrose didn't text again. Callum, with a strange sense of disappointment, put his phone on his bedside table and tried to get some sleep.

Ambrose said Sia was with his dad. Was she working or just sleeping over? Shouldn't she have told them? He wondered if he should go let Lucas and Mick know, but decided against it. He had the strongest desire to cry, but he wouldn't let himself. Everything was going to be okay. It had to be.

And if it wasn't, Callum knew a thing or two about surviving in sub-optimal conditions.

He just didn't want to have to.

CHAPTER 24

CALLUM

Sia came home sporadically and offered no explanations to any of them. Lucas progressively got angrier and grumpier, insisting that he hated her, time and time again.

Callum could never hate her. She gave him so much. But there was a feeling there, of being let down, which he knew he had no right to feel. She wasn't the one who had birthed him. She owed him nothing.

The weather was starting to get chilly. It was a chore getting Mick out of bed to go to school. He always tried to furrow back under the warmth of his blankets.

Dawson started eating with them at the cafeteria almost every day. He would sit next to Callum and, although he was pleasant enough, Callum couldn't help but dislike him more and more as time went on.

He would just say things that rubbed him the wrong way.

Callum did, however, feel a little rush of adrenaline, of satisfaction, when Ambrose would see Dawson take a seat next to him. Sometimes, spite would have Callum turning to Dawson and grinning, as if he were positively delighted to keep his company. At first, Ambrose would rebuttal by scooting closer to Rose. But recently, Liam was sitting between Rose and Ambrose.

Lucas would often be staring over at Rose, his eyebrows pinched together as if he hated the world. As if Rose was the most beautiful person. The most wicked. She rarely gave him the time of day, at least not at school. Callum didn't get it. What was it about Rose that had Ambrose and Lucas so obsessed? That had Ambrose so obsessed that he was willing to look the other way while Rose had affairs with other men.

"Callum? Is that cool?"

Callum turned to Dawson, apologetically. "Sorry, what?"

"Mick says it's cool if I come over after school. We could play some games."

Mick nodded. "Asther is coming over, too."

"So is Rose," Lucas stated.

Callum looked from one cousin to the other, disbelieving. He couldn't really say anything, not in front of Dawson. Lucas understood, though.

"What? Mom won't care. She'll never know." His words were sharp. "She's never fucking home. Do you think tonight, a Friday night, would be any different? She'll be out fucking you-know-who."

Dawson cleared his throat. "Ope."

Mick very obviously kicked his older brother under the table. "Shut up, Lucas. Oh my gosh, just shut up. Your momma's boy jealousy is really showing through."

He rolled his eyes. "Whatever."

Mick turned to Callum. "He's right, though. She probably won't be home. Don't stress it."

Callum's first thought was that he would rather have Ambrose come, not Dawson. But he only nodded.

You stick your nose up at coke. Wasn't that the normal response to cocaine?

"Alright," he said to Dawson, balling his hands into fists under the table.

Callum was a boring person; he was self-aware enough to know that much. At least Dawson would figure that out soon enough, and this problem would resolve itself.

***

That evening, Callum stayed in his room while he waited. Somehow, Lucas had gotten a hold of a decent amount of alcohol and as soon as Rose and Asther showed up, they all started taking shots.

Dawson had texted Mick to say he was on his way. Callum didn't have his number and secretly hoped it would stay that way.

A light knock came on his door before Mick wandered in, followed by Asther. Mick handed him a shot glass filled with a clear liquid. "It's not too awful," he said. "Just have one shot, okay?"

Asther leaned against the doorframe, hands in his pockets.

He never spoke much, but he nodded at Callum, agreeing with Mick.

"I don't know," he hesitated. "I haven't ever really…"

"You've had wine," Mick stated, "and beer. This is just a little stronger," he smiled, "look, you're in our house. With us. It's fine to let loose. We're family."

Callum couldn't refuse after that. He took the shot and downed it, forcing away the grimace. Whatever it was, it was awful, burning all the way down.

"Nice," Callum lied.

"Hurry down," Mick said, walking out of the room. He slipped his hand into Asther's on the way out.

Sia was missing everything. Mick was in love for the first time, and Sia was missing all of it. Callum waited for as long as possible he could before joining them downstairs. Rose made him wildly uncomfortable lately. Maybe because she was blatantly cheating, dating two men at once. Maybe it was something else.

Dawson had arrived and was chilling with the others in the living room. He stood when Callum came in and smiled. He wasn't wearing cowboy boots tonight- some fancy black shoes, and skinny jeans that looked kind of expensive. He was in a nice black t-shirt with a button up, unbuttoned over it. He looked like he was about to be on a date.

Callum was going to sit on the Lazyboy in the corner, but Dawson patted the couch next to him. "Come on," he said. "We are about to start a drinking game."

Callum sat next to him. Dawson's hand lightly grazed his thigh before he turned back to the others. Callum felt like he had misread something, somewhere. Completely. Dawson moved in closer so they were thigh to thigh.

When Lucas handed him another shot, Callum took it without hesitation.

"Oh," Lucas said with a small smile, "that was for the drinking game. Hand it back, lemme refill."

"Sorry," Callum said sheepishly, resisting the urge to get up and run somewhere far away. Subtly, he shifted so that his thigh wasn't touching Dawson's. Dawson just closed the gap again, oblivious.

Asther was frantically texting on his phone. He pocketed it, shot Callum a conspiratorial grin and said, "Alright. What's the game?"

"Spin the bottle?" Dawson suggested.

"What's that?" Callum asked.

Mick started to explain but Callum immediately decided that was a game he didn't want to play.

"Any other ideas?" he asked.

"We could play Never Have I Ever," Rose supplied. She had a manicured hand resting scandalously high on Lucas's leg and the other arm was wrapped around his waist. "Everyone takes a turn saying 'Never Have I Ever' whatever and then if you have done the thing, you take a shot."

"Never have I ever cheated on my boyfriend," Asther deadpanned, his gaze locked on Rose.

Callum shrunk a little, but then Rose laughed, and Asther grinned at her. She took a shot. Callum felt so indignant on behalf of Ambrose. Did all his friends make a habit of joking like this behind his back?

"Never have I ever been in love," Dawson said, stupidly. Everyone in the room took a shot except Callum. All eyes were on him.

"Never?" Rose asked.

"Ever?" Asther chimed in.

"I don't think so," Callum admitted. The room was spinning a little from the two shots he had. He wasn't used to alcohol. He usually avoided it. "I guess I would know if I had."

Asther nodded, seriously.

"Callum might be aromantic," Mick said, "or maybe asexual."

Callum grinned at his little cousin. "Maybe," he lied. Dawson next to him, tensed, briefly.

He remembered the night in Ambrose's Jeep, the funny feeling he had gotten when Ambrose touched him. He doubted he was asexual.

He fished out his phone that he had been keeping close to him more often lately. He felt disappointed when there was nothing. If Asther and Rose could hang around here, why couldn't Ambrose?

Lucas was in the middle of reprimanding Mick. "Stop labelling Callum, dude. He can do it himself if he wants to. You can't just announce to the world what you think his sexuality might be."

"Oh," Mick said, ducking his head, "Yeah, sorry, Callum."

Callum felt mortified, desperately eager to change the conversation to literally anything else, "It's okay, Mick. It's just us. I know you didn't mean any harm."

A knock came at the door.

"I'll get it!" Callum offered, ready to fly off the couch, eager for an excuse to get away from Dawson practically breathing down his neck and the awkwardness that had settled over this previous conversation.

But Mick was already on his way. Asther got up and followed him.

"Man, those two are attached at the hip," Dawson stated.

"It's sweet," Callum said defensively. He didn't look at Dawson, he had been avoiding eye contact since the moment he came into the room. Where had he read this so wrong?

Mick came back, Asther lagging behind a little, with Ambrose.

"I told him to stop by," Asther said with a little grin in Rose's direction, "hope that's okay."

"Why wouldn't it be?" Lucas said through clenched teeth. His hand stayed firmly on Rose's knee. Callum had never in his life, until now, wanted to punch his cousin right in the face.

Ambrose hardly spared Rose a glance. His eyes fell on Callum and then Dawson, who was practically on top of him with how close he was sitting. A strange look flashed in his eyes before he smiled that manic smile. "Well, well. Hope I'm not intruding on couples' night."

"It's not a couples' night," Callum insisted, quickly.

Dawson moved in closer to Callum. Was he stupid?

Ambrose watched, his smile widening. He took a seat in the chair Callum had originally intended to be in. Asther passed Ambrose a shot.

"I thought you weren't supposed to be hanging around us?" Lucas said coolly.

"My watchdog has the night off," Ambrose replied just as coolly. He was still looking at Callum. "And Liam is out of town for the weekend. Asther won't say anything," his gaze landed on Rose, "and she won't either. Right?"

Rose's shoulders seemed to deflate a little. "Of course not, Ambrose. I'm glad you could come."

Dawson shifted. Callum only knew this because he literally felt it. Then he remembered the rumors, the fear Dawson had for Ambrose, and he felt a little bad. Still, he inched away again. At the same time, Dawson stretched and threw an arm behind Callum, resting it on the back of the couch.

There was a tic in Ambrose's jaw. "What are we playing then?" he asked, swirling the contents of his shot glass.

"Never have I ever," Rose supplied. She was being amicable, sweet even. Callum didn't think he would ever understand their dynamic. Rose was literally on another man right now. Liam had said they had a strange relationship. This was very strange. Was it one of those open things?

"Delightful," Ambrose said. "Never have I ever lost a hand."

"Shit," Asther said, with a little grin, "that's fucked up for being this sober."

"It's cool," Dawson said, taking his shot. "I don't think taking a shot is half bad for a penalty."

"Delightful," Ambrose said again, shooting Dawson a cruel smile. He lounged casually, comfortably in the chair. Callum noted that he was wearing black dress pants and a button up, with the top three buttons undone. He must have come from somewhere. His hair was slicked back, neatly.

"No more cruel questions," Rose declared.

"It wasn't cruel," Ambrose defended himself.

Dawson rested his arm fully on Callum's shoulders. Callum resisted the urge to flinch.

"I need some water," he said and got up, making a beeline for the kitchen at a pace he hoped wasn't obviously and desperately fast.

"Me too," he heard Ambrose say, and then Ambrose was there in the kitchen with him.

He leaned on the bar, crossing his arms over his lightly exposed chest. "So, Dawson and you? When did that happen?"

Callum turned the faucet on, filling a glass. He passed it to Ambrose without making eye contact and filled himself one, too.

"I don't know," he said quietly, honestly. "I misread something, I guess."

Ambrose chuckled. It sounded both angry and amused. "I told you. Your gaydar sucks."

"Dawson's gay?"

Ambrose raised a brow. "Yes, Callum, Dawson is gay. He once made a pass at me."

"Is that why he's missing a hand?" Callum asked, and immediately regretted it.

Ambrose's eyes flashed. "Fuck you," he said.

"Fuck you," Callum retorted, even though he wanted to apologize. Still, he was angry about it all.

"Sure," Ambrose said with a wickedly cruel smile. "Come 'ere." he cocked his pointer finger, hopped onto the bar and patted his lap. "I'm a better fuck than Dawson, anyway."

Callum ducked his head, his face red. "Don't be so crass. Anyway, how would you know you were?" and then, "Wait, I don't want to... do it... with anyone."

"Dawson obviously wants to... *do it* with you," Ambrose stated, taking a long sip from the glass of water. Callum watched his throat for a second too long.

"I don't know what to do," he admitted.

"You mean how to fuck a guy? You strike me as a bottom. He'll show you, don't worry," Ambrose spat the words out.

"Oh my gosh, no," Callum said. "I mean, I don't know how to let him down. What is with you? Why are you so angry?"

Ambrose leaned back on the bar, his weight on his palms. "Guess."

"I'm bad at reading people," Callum stated. "I'm bad at understanding them."

"Obviously," Ambrose grinned, slightly.

The change in his mood was so drastic that Callum felt whiplash.

"Fine," Ambrose said, his voice a little too loud. "I'll help you out. Here's what you do. You look him dead in the eyes and say, *I'm not interested.* Tell him you're straight or something."

"So helpful," Callum retorted.

"I do what I can."

Dawson peeked his head around the wall into the kitchen. "You guys coming?" He asked. He sauntered in, standing close to Callum.

Callum took a step, giving a space between them. "Yeah, sorry."

Ambrose hopped off the bar. He took a step toward Dawson. "Dawson," he said, and Callum knew from the tone he used that he was going to be cruel. "How are things?" Ambrose draped an arm over his shoulder and then his other arm over Callum's, shepherding them towards the living room. He sat on the couch between them, grinning delightedly.

"Actually," Dawson cleared his throat, "if you wouldn't mind, I'd like to sit by Callum."

"Oh, what a coincidence," Ambrose declared. "I want to sit by Callum too."

"Oh, for fuck's sake," Lucas snapped, "circle jerk each other outside, would ya?"

Callum stood, facing his cousin. "What is with you, Lucas?" he snapped, surprising even himself. "Why are you being such a dick lately? How can you just sit there with Ambrose's girlfriend and still play the holier than thou card? I don't get you."

The room got deathly quiet.

Mick stood too, placing a hand on Callum's shoulder. "Hey," he said. Lucas was staring at Callum. There was something like hurt *and* pride on his face.

"It's fine," he waved his hand, "Callum's right. I'll do better,"

"This is a really weird party," Dawson said. He was trying to lighten the mood, but Callum wanted to hit him.

"It's delightful," Ambrose stated. "Look at Callum, defending my honor and shit."

Callum turned to Ambrose. "Doesn't it bother you? My cousin and your girlfriend. Right in front of you!"

"Callum," Lucas said gently, "that's enough. You don't understand."

"I really, really don't," he agreed. He felt like he might cry. He felt alone. He was the only person here who seemed totally confused about everything. Besides maybe Dawson, but he wasn't really part of this group.

Ambrose reached up and grabbed Callum's wrist. "Hey, sit back down," He gently pulled him so that Callum was back on the couch, "I can explain it."

Rose cleared her throat. She looked at Dawson and then back at Ambrose. "Now is probably not the right time. You know, Ambrose, for obvious reasons."

"I know," he groaned. "I mean, I'll explain *later*. Let's just play the game." He patted Callum's knee. "Don't worry about it. Everything is fine, I promise."

Dawson cleared his throat.

"Oh, fuck off Dawson," Ambrose snapped. "No one wants you here."

"Hey, he's my friend," he lied, "and you're in my house. Don't be a jerk." Callum wasn't sure why he did it, but he stood, walked over to the other side of the couch, and sat back down by Dawson.

Dawson shot Ambrose a triumphant grin. Callum really, really didn't want Dawson here. Ambrose was right. No one wanted him here. But he was talking anyway because he had to be fair. *He* was the one who had originally pursued a friendship with Dawson. "Never have I ever committed a crime."

Everyone in the room took a shot except Callum.

"Mick, explain," Callum and Lucas said simultaneously.

Mick put his hands up. "Hey, those aren't the rules."

Asther filled every one's shot glasses back up before stating, calmly, "Never have I ever had sex in the backseat of a car."

Mick's whole face was practically red as he took the shot with Asther, and then Lucas and Rose, and then Dawson. Ambrose didn't drink his, which, in Callum's opinion, made the Rose thing really, really awkward. But again, no one else batted an eye at it.

"So, you two are having sex?" Rose directed to Mick and Asther playfully.

"I hope you're safe," Callum said, feeling a strange sense of... something bubbling in his chest. Mick was growing up. Callum was literally only a few months older than him, but he always felt like Mick was so much younger.

"Wow, okay, yes Mom," Mick stated with a groan.

"Never have I ever had sex," Dawson interjected, eyes on Callum.

"It's not your turn," Ambrose stated. He languidly leaned back, kicking his feet up on the coffee table and crossing his ankles.

"There aren't any rules," Dawson retorted. So much for being afraid of Ambrose. Though alcohol was powerful that way.

"Fine," Callum said, taking the shot. He was progressively becoming more and more annoyed with Dawson. Did he not hear a word Mick had said earlier? It's like he had tuned out the words *asexual* and *aromantic.* They probably weren't words he would use to identify himself with, but Dawson didn't know that. How had Callum ever thought that Dawson was some shy and sweet misunderstood person?

"Oh. really?" Rose asked. It wasn't mean, but still, Callum was annoyed with her too.

"Yeah, really," Callum spoke a little defensively, "I'm almost eighteen and I'm a virgin. We *do* exist, believe it or not."

Ambrose's eyes were lit up, a grin on his face. He was swirling the contents of his shot glass around and around. "There is nothing wrong with being a virgin," he agreed, though to Callum his tone almost sounded mocking.

"Dang," Dawson chimed in. His arm found itself to

Callum's shoulders again. "Honestly, that's super-hot."

Ambrose chuckled darkly. "You think you'll get to take his virginity? I'd think again."

"Woah, woah, woah," Callum felt this night could not get worse. "Who's talking about," he cleared his throat, his face going red, "taking my virginity? That's... no. Let's stop. Let's," he turned to Lucas, "your turn." it was practically a plea.

Lucas stated, "never have I ever killed someone."

Callum's eyes shot to Ambrose, who had a decidedly unamused look on his face. Rose said, "Lucas, stop."

Her voice was cold.

Dawson cleared his throat. "Guys, maybe we should play another game."

"Yes," Ambrose agreed amicably, "how about the one where you fuck off?"

Callum buried his head in his hands with a groan.

"Whatever, man," Dawson was standing, reaching for his coat resting on the back of the couch. "Callum, I'm going to bounce. Call me, okay?"

"Okay," Callum lied, standing too, "I'll walk you out."

He knew he should say something like *oh, don't go,* or, *Ambrose, you should be the one to leave,* but he said neither of those things, just trailed Dawson to the door. He had a pounding headache and was feeling the alcohol in ways he didn't love, like the slight spinning of the room and the strong desire to be touched. Was that what he was feeling?

He hated drinking. Even though he never drank, he knew

what drinking did to people. What drinking meant. That was, bad decisions and revealed truths better left buried for good.

Dawson turned to him at the door. He smiled, a little dejectedly. "Kinda wish the buzz kill hadn't showed up."

"I'm sorry," Callum lied again, "this wasn't how I expected the night to go."

"You're cute," Dawson stated.

"Thank you," Callum returned, awkwardly. Even with his senses blurred, he knew he wanted to be touched, but just not by Dawson. He had this strange mix of feelings of fondness and repulsion for him that he couldn't explain even to himself.

Dawson leaned forward slightly. Shouting from the living room jolted him back. Everyone was shouting. Dawson sighed. "I'll be going then. You sure you don't want to leave with me? Sounds messy in there."

Callum shook his head. "I better go see what's happening. See you at school on Monday."

Dawson furrowed his brows. "Text me before then."

Callum nodded, shutting the door behind Dawson as he left and returning to the living room. Lucas was practically at Ambrose's throat. "Just tell Callum then and make all of our lives easier!"

"Tell me what?" Callum asked, leaning on the wall, crossing his arms. He felt tired and a little too fuzzy to stand on his own.

"Nothing," Lucas said too quickly, a mix of shame and horror on his face.

Ambrose turned on Rose, who was standing beside Lucas,

his tone fierce. "You should never have told Lucas. Because you wanted to fuck him I get to be in this situation!"

"Hey," Asther said, to everyone's surprise, standing, pulling Mick up with him. "Everyone, cool it. Ambrose, don't be too hard on Rose, please? Rose, you should stop telling secrets that aren't yours to tell. Now, Mick and I are heading up to bed," he pulled on Mick's hand, heading towards the stairs, "have fun with this."

"Sh—should he be staying the night?" Callum asked Lucas. He couldn't bring himself to look at Ambrose, not right now, for whatever reason.

"It's fine," Lucas passed a tired hand over his face with a sigh. "Rose and I are heading up, too." He turned to Ambrose. "I'm sorry. It isn't Rose's fault. It's mine. I'm sorry."

Ambrose shrugged. Callum could feel that he was looking at *him,* as Rose and Lucas also went upstairs, but he felt so awkward. He was a little too dizzy to stand, so he took the nearest seat, the couch. He looked at his shoes.

"Hey," Ambrose said, sitting right next to him, "sorry if I ruined your night. I was completely out of line." He sounded about as apologetic as an emotionless cow.

"You didn't. Not really. But you *were* out of line."

Ambrose smiled. "Dawson just irritates me. He totally wants to fuck you, you know."

Callum swallowed. "I guess I've been figuring that out tonight. I..." he looked at Ambrose, "don't want to..."

"Fuck him?" Ambrose supplied, leaning back casually.

"Yes. That."

"Good," Ambrose said, satisfied. "I don't approve."

"Why should I care if you do or don't?" Callum huffed. "*You* made it clear we weren't to be friends."

He didn't want to sound bothered by it, but the truth was clear in his tone. It caused Ambrose delight.

"I thought it was best that we weren't. But friendship is more fun when it's forbidden anyway." He winked at Callum.

"You frustrate me," Callum stated truthfully. "Maybe *I* don't want to be your friend anymore."

Ambrose almost sounded dejected when he responded. "Is that true?"

"No."

Silence settled between them. Callum stared at his shoes. Ambrose cleared his throat after a while. "Well, I should be off. How about we just give it a try again? Being friends."

Callum nodded. "Should you be driving? You've had some drinks."

Ambrose barked out a laugh. "Hardly. Besides, I can just ring up my bodyguard if I need to."

"Bodyguard?" Callum almost balked.

"Have you forgotten I'm in the Mafia? Selective memory perhaps?"

Despite himself, Callum grinned. Of course, it was something he couldn't forget. It kept him up lately, it left him with a thousand questions, it *terrified* him. Hearing that Ambrose had a bodyguard just made it even more real.

He walked Ambrose, quite wobbly, to the front door. Some strange voice in his head wanted to ask him to stay. He ignored that one but humored the voice that said *touch*. In a fuzzy haze, he reached out a hand and lightly touched Ambrose's shoulder. Ambrose froze.

Callum pulled his hand back awkwardly. "Goodnight then. See you at school." He practically shut the door in his face and then rushed up the stairs to his room. He heard Mick laughing about something. He heard the muffled voices of Rose and Lucas.

He tried to sleep. After what felt like hours, he found his phone and texted Ambrose.

Callum: *Doesn't it bother you?*

Ambrose: *What?*

Callum: *Rose and my cousin. Right in front of your face.*

Ambrose: *It's complicated. I guess the best way to describe it is an open relationship.*

Ambrose: *Anyway, don't worry about me ;) I'm not completely innocent either.*

Callum had a vague idea of what it meant, but still he Googled *open relationships* and then felt his face grow hot. He imagined Ambrose with other women and shook his head. His first impression of Ambrose and Rose had been that they were madly in love; even their names matched. Everything about them had been perfect in his mind. And Ambrose didn't seem like the type to share.

Suddenly, he got images of that night in the Jeep, of Ambrose touching his thigh. That same sensation pooled in his stomach as he buried his face in the pillow, trying desperately to sleep. People were too confusing. His mind was a jumbled mess of thoughts as he finally fell into a fitful sleep.

CHAPTER 25

CALLUM

The next Saturday, Sia texted them that they would be having dinner together.

"What do you know?" Lucas stated from his spot on the couch. "She must have remembered we existed or something."

"Lucas," Mick pleaded, "can we please have one nice dinner with her? We don't know her side of things. Just... be civil."

Lucas rolled his eyes. Callum hadn't seen his aunt in days. The last time he *had* seen her, it was so brief it couldn't even count.

"Let's just confront her about everything," Lucas said.

"Absolutely not," Mick stated.

"Callum?"

He looked up from his book to see his cousins looking at him expectantly. "Oh," he mused on it for a second, "probably not a good idea. Ambrose's dad doesn't really seem like someone we just... disobey."

Lucas scoffed. "He's just a stuffed-up prick."

"Sounds familiar," Mick said, grinning over at Callum.

"What sounds familiar?" Sia asked, walking in through the

front door, a smile on her face. Callum felt the three of them collectively deflate a little with relief. No matter what hothead thing Lucas said, they all idolized Sia and to see her again was good. He was sure they all had the same fear; would she not make it home one day? None of them had any mafia experience to speak of, obviously, but if it was anything like the books or movies depicted, then it wasn't exactly a cushy job. Mick rushed over to her, throwing his arms around her in a hug. What shocked everyone was Lucas hugging her next. He held on to her for a while.

She patted his back. "Now, what's this about?" Concern flitted across her features and Callum couldn't blame her. Lucas was not being subtle; he was not the hugging type.

"I just miss you," he said. Any of his tough guy act had gone out the window now that she was there.

Her face fell. "I've been a terrible mom. I need to be present more. I'm really sorry, boys." She walked over to Callum and gave him a quick hug. "All three of you deserve better."

"It's okay," Callum said quickly, "we understand."

She sighed. "There's Chinese takeout in the car. Lucas, would you grab it? I'll set out the table."

When he left, Sia turned on the two. "Explain that. Is Lucas okay? Is this really because I've been absent? Gosh, I can't even remember the last time he ever hugged me."

Callum shifted, never very good at lying.

Mick saved them. "He's just having a tough time lately. Girl problems. School problems. The works."

Callum nodded vigorously. "The works."

Lucas came back in, boxes in hand, and they all sat around the table, falling back into the rhythm of how things used to be.

Sia hedged, "Lucas, how is the girl you are seeing?"

"She's fine," he said and smiled. "It's going really great."

Sia shot a look at Mick, and he and Callum just shrugged.

"Can I meet her?" The table got really quiet. "Or not." Sia quickly added, "I don't want to make you uncomfortable."

For the briefest moment, it looked like Lucas was about to shatter whatever tentative peace they had at the table, but he only sighed. "Maybe. It's complicated."

She arched her brow. "Is it going really great, or is it complicated?"

Before he could respond, Sia's phone started ringing. She pursed her lips as she checked the caller ID. "I have to take this," she said, moving to stand.

"Are you fucking kidding me?" Lucas snapped.

Sia flinched. "Excuse me? Watch your language at the dinner table. Lucas, it's work. I have to."

"That is rich," he responded, wide-eyed, even as Callum and Mick simultaneously kicked at him under the table. He astutely ignored them. "Work? Mom, really?"

She slammed her hand down on the table. "What is with this attitude? Yes. Really."

Her phone started buzzing again, and she shook her head. "We will continue this when I bet back."

She started to walk away, but Lucas couldn't leave well enough alone. "It's okay, mom, we get it. Fucking around with a Mafia man is probably a real thrill. Don't worry about us. We'll just sit here and wait for you to remember we exist again."

Mick started choking on his water. But then, the silence was so loud it screamed.

"What did you just say to me?" Sia clipped out after what felt like an eternity. Callum sank lower into his seat, willing himself to be invisible. Mick seemed to do the same. Lucas, like the peacock that he was, puffed himself out.

"I think you heard me."

There was genuine fear in Sia's voice when she spoke again. "You do not understand what you are saying. Lucas Botan Takagi, watch what comes out of your mouth."

Lucas snorted. "It's true though." He nodded in Callum and Mick's direction. "We know everything."

"Don't drag us into this, Dick," Mick snapped.

Sia stood still for a moment before sinking back into her chair. She buried her head in her hands and then started sobbing. She was wailing and muttering things that were completely indiscernible.

"M—mom," Lucas stammered, suddenly at a loss for words.

Mick went over to her, shooting Lucas the meanest look Callum had ever seen and that was saying a lot.

"Mom," Mick said, rubbing soothing circles on her back. "Lucas is being a jerk. We don't know anything. Do you understand what I'm saying? We *don't know anything.*"

Lucas nodded. "He's right."

She shook her head and took a deep breath, gracelessly blowing her nose into her sleeve. "Fuck," she said, causing Callum to feel the urge to laugh. She summed it up perfectly.

She stared at a spot on the table as she went on. "You were never supposed to know anything. But I don't know what I was thinking. You go to the same damn school as his son."

Callum swallowed.

"I had no choice," she went on, still staring at nothing on the table, an emptiness in her eyes and a hollowness in her voice. "We were so broke. We lost our house, you know?"

"I didn't know that," Lucas said, fully ashamed.

"I got this offer that I couldn't refuse. Desperation is exactly what people like them look for because only the desperate would be so foolish."

She shook her head, gnawed at her lower lip. "But... you were safe. I had it all worked out to where you would all be safe and only myself would be at risk. How stupid was I? Look what I've done," she spat out angrily. "I've put my three boys in danger. Look what I've done."

"We're fine," Mick said, though no one really believed him. "Mom, we are going to be fine."

Her phone started buzzing again. She wiped her eyes. "I have to take this. Don't go anywhere."

When she was out of earshot, Mick turned on Lucas. "Why are you like this? Literally, what the fuck is wrong with you?"

Callum cleared his throat, "Hey—"

"He's right," Lucas said. "I can never keep my mouth shut. You guys didn't know him very well, but I remember dad and I'm just like him. I can't just keep my mouth shut."

"Shut up," Mick stated, angrier even still, "you are nothing like our sperm donor. Don't say that. You're here."

Lucas sighed and then leaned over and ruffled Mick's hair. "This is a mess, little buddy."

"Should we tell her the rest?" Mick hedged, crossing his arms over his chest. "Like that we are all dating Mafia members?"

Callum snorted. "I'm not."

Mick rolled his eyes, but he grinned, and that was a small victory. "Give it time."

"I don't know what that means," Callum said stubbornly as Sia came back into the room, pocketing her phone. Her posture was straight again, her eyes dry, and she spoke with confidence.

"New plan," she stated. "We are all going to the Romano estate for dinner. Go get changed, wear dinner clothes." She spoke more sternly when she added. "I'm warning you to show Tomas respect. Lucas, you especially. He is powerful. And he is dangerous."

***

Callum pulled at the collar of his black button up as they were ushered into the estate by a man in a suit. He wasn't quite sure what Sia had meant by dinner clothes, so he settled on a button up and a pair of jeans with no rips. To be safe, and for no other reason, he spritzed a bit of cologne on his wrists.

Sia had briefed them in the car about what was happening. Tomas insisted that since they all knew that they come together to form a plan of action. Tomas knew all along that they knew which Callum, of course, refrained from mentioning to Sia, but he disliked the man a little more for his sliminess.

"Always respond with Sir," Sia had told them. "And don't make any jokes. He's a serious man. Take everything seriously."

"Sounds like a prick," Lucas had said, and she reached over to the passenger side and pulled on his ear.

"Start practicing being a meek person," she had snapped.

And here they were. One big happy family.

Tomas was waiting for them in a grand dining room, Ambrose seated to his right. His gaze flitted to Callum, expression unreadable. The man who had escorted them in literally assigned them to seats; Lucas next to Ambrose, Sia next to Tomas- who had everyone repulsed when he leaned over to kiss her- Callum next to Sia across from Ambrose and then Mick next to Callum.

Tomas cleared his throat. "I'll lead us in prayer before they bring the courses and then we can get down to business."

Callum held his breath, waiting just waiting for Lucas to have some snarky comment about Mafia men praying and hypocrisy, but by some miracle he was perfectly meek.

Callum watched as Tomas made the sign on the cross, Ambrose his perfect mirror. Tomas recited, "Bless us, Oh Lord, and these thy gifts which we are about to receive from thy bounty, through Christ, Our Lord. Amen."

"Amen," Sia and Ambrose said simultaneously and Sia shot the boys a look so they said it too.

Callum raised a subtle brow in Ambrose's direction, but Ambrose kept his face completely neutral, his hands folded in his lap. The perfect little son. Callum felt annoyed for no reason.

"Well then," Tomas said, clearing his throat and spreading a cloth napkin over his lap.

Servers brought the first course; placing a plate in front of each person; some delicate-looking salad with tomatoes, which Callum absolutely hated. He wondered if Tomas would take offense if he ate around them.

Tomas continued speaking, his voice deep and commanding, "I guess the cat's out of the bag," he shot a dark look briefly in Ambrose's direction. Ambrose astutely picked at his greens. "So there is no point beating around the bush. Things will be different now. You are fully under my protection for your safety. You are dear to Sia, therefore you are dear to me and from now on we will be having dinner together every Saturday." He paused to take a bite of salad, chewing it slowly before continuing. "You will not miss it. No excuses."

"Yes, Sir," the three of them said in unison. Callum thought he caught Ambrose rolling his eyes, but then his face was back to the previous lifeless expression. He thought to himself, *weren't they always dear to Sia*? Why was it just now that they were getting his *full protection?*

"I've assigned a tail to you boys," he went on, "you won't even know he's around. He's excellent at his job and he is merely a precaution. Lionel, come in here!"

The tallest man Callum had ever seen walked into the room, with shoulders so wide they were impressive. Ambrose towered over Callum's own short height, but this man definitely towered over Ambrose. How were they expected not to notice him? He must be *really* good at his job.

"Lionel, these are the boys, Lucas, Callum and Mick. Boys, this is Lionel. No need to ever speak to him. He's simply going to always have tracking on you and he'll tail you when necessary. Understood?"

"Yes, Sir."

Callum hated this. He really wished Lucas hadn't opened his loudmouth just for once and they could go on pretending like they didn't know a thing and not have to be subjected to incredibly weird shit like this. Having a tail sounded horrible; would they ever have any privacy again? It almost seemed to him like Tomas did it more to keep an eye on them than anything else. After all, they knew too much.

"Ambrose," Tomas turned to his son. Callum swore he flinched, barely perceptible. He clenched his fists under the table.

"Yes, *Sir?*" Ambrose asked.

"When we are done here, show them around the estate. Be a good host. Then show them each to a room."

He turned back to the three. "You will each have a room

here. There may be instances where you will have to stay under my roof. Feel free to bring some things next Saturday to leave behind in your drawers." He smiled over to Sia, a shockingly loving and genuine thing, out of place on his face. "Mostly, be comfortable. What's mine is yours."

Callum felt the strangest urge to laugh. Comfortable? Nothing about this was ever going to be comfortable. Everything he said to them felt so transactional. Even when he spoke to his own son, it seemed to be business, business, business. The only person in the room that Tomas was kind to was Sia.

The second course was a gnocchi soup of sorts, but Callum was struggling to find any appetite. He glanced over at Ambrose. Briefly, Ambrose met his gaze and then looked away.

They finished the meal in relative silence, though Tomas often spoke to Sia. The main course was steak and potatoes, and by the end of it, Callum never wanted to see food again. Did they eat like this every night? Enough was enough.

Tomas made them pray again in thanksgiving, and then he stood, Sia following suit. Callum willed Lucas to leave it be because he could see his cousin practically seething with annoyance. They weren't a religious family, never had been, but they especially weren't a fan of Catholics. That was until now, it appeared. Sia went along with Tomas as he had prayed, her own head bowed in devotion. Even Callum felt uneasy about it. Thankfully, Lucas said nothing. He did look at Sia with disgust, which might have been worse.

"Your mother and I have work to discuss. Ambrose, I will leave you to it. Be a gracious host."

The last part sounded strangely like a threat.

The minute he was out of the room, Ambrose transformed. His shoulders relaxed, and he stuffed his hands into the pockets of his slacks. "Good god I thought that would never end."

Lucas found his snarky voice again. "Your dad is a prick, capital P. This sucks."

"Imagine me," Ambrose said, no sympathy in his tone, "this is how I live. And not just on Saturdays."

"It's all very... awkward," Callum supplied.

"The question is, how the fuck did this happen?" Ambrose's accusatory gaze landed, rightfully, on Lucas.

"Does it matter?" Lucas responded. "It happened. Here we are. A big, happy family. Praise the Lord or whatever prayer you say."

Ambrose rolled his eyes. "Anyway, let me give you the grand tour." Ambrose stood, brushing past Callum. He was acting strange. Or maybe he wasn't. What did Callum know? It just felt like he was upset with him almost, like him being here was making Ambrose angry.

Callum recalled the birthday party and how Tomas had commanded him never to set foot on the estate again. But here they were. All playacting. All fake, tight smiles.

Ambrose sauntered through the massive estate, showing them different rooms, many of which they had already seen at the party. There was an excessive number of men in suits scattered around the house, and they would dip their chins at Ambrose as he walked by.

Ambrose finally led them to the second floor. "My room is the second door," he stated, "and my dad's is the first. Guest rooms are here, down the hall. Pick whichever I guess."

"Do we have to?" Lucas hedged. "Seems a bit much."

"I mean, if you like living," Ambrose deadpanned. Callum was pretty sure he was joking, but couldn't actually tell.

"I'll just take whatever," he said. "Mick, I can bunk with you."

Ambrose tsk-ed, "I'm sure Mick wants to leave the door open for Asther. Come now, Callum. Don't be thoughtless."

Mick ducked his head, embarrassed.

"Oh. Does Asther come here?" Callum asked.

"He practically lives here. His dad works with my dad. For my dad. Whatever. Rose is here a lot too," he said, directing that part towards Lucas.

Callum would never ever get used to Lucas and Ambrose sharing a girlfriend.

"Mom doesn't know we're dating them," Mick stated. "We should probably wait a bit to break that bombshell."

Ambrose shrugged as if he couldn't care less. "I'll show you our pool. It's in the basement."

"Oh, hell yeah," Mick said enthused.

The lower level had a massive gym and an even bigger heated pool with an adjoining hot tub. Said hot tub was occupied by Rose, Liam, and Asther. The latter lit up when he saw

Mick bounding over, his shorts swung low and water dripped down his bare chest. "Well, how did it go?" he asked, wrapping himself around Mick, not caring that he was sopping wet.

"Not as bad as I expected, honestly," Mick told him. "But I'm dying to get into that hot tub."

"Come in then," Asther said, a devilish glint in his eyes. Callum felt uncomfortable for whatever reason and had the strangest urge to blush at their intimacy.

"Come too!" Rose called over in their direction, either to Ambrose or Lucas. Callum wasn't sure.

"There's a bunch of shorts in that locker," Ambrose pointed, "knock yourself out."

Lucas and Mick left to join them.

"You?" Ambrose asked Callum, his eyebrow raised.

"Not a huge fan of water."

Ambrose chuckled. He was more himself again, but there was still a strain.

Callum knew he wasn't imagining it. "I'm bored of it." He turned around, his hands back in his pockets, and started walking away. Callum watched him, confused, before he turned around and said, "Well? Coming?"

"Where are we headed?" he asked when he caught up.

"The fuck out of this house," Ambrose said with a grin.

Ambrose brought him to his Jeep and drove on a dirt road a few miles into the property. He killed the engine and reached into the backseat, tossing a blanket at Callum.

"I just need to be out of the house," he said. "Dad's not

pleased."

"Because he has to include us in Saturday dinners?" Callum asked, wrapping the blanket around himself.

Ambrose raised an eyebrow. "That was to share."

Callum rolled his eyes, followed by a small smile. "You are so different around your dad," he finally said, ignoring Ambrose's plea to share as he grabbed another throw blanket from his backseat.

"Yeah. You have no idea."

Callum had never heard Ambrose sound so bitter.

"He seems to really love you," he offered. "Are you sure you have to change around him?"

"You don't understand." Ambrose waved a hand. It was just chilly enough that their breath came out in little puffs of smoke. "He loves the version I give him."

Ambrose looked out the window. "I've seen what it would be like if I gave the real me. It's not pretty."

Callum said nothing. There was nothing really to say. He knew a thing or two about shit dads. He could understand in silence.

"He can't ever know about Asther and Mick," Ambrose stated matter-of-factly. "Never."

"They are probably making out right now in his hot tub." Callum grinned.

"No," Ambrose snapped. "I'm not kidding, Callum. The last time someone in his circle was openly gay, he disappeared. I'm like 99% sure my dad killed him. And that was his own nephew."

Callum didn't move. "What the hell, Ambrose?" he finally said.

Ambrose laughed. It was unhinged. "Did you think this was all going to be okay because he's fucking your mom and we have family dinners now? It's not okay, Callum. Everything is fucking fucked now. Do you get that?" he asked, leaning closer, viciously enunciating each word as if Callum were simple. "He's dangerous, he's calloused, and he's cruel. Everything's different now." Ambrose slammed a fist down on the steering wheel, startling Callum.

Callum stared at him, a sinking sensation in the pit of his stomach. His wild, dark hair hung at his neck and over his eyes, almost hiding the anger simmering in them. "Why are you lashing out at me?" Callum snapped. He felt hurt and annoyed. He had never asked for any of this. He was a fish out of water here.

"Because," Ambrose snapped back, "everything was fine. But then you came and you're ruining my life."

Callum felt like he had been punched right in the stomach. He wasn't sure if he was breathing.

"Shit," Ambrose said, leaning back, "I didn't mean that. I was angry."

"Take me back," Callum said quietly.

Ambrose reached over and grabbed Callum's wrist. There was an urgency in his tone when he spoke. "I didn't mean it. God, I take it back."

Callum pulled his wrist away and stared blankly ahead. *Too late,* he thought, that crushing sensation strengthening. He was a burden to everyone. He already knew that. Sia, his cousins. He came in and disrupted their life by existing. They were a family, though. Ambrose was different. Maybe that's why it was more disappointing.

"Drive me back. I'm tired and Sia might get worried," he said, leaning on his window and gazing out at the property, the stars speckling the sky. He wanted to throw up. At the same time, he wanted to appear unbothered.

Ambrose was about to argue but seemed to think better of it. He sighed, turned his Jeep back on, and they drove back in silence. When they pulled up, Sia was waiting with the boys and Callum got out of the Jeep without a word. He slammed the door without even thinking and walked away.

CHAPTER 26

CALLUM

Mick flopped onto Callum's bed. "We're going to a party," he stated. Lucas ambled in after his little brother.

Callum was glad they were back on good terms, but he looked sceptically at the clock on his nightstand. "It's 11pm."

Mick laughed. "That's when parties start getting fun." He poked Callum in his ribcage, playfully. "Come with us."

He hesitated.

"It's great payback for Ambrose being such a dick," Lucas said from the doorway.

Callum's head shot up. "What do you mean? How did you know?"

Mick had the decency to look guilty. "Ambrose whined to Asther. I told Lucas." He leaned forward and clasped Callum's shoulder, "You know he was a dick to say that. He's torn up about it pretty bad, but, I mean, who cares about him right now? Come party with us. The gang back together. It'll be fun!"

Callum would never say no to Mick on anything. No one would really. That was his power. He was delightful and spoiled, but not at all obnoxious about it.

"Fine," Callum said. "Where's the party?"

***

The party was at one of Lucas's classmate's homes. The parents were away for the weekend and in typical teenage fashion that was taking advantage of for the purpose of illicit fun. It was crowded when they got there, the music booming at a volume unnecessarily loud, bodies pressed together in the cleared out living room, dancing with red solo cups in hand.

"This is awesome," Mick said, adoration in his eyes.

Dawson spotted them from the dance floor and immediately made his way over.

"Hey!" he shouted over the music. He was back in cowboy boots and wrangler jeans, a long-sleeved sweater, cup in his hand. "You never called."

Lucas said, "have fun," and immediately left. Mick shot Callum an apologetic look and subtly shrugged.

"Sorry," Callum lied.

"Want a drink?" Dawson yelled, and just for the sake of getting him away, Callum agreed.

"There's Asther," Mick said, pulling Callum over to the next room. It was slightly less loud and there wasn't dancing; plenty of bodies mingling around more lazily. Callum saw them passing around a blunt. Asther lazily patted at a space beside him where he sat on a couch and Mick dragged Callum over.

As they squished into the minimal space, Callum remembered Ambrose's warning about his dad never finding out about the two of them. He felt sad about it as he watched Asther slip an arm around Mick's waist, painted black nails tapping a rhythm on his side. If Tomas could never know, Sia probably couldn't know. That was such a shame.

"Why do you look so glum?" Asther asked. Callum always startled a little when Asther spoke. He wasn't even sure why. He didn't talk much.

"Oh," Callum shifted subtly when he saw Dawson searching for him, finding him and walking toward him. He held one cup in his hand, the other with his teeth. Callum felt a twinge of guilt, but he quickly said, before Dawson could hear, "I just hope you two are being safe. Around Ambrose's dad."

Mick grinned. "You're worried. How positively big bro of you."

Asther accepted a blunt passed to him by some random person, took a hit and said, as he exhaled, "Don't worry. We know how to work around Tomas."

Dawson was there, handing the cup to Callum. He opened his mouth, letting the other cup drop into his now free hand. "It's jungle juice," he stated.

"Cool, thanks," Callum said. Asther scooted down on the couch, pulling Mick with him so there was an obvious space next to Callum. Asther shot Callum a devilish grin before placing said grin right on Mick's mouth.

Callum looked away as Dawson took the seat, leaving absolutely no breathing room. He saw Ambrose amble in, Liam at his side. He had changed from slacks into rich jeans with a black tee and a blazer effortlessly thrown over. Their gazes met and Ambrose tented his brows in annoyance when he saw Dawson. Callum was immediately indignant. Ambrose had no right to be annoyed about anything. In an extremely petty move, perhaps the pettiest move of his life, Callum placed a hand on Dawson's knee and grinned up at him.

Dawson couldn't just leave Callum's fake advances be. His face lit up, and he leaned in, whispering, "Now it's a party."

Callum had to refrain from rolling his eyes. That would be really unfair, seeing as he was the one who was encouraging this. Briefly, he checked to see if Ambrose was still watching. He couldn't even believe how petty he was being right now, but he was already committed, and the look on Ambrose's face was like a tiny victory. Ambrose really did not like Dawson.

The weight shifted on the couch as Asther and Mick stood up.

"We are gonna go somewhere private, if you know what I mean," Mick shamelessly said. They walked past, but Asther paused and leaned over to whisper so only Callum could hear, "rub it in for a while longer. Ambrose needs it." He winked and then slid his hand into Mick's, pulling him close and kissing his neck as they walked away.

"Those two," Dawson said, "literally never see them not touching each other."

"So?" Callum said, defensively.

Dawson laughed. It was a perfectly nice laugh. Callum hated it. "No, no, I mean it's adorable."

"Oh," Callum said, his eyes scanning the room for Ambrose. He found him across the room, talking in a group with Liam. He was laughing and smiling at something some tall blonde girl was saying. He had a type. Callum rolled his eyes. Ambrose looked over at that very moment and Callum returned his whole focus to Dawson, all ears for whatever stupid thing he had to say.

"So why is it?"

"Why is what?" Callum asked. "Sorry, I missed it." Callum took a sip of the jungle juice. Apparently, jungle juice was just throwing together a bunch of different alcohols and calling it a drink. It was disgusting. He took another sip.

"Yeah, it's a little loud in here." Dawson said. "Let's find a quiet place." Dawson stood, bit the rim of his cup to hold in and held out his hand, pulling Callum from the couch. He did not let go of his hand, to Callum's chagrin, as he pulled him through the throngs of teenagers, right past Ambrose, to find a "quiet place." Ambrose raised a brow at Callum before returning his attention to the blonde girl.

Callum felt irrationally angry. He took a big sip from the disgusting jungle juice and, because he was especially stupid this night, squeezed Dawson's hand. Dawson started walking faster. He led Callum out of the house, into the freezing cold, to a small area on the back patio. Some people were scattered around, but the cold dissuaded most. The few that were out were otherwise occupied, keeping themselves warm with each other's body heat.

It was all incredibly overwhelming to Callum suddenly. He pulled his hand away from Dawson and took a drink. And kept drinking. And drinking, until his cup was empty, and he dropped it. Immediately feeling a pang of guilt for the environment, he picked it up and crunched in his hands.

"That stuff is really strong," Dawson said.

"Yeah, I gathered," Callum said, leaning against the rail for some support, his head slightly spinning.

Dawson leaned next to him, shoulders brushing. "Callum," he said with a light chuckle, "you're a delight."

How could he possibly think that? He brought out the douchiest side of Callum. Or maybe that was his type all along. Maybe Callum should start being nice to him and he would lose interest.

Dawson threw his arm over Callum's shoulders, handing him his own cup. "Here, have some more. I've had plenty."

Astutely blocking the fact that he had his mouth all over the cup, Callum took it and chugged. He hated alcohol. With his whole heart. He wasn't even sure why he was doing this. He wanted to scream. He never acted this irrationally before moving to Kansas, before meeting Ambrose. Ambrose was a specific type of infuriating.

"Thanks," he offered Dawson a smile, angling his body towards him a little. Dawson wasn't so bad, was he? Callum felt heady, a buzz building. Maybe he would try kissing Dawson. It probably wouldn't be terrible. He had never kissed anyone. Maybe it was time to try.

"There, doesn't taste so bad after you've had enough?" Dawson asked him with a wink. He handed Callum another cup. Callum had no idea where he got it from. His usual sensibilities and germ-aversions were lost to him currently, and he drank some more.

"There's two of you," he told Dawson with a giggle. Wait, did he actually just giggle? The thought of it had him giggle more. He lost his balance a little and ended up falling into Dawson.

Dawson wrapped his arms around Callum, a grin on his face, patting his back with his hand. "Man, you are adorable."

Callum smiled. With the alcohol running through his veins, with all the events of the last twenty-four hours, with his insecurities, it was nice to hear.

Dawson leaned in close, whispering, "I'm going to kiss you now."

Before Callum could process, Dawson was jerked back by his coat. "Like hell you are," Ambrose snapped, literally tossing him to the side in an impressive show of strength. Callum whistled,

"That's quite the strong stuff you got there," he said, as Dawson picked himself up angrily.

"Oh my God, Callum, you are completely wasted." Ambrose whirled on Dawson. "You think it's cool to mess around with drunk people half your size, man?!"

Liam was at Ambrose's side. He looked over at Callum, concern briefly flashing across his features. Callum felt oddly touched as he swayed on his own two feet; he had always had the impression Liam disliked him. "Hey, leave my size outta this," Callum slurred, too quietly for anyone to hear.

Dawson spat back at Ambrose. "Would you fuck off, man? We can never have a moment's peace without you lurking around. It's creepy."

Ambrose laughed. It was the opposite of Dawson's laugh in every way; disturbed and manic, and Callum loved the sound of it. "You're the one who won't leave Callum alone. Take a hint, dude. He doesn't want to fuck you."

Dawson shook his head, disbelieving. "Doesn't look that way to me."

Ambrose took a step closer to Dawson. His voice was dark, low. "He's fucking trashed you piece of shit. Haven't you noticed? The only time he flirts with you is when he's had a poisonous amount of alcohol."

Dawson turned to Callum. "Well? Why don't you call off your watchdog?"

"Hey now," Callum said, throwing up his hands. Bad idea, he realized quickly as he almost face planted the floor, so he quickly put his hands back on the rail of the porch. Lucas was coming toward them. "He's not my watchdog. He *is* really strong though, but you saw that. Felt that. Well, you know. Oh, and tall. Look how tall he is." Callum looked up at

Ambrose, demonstrating his point.

"What the fuck?" Lucas said, approaching them.

"Dawson got him really drunk," Liam explained, helpfully.

"I didn't force him to drink anything, man! He drank on his own."

Callum nodded in what felt like a professional and controlled manner. "Yes, that is true. He kept handing me cup after cup and I just kept drinking them."

Dawson's eyes widened. "Well..."

Lucas had his hands balled into fists at his sides. "Dawson. Come on. Seriously? You know he can't hold his alcohol. That was literally a major part of the conversation the last time you were over."

Dawson huffed, losing patience. "Is Callum twelve? Is he some precious prince you all bend over backwards to protect? What the fuck, man, I'm so over this! You act like he had no part in this at all! The flirting wasn't just on my side!"

Dawson shook his head, briefly glancing at Callum, and then shook his head again. He started to walk off. Ambrose grabbed the back of his coat again and pulled him back. He punctuated each word dramatically. "Don't pull this shit again, Dawson. I am losing my patience with you."

Ambrose let him go with a not so gentle shove.

Dawson left, mumbling. "Such a fucking prick."

Lucas threw an arm around Callum. "Are you okay?"

Callum nodded, "Oh yeah. You know, I think he was going to kiss me. I'm glad you came. I would have probably kissed him, and I don't think I want to. Everything is really, *really* weird in my head right now."

Lucas made a face. It looked like he was trying not to laugh. "Well, yeah, you are pretty drunk."

Ambrose made a sound like clearing his throat. Callum looked over at him. "Oh yeah, thank you," he leaned over Lucas and squeezed Ambrose's arms, "that was, wow, yeah, you really use that gym in your basement, don't you?"

Liam rolled his eyes affectionately. "Don't tell him these things. He'll be insufferable."

"He's already insufferable," Callum slurred, and then giggled.

Ambrose chuckled, but before he could respond, his phone started buzzing. He made a face when he looked at the ID and then left, answering it with a stiff *hello,* the ones reserved for his father.

"What a guy," Callum said.

Liam shook his head with a little grin. "Honestly."

"He irritates me," Callum said, feeling the urge to be honest and share everything in that moment.

"He irritates everyone," Liam agreed amicably, "that's part of his charm."

Callum started to explain, "He really hurt my feelings earlier—"

Ambrose came rushing back. His face was completely pale, and his hands were shaking. Callum gripped tighter onto Lucas, suddenly afraid.

"Liam, find Asther and Mick," Ambrose said, desperation in his tone. "We all have to get to the estate. Right the fuck now."

Ambrose's bodyguard was waiting by his Jeep. At least, Callum assumed it was his bodyguard. Ambrose insisted that they all pile in his Jeep and they would get Lucas' car later and he seemed scared and panicked enough about something that everyone went along.

"What's happening?" Asther asked, sliding into the back. With the bodyguard, there was limited space, so he pulled Mick onto his lap. Lucas and Liam squished in.

"Do I need to call Rose?" Lucas asked.

"Already did," Ambrose said, helping Callum into the passenger side. The bodyguard was driving, so Ambrose squeezed in next to Callum.

"Devin," he said to the driver, "I don't know what to do."

Callum startled. Ambrose sounded terrified. Callum leaned his shoulder on his as Devin pulled out and responded, "Sit tight, boss. Tomas will fix this."

"Fix what?" Callum asked. He tapped Ambrose's hand over and over again. "What's wrong?"

Ambrose sighed, shook his head, and pulled his hand out of reach from Callum's incessant tapping. Callum made a face.

"I—in Boston. It's something I did in Boston." He clenched his teeth. "Something none of us knew would have some pretty dire fucking consequences."

"Oh shit," Asther and Liam said from the back at the same time. Then Liam added, "Was he... who was he?"

Ambrose spat out, "Apparently, he wasn't just Mat Belleno. He was *Mattio* Belleno *Campano. The* Mattio Campano."

Callum didn't understand why it became deathly quiet in the Jeep. Why Asther started shaking his head, subtly pulling Mick closer to him. Why Liam and even Lucas were so shocked they were frozen.

"Who is Mattio?" Callum asked, stupidly. "Is he your dad's friend?"

Ambrose barked out a laugh. He didn't stop laughing. When he finally caught his breath, he wiped away tears that had streamed down his eyes. Callum smiled brightly. He didn't know what in the world was going on, but he liked when Ambrose laughed. Even though he knew it unsettled most people, it was becoming one of his favorite sounds.

Ambrose looked at Callum and then smiled, too. He rested his hand above Callum's knee. Callum remembered the night in the Jeep with Rose and cocked his head as some sort of realization dawned. He felt the strange sensation building in his lower belly.

"I'll explain everything in the morning," Ambrose said.

At the estate, things were in an uproar. Sia was waiting for them on the porch, frantically ringing her hands. Men in black suits were coming in and out, armed to the teeth.

"Woah," Callum said,

"He's drunk," Lucas warned Sia.

She sighed in relief as she ushered them into the house. Tomas surprised everyone by wrapping Ambrose in a hug the moment he walked through the door.

It was brief before he pulled away and started barking orders. "Everyone is here! Lockdown the house!" he turned to the group of them. Rose rushed over from where she was waiting on the stairs.

"Alright, here's the deal," Tomas stated matter-of-factly. "No one leaves this house until we can be assured there will be no return attack."

Callum registered the words, dimly. There were other people in the house whom he assumed were Asther's parents, the way a tall woman was hugging him over and over and the man next to her looked exactly like him. Maybe the other man was Rose's dad, though he didn't seem to harbor much concern.

Callum was still confused, but Ambrose had said he would explain so he waited.

Tomas went on, "There are plenty of rooms for everyone. My men will be on the perimeter. You are safe here."

Sia nodded in agreement and solidarity. She left with Tomas to make *an international call.* Callum thought that was pretty cool.

Ambrose sighed, his shaky hands running through his hair. "You guys can head to your rooms. They'll be guarded. I'll help Callum."

Rose subtly inclined her head towards Tomas' office. "Are you sure, Ambrose? Shouldn't I stay with you tonight?"

"Dad's pretty distracted right now, Rose," Ambrose said in a surprisingly condescending tone. "I don't know whether or not we are actually fucking is going to be on his list of priorities."

She rolled her eyes. "I get it. You don't have to be a prick."

With that, she went over to the stairs to head up. The man Callum assumed was her dad stopped her on the way. "Rose." Callum heard every word he said because he made no effort to lower his voice. In fact, he seemed to purposely pitch it high enough for everyone to hear. "Were you being disrespectful to Ambrose?"

"She was not," Ambrose called out, annoyed, "just a little lovers' spat. Happens to the best of us." He winked at Rose and smiled. It was the smile Callum associated between the two from the beginning, completely adoring. "Headon up, babe," he called to her, "I'll be right there."

She shot him a grateful look before calling back, "Love you," as she walked up the stairs.

"I love you," he returned.

Callum swallowed.

Rose's dad grinned over at Ambrose and then walked over to another room, pulling a pen from behind his ear and a notebook from his back pocket.

"I hate that man," Ambrose told Callum.

"I hate him too," Callum said in solidarity. Ambrose grinned again. It was a relief.

"Let me help you upstairs." He walked with Callum up the stairs, to the very end of the hall, the last bedroom.

It was a small room, but the bed looked big and comfortable.

"So many rooms," Callum mused. He let himself very

gracelessly onto the bed. The muted brown comforter felt like a cloud and he sighed, contended.

Ambrose shut the door and leaned against it. He watched Callum like he was the most interesting person in the world. Callum recalled the mean things Ambrose said earlier, the words playing again and again in his head and he made a face.

"What's that about?"

"How am I ruining your life?" Callum asked bluntly. He rolled onto his stomach and propped his chin up with his hands.

Ambrose winced, sliding down to the floor, his back against the door. "I was angry. I was worried. You have to believe me when I say that is the furthest thing from the truth."

Callum was quiet. After a while, Ambrose said simply, "I'm really scared, Callum."

"Because of Mattio?"

Ambrose winced. "Yeah."

"Did you kill him?"

Ambrose winced again. He didn't look at Callum when he replied, "Yes."

Callum already knew that, deep down. He was surprised that he didn't feel disgusted, annoyed, or upset. Maybe it would be different in the morning when the cursed jungle juice wasn't blurring his senses. But Ambrose didn't want any of this. That much was obvious.

"Why?" Callum asked, keeping any sort of accusation or judgement from his tone.

Ambrose briefly looked over at him before looking back at his shoes. "It's like an initiation. It's a Lastra tradition. When a member of the family turns eighteen, they kill a prisoner. I didn't want to. I throw up every night when I think about it."

"And Mattio. He was important?"

Ambrose scoffed. "He was the grandfather of the Campano branch. The literal Patriarch. Someone, somewhere, really fucked up with that. The Campano's and Lastras already have such a tentative peace as it is. And I fucking cut them off at the head."

Callum's eyes widened suddenly, afraid. Not for himself.

"Will they come for you?"

Ambrose finally looked at him. His eyes had a gleam to them, suspiciously wet. "Yes, Callum. And they won't stop until they feel they have their eye for an eye."

"Come here," Callum said, patting the space next to him.

Ambrose hesitated before straightening and walking over. He laid on the bed, a space between them. Callum rolled onto his back so they were both looking at the ceiling.

"I don't ever sleep," Ambrose said. "I just can't. Ever since I shot him, I can barely ever sleep."

"I'm sorry."

Callum searched for something to say. He was desperate for Ambrose to know that he wasn't looking down on him. That he couldn't find it in him.

"Don't be sorry," Ambrose demanded. "Don't ever be sorry. I should never sleep again. I mean, the gravity of it. I took a man's life. Just took it like it was nothing."

"It obviously wasn't nothing to you," Callum defended.

"I thought you would be mad," Ambrose admitted softly.

"I'm not."

Ambrose chuckled; Callum was close enough to feel his body shake with it. "Because you're so drunk."

"Not anymore," Callum lied, "at least not as much."

Ambrose rolled to his side, facing Callum. "I have to tell you something."

Callum rolled to his side too. "What?"

"I'm not—"

There was a knock on the door, and Ambrose practically flew out of the bed. He smoothed down his shirt and opened it, leaning out before letting Lucas in.

"Rose is in your room," Lucas said quietly. "She needs to talk to you."

Ambrose sighed but left, closing the door behind him, not saying another word.

Callum felt disappointment. Annoyance. Lucas was about to say something but just shook his head and left, too. Callum rolled onto his back again and stared at the ceiling.

CHAPTER 27

AMBROSE

Ambrose shifted in his seat, scrutinized by his father seated across from him. Sia was present, standing behind his father like a shadow. Ambrose never knew how to feel about Sia. She was kind, and she was obviously a genius lawyer—some of the messes she made disappear were incredible. But she had to be stupid in every other aspect to get in bed with his father. She had to be.

"We may have a solution to this mess," his father said finally.

Oh, you mean this delightful mess you *created by handing your eighteen-year-old a gun and telling him to shoot?* "Oh, yeah?"

Tomas sighed. "It's just... I don't like it." He turned to Sia.

She nodded. "It involves you, Ambrose. Since you were the one to pull the trigger, they want you to pull the trigger again. But for them."

"Umm," Ambrose stated. "I think I'll pass."

Tomas shot him a warning look. He hated to be disrespected, but he especially loathed it with an audience. It had to be triple bad if that audience happened to be his little fuck buddy.

Ambrose took delight in this, but he toned it down, anyway. *He* wasn't stupid. He wasn't about to piss off his dad.

"If you don't do this," his dad said. "You will be hunted by them. And they won't stop until you are dead. You know our line of business, son. An eye for an eye. It's only fair."

Ambrose choked down his scoff. "How was he the man chosen in the first place?" He tried to block out the memory of that night, drowning it out with a smile, forever out of place on his face. "Why was I killing a member of the Campano family to begin with?"

"It was less of a mishap," his father said seriously, "and more of a plant. This was done purposefully, to push the families into war. Luckily, the Campano's can be reasoned with. When they understood this, they were willing to make a deal."

"Who did this?" Ambrose asked, indignant at being a part of it, dragged into this stupid mess by being born. And never in his eighteen years of life had his father put the words *reason* and *Campano* in the same sentence.

"You don't need to worry about that," his father said, shifting. Ambrose's pulse picked up when he realized his father was uncomfortable. Which meant he was having a strange bout of protectiveness.

"Who was it?" Ambrose snapped.

Sia laid a hand on Tomas' shoulder, as if to support him.

Tomas gritted out, "I said none of your concern. We have more pressing matters. We need to settle this. Things are already tense with the Campano's. We can't afford an all-out war."

"So, let me see if I have this right." Ambrose leaned forward in his chair, elbows on his knees, hands clasped at his chin. "I killed Big Daddy Campano and they are willing to forget it all, so long as I kill their mark? As simple as that?"

Simple was laughable. Ambrose never wanted to kill again. He had sworn to himself he would never kill again.

"It is as you say," Tomas said, leaning back in his own chair, into Sia's touch. "I wish there was another way. Do you want to know the mark?"

Ambrose threw up his hands. "Absolutely dying to know."

Ignoring the quip, Tomas explained, "Do you remember Damian Magento?"

"Eccentric millionaire. Lives in a castle alone in the middle of California," Ambrose said, chest sinking. Also, someone whom Ambrose had found memories of. His father had done some business with him when Ambrose was much younger and he remembered running through the halls of Damian's castle, overjoyed. Pretending it was a different world, and he was a prince, a real prince. Damian had allowed him to explore everywhere, anywhere. Nothing was closed off or off limits because he was a child.

"That's him," Tomas said, "and thankfully, we have connections with him already. Getting him to you won't be a problem," he hesitated, "well not much of one."

Sia urged him to continue with a squeeze to his shoulder.

"You know, I wish I didn't have to do this, Ambrose. At

least you won't go alone. Devin will be with you every step of the way. He'll help you anyway he can. You will go over the winter break. No need to miss any school over this."

"How practical," Ambrose deadpanned.

"Sia and I discussed it. This mission is perfectly safe. Damian is a recluse, alone. He's making this all too easy. So, she is not averse to you taking along Lucas if you want. For company."

"I'll pass," Ambrose said. He would love to take Callum, but shame creeped in, turning his stomach sour. He was going to kill a man. A man he knew and genuinely liked. There was no way he would subject Callum to that.

"What's their deal with Damian?" Ambrose asked suddenly. "He was always good at keeping nice with the five families. What happened?"

"I don't know, and I don't care," Tomas said. "Better not to get too involved in the reasons and make this harder."

Ambrose sighed.

"We have everything in order. Damian thinks you are coming to discuss business. Over the next few weeks, I'll brief you on it. Take your time when you get to Damian. Get close to him. Get his guard down. Even though he is a recluse, he will surely have some guards. He works with too many important people not to. Devin will take care of them. But, and Ambrose, this is important, you must be the one to end Damian. You."

"Delightful," Ambrose said with a smile that conveyed the opposite.

Sia gave him a sympathetic look as he left the room, feeling defeated.

CHAPTER 28

CALLUM

The next week's Saturday dinner was equally unpleasant for Callum. The entire week had been strange; Ambrose was dejected, moody and stand-offish. None of those traits fit him. It was so jarring.

At the table, their seating was the same. The courses were pretty much the same. Callum watched as Ambrose shoved his salad around with a fork, never taking a bite.

Tomas cleared his throat. "Since we are doing this, I think it's best we are always transparent with each other. Next Friday, when winter break starts, Ambrose will be leaving for California to resolve... the problem."

Callum jerked his head up. Ambrose had astutely avoided this topic with everyone. They assumed something had been done because everyone was permitted to leave the premises and life could go on as usual.

"Alone?" Callum asked, surprising even himself. He purposefully kept quiet at these dinners, afraid to step out of line in any way and put Sia in an uncomfortable situation.

Sia answered, "Well, I said he could ask Lucas for company.

He wants to go alone."

Ambrose shot Sia a funny look. Callum *felt* funny. So he wanted to go alone. Who cares?

"Ahh," Lucas said, "no offense taken."

"None intended, truly," Ambrose said, a hand to his heart.

Callum stabbed at a stupid tomato in his stupid stuffy salad. Ambrose watched him, a tiny grin on his face. Callum wanted to punch him. That reaction always surprised him. Ever since he met Ambrose, he had the strangest urges and feelings that he never experienced before. Like extreme irritation, for example.

"It's better if I go alone," Ambrose told the table, his eyes never leaving Callum. "No point involving anyone else in what I have to do."

"Commendable," Sia told him with an encouraging smile.

"Dang, what is it you have to do?" Mick asked, wide-eyed.

Tomas cleared his throat, and Mick actually jumped a little out of his chair. Mick was really shifty around Tomas, more so than the rest of them, and Callum had to wonder if it was because of Asther. They had to keep their relationship completely private from him. Callum could never be angry with Sia, but there was a little annoyance directed at her for choosing to love another problematic man. Mick shouldn't be put in a situation where he was this uncomfortable. This was the most concerning thing to Callum about their new life, about Sia now. Mick was her baby. She was always like a mother bear when it came to him, extremely defensive and protective. Lately, she either did not notice his turmoil or chose to ignore it. The latter would be quite disappointing. But as he thought about it, so would the former.

"We don't discuss things like this at dinner. I only wanted to inform you the problem is taken care of and that there is nothing to be afraid of. No more business at the table." Tomas clipped.

"Yes, sir," Mick answered, his face red.

Sia asked, "Mick, how is school?"

A little more annoyance bubbled inside Callum. She was swiftly changing the topic, eager to keep things cool.

"It's good," Mick said quickly.

Surely that was odd to Sia? Mick never shut up on the worst of days.

"Wonderful," she beamed.

"Ambrose," Tomas asked, in between bites, "how are your grades?"

"Adequate," Ambrose replied, still pushing around his greens, never eating.

"They had better be more than adequate," Tomas stated coolly.

Ambrose sighed, setting his fork down. More like throwing it down. Callum was instantly concerned for him when he saw the look that flashed in Tomas' eyes.

"Why?" Ambrose had frustration in his tone. "There is no point. Not in my line of work."

Callum wanted to interject, tell Tomas that Ambrose had stellar grades. He was always getting perfect scores in everything, even if it seemed like he didn't try. He was one of the top scorers in the entire school. He shouldn't downplay it to his father.

Tomas' tone was ice. "It matters. I will not have my heir lacking in any sense. Are we clear?"

There was silence at the table, the most awkward kind.

Ambrose smiled, ear to ear. "Oh, yes sir, absolutely. I would never want to reflect poorly on *you.*"

Tomas threw his own fork down. "My office. Now."

Ambrose actually rolled his eyes. Apparently, all previous fear of his father lost to him, pushed his chair out and stormed away, followed by a very angry Tomas.

Sia stood. "I'm going to try and cool him down."

Hurt flashed in Mick's face. Callum saw it. You couldn't miss it. Like she would defend Ambrose, but not her own son.

"Welllllll, this is an absolute delight," Lucas declared when they were alone, save for the suited men that were sprinkled everywhere. Ambrose was raised in such a way that privacy was a foreign concept to him. Callum pitied him.

Mick's eyes glistened slightly. He said nothing.

"Hey," Callum said, "you know what, Mick? Let's do something tonight. Something fun. Whatever you want."

Mick smiled slightly. "You don't have to do that."

"Do what?"

"Baby me. I'm fine. I'm a big boy now. I can grow up."

Lucas and Callum exchanged a look. That sounded awful. Callum never wanted Mick to change; he assumed Mick would always be Mick, never daunted or deterred by anything.

"No," Lucas stated firmly. "We *are* doing something tonight. The three of us."

"Okay," Mick said. Sia returned moments later, flushed.

"Boys, let's call it a night. Ambrose needs some rest."

"What the fuck?" Lucas snapped. "Why?"

Sia hissed. "Watch your tone, son. You can't begin to understand how these things work. Take your brothers home. I'll see you soon."

She walked back out before anyone had the time to say anything.

"I hate her," Lucas stated.

Mick sighed, standing up. "No. You don't. Let's just go."

Callum followed them out. In the hall, getting their coats, Callum spotted Ambrose creeping out of the office and towards the stairs, his head down. Annoyance turned to pure anger.

Ambrose was limping, blood dripping from his leg, a tear in his jeans. Ever so briefly, before he turned, Callum saw there was a gash on his thigh, the source of the dripping blood. Did his father actually stab him?

Callum started in his direction, but Sia appeared at his side, her hand grabbing his arm. She whispered urgently, "Don't make this worse for him, Callum. Leave before I can't salvage this."

He looked at his aunt, startled. That's when he realized he had had it all wrong.

Sia wasn't happy in love.

He now recognized the emotion on her face. It was so similar to Ambrose's, the way his smiles were so strange.

No, Sia wasn't happy. She was terrified.

***

After what they saw, the three of them didn't feel like doing much, so they settled on staying in and watching a movie together.

Callum couldn't focus.

Had Ambrose's father actually cut him over some backtalk? Callum's own dad could win father of the year at this point.

The three of them sat together on the couch, Mick in the middle, snacks scattered over the end table.

"Lord of the Rings is losing its charm," Lucas admitted, stuffing some popcorn into his face.

"Never say that again!" Mick declared. "Legolas. That is all."

Amused, Lucas and Callum shared a look.

How had Callum ever thought Mick was straight? How had any of them? Mick had always had this massive, overblown crush on Orlando Bloom and any character he played. He would have to lie awake after any of those movies, listening to Mick talk about him for hours.

But Callum couldn't even begin to focus on Lord of the Rings right now.

He pulled his phone out of his pocket and thought for an

eternity before sending.

Callum: *Is everything okay?*

Stupid, really. Of course, nothing was okay.

It was an hour before he got a response.

Ambrose: *Of course. :) just peachy :)*

He could feel the sarcasm through the text. He shifted, gnawing on his lower lip, trying to pose his next question in a way Ambrose couldn't refuse.

Callum: *I need to see you. It's important. Can I come over?*

The Fellowship of the Ring was almost over by the time he got a response.

Ambrose: *Sure. Dad's gone. Just come on up.*

Callum breathed a sigh of relief. He sat with Lucas and Mick for a while after the credits rolled, just happy to have each other. If nothing else, there was always them. Three parts to a whole.

Asther showed up a little later. Lucas was going to see Rose anyway, so Callum had him drop him off on the way.

Callum entered the estate easily. Tomas hadn't lied when he said they were welcome anytime. The guards dipped their chins in greeting as Callum made his way straight to Ambrose's room, his stomach in his throat.

Ambrose was sitting languidly on a plush chair beside his bed. He looked perfectly fine, a smile on his face, and a fresh pair of jeans.

"Hey," Callum said, pinching his brows together.

"Hey," Ambrose said. He patted his bed. "Make yourself comfortable."

"How'd it go with your dad?" Callum hedged.

Ambrose smirked. "He's all bark and no bite. A little slap on the wrist. No big deal at all."

The blatant lie shocked Callum. But he understood pride, so he shelved that topic momentarily, for the reason he was here.

"Let me go with you."

Ambrose looked shocked for the briefest moment. Then his effortless smile, his terrifying smile, was back on his face. "Honored though I am, I must decline."

Callum sighed, leaning back on the palms of his hands. "Why are you being like this?"

Ambrose chuckled. "How am I being?"

"Weird. Ever since the party. Are you angry with me?"

"Of course not." Ambrose rubbed at his thigh, almost absentmindedly, then winced. Callum clenched his fists.

"Then why can't I go with you? Are you... bored with me?" Ambrose shook his head, a bite to his tone. "There is nothing boring about you." He turned his hand away from Callum, staring at the wall. "Look, it's... I am humiliated. Ashamed. I don't want you there because then you will know what I have to do."

"You have to kill him," Callum stated.

Ambrose's eyes widened. "Did Sia tell you?"

He scoffed. "No. I just figured. I'm not clueless."

Ambrose pursed his lips. "On certain things, you are very clueless."

"Whatever," Callum said, refusing to be deterred. "So, you

have to kill someone. I know you don't want to."

"I *have* to," he clipped out, "unless you think I should just meekly sit back and accept death?" here he showed vulnerability for a split second. "News flash, Callum, I'm human. I don't want to die."

Callum patiently shook his head. "No. What I am trying to say is I know this is hard for you. So let me go with you."

Callum hoped that Ambrose wanted him around, doubts again bubbling up, but he went on. "Let me help you through it."

Ambrose seemed stunned into silence. He crossed an ankle over his knee, apparently forgetting about his injury, winced, and shifted it back.

"Help me through it? *I* am the one going off to kill someone. Someone who I know, by the way, and has always been very kind to me. I should not have anyone's support, least of all yours."

"What does that mean?" Callum asked. "'Least of all not mine?' Why least of all not mine?"

"Because," Ambrose said bluntly, "you are good."

Callum barked out a laugh.

Ambrose's face shifted. "Wow," he breathed.

"What?"

Callum couldn't believe it, but Ambrose might have actually blushed. Pink tinged his ears, and he shook his head.

"I'm not good," Callum said. "I just am."

After a pause, "Take me with you."

He would beg if he had to, he realized. He understood now, had understood for a while what was happening inside of himself. Something he would never admit aloud, but something he could hold and cherish silently inside.

Ambrose almost looked relieved. "Are you sure?"

"I am."

Ambrose smiled. "I think you'll regret it."

There was a commotion from downstairs. Callum raised a brow in question.

"Probably dear old dad," Ambrose said bitterly, "and Sia. They left for a while."

"Where did they go?" Callum wanted to approach the topic of what he had seen, of the blood that had been seeping from Ambrose's leg, but he didn't want Ambrose to feel pushed in a corner. Now that he was going with him, he would have time.

Ambrose was silent for a beat too long before saying, eyes averted from Callum's, hand absently rubbing at the spot on his thigh, "Sia did it. She took him away. She does it sometimes. To cool him down."

Callum was hit by the strangest sensation of relief paired with hurt. Relief that Sia was there to stop things from getting too bad for Ambrose and hurt because that meant Callum and his cousins were pushed to the back burner more and more. It must have shown on his face.

Ambrose looked away again. "I'm sorry."

"There's nothing to be sorry for," Callum said, though he didn't believe it. There was just nothing for *Ambrose* to feel sorry for.

Ambrose's phone pinged. His brows furrowed at whatever the text was before he placed the phone back on the arm of the chair. "Rose is coming."

"I don't know if I should feel indignant for you or for Lucas," Callum admitted, a sick feeling twisting inside his chest. "The entire arrangement confuses me."

Ambrose scoffed, delighted. "Like I said. You are clueless about certain things."

Callum rolled his eyes. "I think a lot of people would be confused. I'm not an outlier, not on this."

"I wish I could explain it," Ambrose said, looking at Callum intently. "I almost did when you were wasted."

"I'm not wasted now," Callum replied, flushed a little, remembering that night. Had he really almost kissed Dawson?

Ambrose shook his head. "I can't. You are literally the last person I should tell. Callum, I wish I could." Ambrose stood then; the struggle apparent on his face though he tried to hide it. He made it to the bed in one step and sat next to Callum.

"Why?" Callum asked, trying to keep the hurt from his voice. "And don't say it's because I'm good."

Ambrose bumped his shoulder against Callum's and grinned. "Maybe one day you'll figure it out. Then you'll understand." He leaned back and sighed. "When Rose comes, she's gonna make out with me. Don't leave." The next word he whispered. "Please."

"Oh," Callum said, shifting slightly, "Okay. I won't." He

thought of Lucas. At first, he had been so angry with Lucas for the sake of Ambrose, sneaking around with his girlfriend. But now he was angry with them both. He was angry at Rose. He was confused.

Sure enough, when she came into the room, her gaze landed on Callum and determination set in her jaw. She walked over to Ambrose, sat next to him on the bed.

Three's a crowd, Callum thought.

"How are you?" Rose asked gently. Ambrose subtly shook his head, but Callum saw. He wanted to laugh. He had nothing to hide, Callum had seen.

"Poor baby," Rose said and then her lips were on Ambrose's, her hands were in his hair.

Callum found himself remembering that day in the Jeep and suddenly that was all he could think about. Almost as if he read his mind, Ambrose knotted one hand through Rose's hair and with the other, he reached over, placing it on Callum's thigh. Rose kept kissing Ambrose, and this time, Callum hoped she would never stop, as Ambrose's hand on his thigh rubbed up and down. Every time he rubbed upwards, he inched higher.

Callum shifted, embarrassed, as he hardened. Ambrose moaned into Rose's mouth.

Never in his entire life had this happened over the actions of another. Callum had relieved himself, sure, he was human, but it was always just like a necessity, going through the motions. Now, he felt like he was on fire because Ambrose's slender fingers were touching him.

A knock sounded on the door. Quick as a flash and surprisingly subtle, Ambrose tossed a pillow onto Callum's lap right as Tomas walked in.

Callum leaned his elbows into the pillow, trying to think of something, anything, to fix this. He didn't know what other people did in this situation. He wasn't used to situations like this.

Tomas was saying something, but Callum couldn't pay attention if he tried. What did this mean? Did Ambrose sense the turmoil in Callum's head and simply want to torture him? This was the second time. Was it a fuck you to Rose?

Rose had her arm slung over Ambrose's shoulder, nodding, and agreeing with whatever Tomas was saying, but there was a stiffness in her posture. She hated the man. She had come here asking if Ambrose was alright. She knew what had happened, Ambrose must have confided in her.

Why did that sting? She was his girlfriend, after all. As incredibly confusing as their relationship was to Callum, there had to be some love between them.

Callum realized that Tomas was leaving. He had literally not registered a word of what was said. His head was spinning.

Rose blew out a breath. "Well. Since you are alright and he saw enough, I'll leave." She wrapped her arms around Ambrose. "I'm really sorry, Am."

Am? Bleh.

Ambrose returned the hug. "Thank you, Rose. Really."

Callum was no longer in *the* situation. He tossed the pillow to the side. Rose looked at him, and it was a mixture of fondness and annoyance. "Bye, Callum. See you around."

"Yeah, bye," Callum said, not too kindly.

When the door clicked shut behind her, Ambrose turned to Callum. Briefly, his eyes wandered down before flicking back up to Callum's face, pupils strangely dilated. "You don't like her. Everyone likes Rose."

Callum kept his tone neutral. "I don't really know her."

Ambrose smiled. "Be fair now, Callum. If it's because of the Lucas-me-Rose situation, then there are three consenting adults involved. You can't put the blame on Rose."

Callum startled at this. Ambrose was right, of course. But then, that wasn't really his issue with Rose. He couldn't say anything on that so instead.

"Liam said she cheats a lot," he blurted, protecting himself from revealing something damning. Ambrose obviously loved Rose more that she loved him if he let those things slide. That irritated Callum. There should be equal love and obsession in a relationship, otherwise what was the point?

Ambrose laughed. "Liam says a lot of stupid shit. Haven't you realised? He means well, but he's just an idiot." There was a fondness in Ambrose's tone.

"You have odd friends."

"Hey now. You are one of them."

Callum felt a headache forming at his temples. Did they just act like nothing happened two minutes earlier? He was embarrassed, mingled in with shame he didn't understand.

Was it just a game to Ambrose?

Suddenly, Callum was annoyed. Feeling like he had just been played with and discarded, he stood. "I better get back."

Ambrose's face fell. He stood too, keeping the weight off his left leg.

"Callum," his voice was husky.

Callum waited, but Ambrose said nothing else. He just stood there, waiting too, as if he dared Callum to be the one to bring it up.

"See you Monday," Callum said, and he quickly turned away. He knew Ambrose wouldn't follow. He couldn't follow.

***

He hadn't really thought this through. He had been on a plane once in his life and he had planned on it being the last. Something about flying in a small helicopter was even more terrifying.

Ambrose approached him, a messenger bag hanging at his side, casual in grey sweats, and a white fitted tee. His limp was almost entirely gone. The whole week he had hardly seen him at all; he avoided him when he could, and he had a feeling Ambrose had been doing the same. Callum's reason was embarrassment; Ambrose had gotten him hard and then acted as if it were nothing. Another day in his life. He figured Ambrose's reason was guilt, not over that, but the impending murder he would have to commit.

Tomas and Sia came to see them off, and Devin and another, Vincent. Vincent was assigned to Callum, making him feel entirely out of his element. Never in his life could he have imagined a version of himself that needed a bodyguard.

Sia embraced him. "Be careful," she told him, a little worry in her eyes. It became apparent to Callum that when he told her he would go with Ambrose that she had never intended for any of the boys to actually go along. She had offered Lucas as an offering she knew would be refused. An empty gesture.

Callum swallowed.

"I know you hate planes," her voice dropped to a whisper so only he could hear. Tomas was absorbed anyway, hammering more details into Ambrose.

Callum could never like the man. Never in a million years.

Sia went on, "Helicopters are so much safer, and Harry has been a pilot for many years. You are in the best hands."

"Okay," he said, his hands nervous with sweat at his sides.

"Last chance," she said, "you can stay here. With me. Where you belong."

Belong.

There was pleading in her eyes.

Strangely, even if this were just a month ago, Callum's heart would have somersaulted. He would have been overjoyed. Now, he was happy, yes, but he had grown. He realized that there was nothing he could do that would make him not part of their family. He was their family. He didn't have to walk on eggshells or constantly try to please them, even if the urge was still there.

"Ambrose shouldn't go alone," he said.

Sia made a strange face, nodding. She squeezed his shoulder. "You are such a good friend. You two are quite the pair."

Callum grinned slightly, and Ambrose ambled over with a smile on his face. His manic smile was tinged with the undeniable hint of worry. What was ahead of them was madness. Callum could hardly believe he had decided to come, to be a part of it.

"Ready?" Ambrose asked him.

"Ready." Callum followed Ambrose into the helicopter. It was more cramped than cosy and Ambrose showed him how to get situated, giving him a head and mouthpiece. They would need to communicate over the sound.

Ambrose winked at Callum, pulling out a little pill bottle.

"I hate flying," He admitted. "So I have no shame popping one of these and sleeping the whole time. You in?"

While it wasn't exactly awkward between the two, it was different, terse.

"Yes," Callum said without hesitation, eliciting a chuckle from Ambrose. He passed him a little yellow pill. Callum didn't even care what it was. He trusted Ambrose enough to not give him something dangerous. He swallowed.

The next thing he remembered, he was waking up, body uncomfortably hunched over in the seat, the copter landing.

CHAPTER 29

AMBROSE

Ambrose was livid. Over the past few years, Damian must have had a complete personality change. When they approached the castle, landing on the jet pad a few miles south, then driving in an all-road vehicle left for their purpose, they arrived to quite the shock.

Back when Ambrose was young, Damian had been a recluse, keeping to himself in the castle like his life depended on it. Which, looking back, maybe it had. Ambrose had been too young to understand much of the business.

The castle was much the same, grand stone, looking like something straight from medieval times. It was delightful to watch Callum take it in, his throat working as he sighed in awe. Ambrose almost blushed, had been almost blushing every time he caught a glimpse of Callum lately. The memory of that night, one week ago, burned hot in his mind, encouraging worthlessly stupid hope. Hope that he had to douse before he made a mistake before he put both of them in danger.

Damian hadn't greeted them at the gates. A young man, thirty at best, introduced himself as Benedict, one of Damian's many manservants. He led them through the first room, The Great Hall. Callum silently took in every detail, and Ambrose silently took in Callum.

They were led through a door at the end of the Hall that brought them to an office, startling and out of place in its modernism. Damian sat at a large steel desk, looking not a day older, lost to something on his laptop.

Benedict cleared his throat.

"What is it, Benedi—" he started in a tone that could not be considered kind. He stopped himself mid-sentence when he looked up to see Ambrose and Callum, accompanied by two guards. His tone changed, a bright, mesmerizing smile on his lips. "Ambrose Romano," he cooed, standing. "My, how you have grown."

Damian wrapped Ambrose in an intrusive, unexpected embrace. He smelled like too much cologne. Nostalgia had Ambrose returning the embrace, wrapping his arms around a body that definitely spent time in a gym.

"I'm so glad your father sent you!" he said delightedly, stepping back to give Ambrose a once over. Ambrose tried not to shift under the scrutiny, keeping a smile on his face. "I remember you so fondly," in a conspirator whisper he added, "your father, not so much. Quite *difficult,* that one. Never very kind to those of us who weren't straight edge heteros."

Callum shifted next to Ambrose, catching Damian's attention. Ambrose was stuck on the last words he had spoken; was Damian gay then? That would explain the lack of communication between his father and him over the years.

"And who is this?" Damian asked, bringing Ambrose back.

"Callum. My friend." He didn't introduce the bodyguards. It felt gross not to, but it was considered inappropriate; they were there to silently observe and to protect when needed. A bodyguard left their persona behind when they clocked in and they were often treated as such. Ambrose had a fondness for Devin, even Vincent. But Ambrose had a problem with forming attachments to anything that breathed. His father often bemoaned the fact.

"Interesting," Damian said, raising a light eyebrow. "You bring a friend along in this kind of work."

Ambrose clarified. "He's the son of my father's lawyer. The family is very involved... in the work, as you put it."

He stuffed his hands into the pockets of his sweats out of habit, adopting a causal stance.

"Nice to meet you," Callum said, though Damian's attention had long left him, his eyes back on Ambrose. Ambrose, too, felt drawn into Damian's orbit in the way a nephew might towards an uncle they hadn't seen in some time. Fondness swelled in his chest looking at him, well into his forties, maybe fifties, looking not a day over thirty, rich dark blonde hair and eyes.

"Well, let me get you boys settled. I'm afraid we are running out of space; I wasn't expecting Callum. I hope you don't mind sharing a room?"

Ambrose made a strange sound before clearing his throat. Callum shifted.

"I recall you having plenty of rooms," Ambrose said, keeping his voice light. Did he imagine Callum stiffening? Why did Ambrose always insist on being an idiot, on doing stupid shit like touching Callum while he kissed Rose, when he was supposed to be appearing straight?

Delighted, Damian tapped his own nose. "You see, I am having a weekend. Quite the weekend. An event, a medieval style party. Think of it as in your honor."

He started walking, expecting them to follow.

Callum fell in line with Ambrose. Ambrose's stomach twisted, new nerves making themselves known at the thought of a castle crowded with people. More bodies meant more witnesses meant higher risk. His head was swimming.

"You don't mind?" Damian asked, stopping when they reached the stairs. Ambrose almost ran into him, lost in thought, trying not to panic. He had brought Callum into this.

"Oh sorry," Ambrose said, screeching to a halt. "What was the question?"

Damian chuckled, good naturally. "I was saying it's going to be a full house for the first few days of your visit. You don't mind, do you?"

"Nah," Ambrose said, casually. "I remember you as sort of a recluse, though. I'm surprised."

Damian nodded, hand on the banister as he ascended the impressive stairs. "I was struggling in my twenties and thirties. Denying who I really was and hating life because of it. When I came into my own skin, got comfortable with my preferences, everything changed." He turned back, flashing a grin at them as he continued up. "Life is grand now, every day a party!"

Callum didn't say a word, adjusting his backpack and keeping his eyes lowered. He seemed wildly uncomfortable, and Ambrose realized with a sinking feeling that he was probably regretting coming.

"I see," he replied, forcing himself to smile. "That's wonderful. Glad you can be yourself."

There was almost a bitterness for Damian now, mingled with the fondness. A sick jealousy of sorts. Ambrose couldn't see a future where he could ever comfortably be who he was. Briefly, his eyes flitted to Callum.

They reached a landing, with a sprawling red carpet, doors on either side of a long hall. Ambrose figured the bedrooms totalled fifty at a minimum, so the party was a bit of an understatement.

"Some of the guests have already arrived," Damian was saying, stopping at the very first door on the right, digging for a key in his pocket and unlocking. It opened to a room the size of a home, with a grand four-poster bed, dark reds lined with gold everywhere he looked. The bed. The bed he was going to share with Callum. He swallowed. It looked massive; at least there was that. He was both relieved and acutely disappointed.

Callum stared at the bed. Ambrose watched as he swallowed, Adam's apple bobbing. He tightened his grip on his messenger bag and turned to Damian. "It's lovely. Thank you."

Damian waved a hand dismissively. "Don't mention it, my

boy. We will get to the business side of things, don't worry. But I think pleasure should always come first."

"I like the way you think," Ambrose returned with a grin.

CHAPTER 30

CALLUM

When Damian left, Callum felt like he could breathe again. He tossed his bag to the side. Vincent and Devin had left the room, taking up guard on the other side.

Ambrose placed his bag on a rough-looking chair–everything in this place looked like it was authentic from the past, and Callum hated it.

"Devin will grab our other bags later," Ambrose said, plopping onto the bed, kicking off his shoes, never looking directly at Callum.

"Oh," Callum said, looking at his own bag, "this is all I have."

Ambrose laughed, closing his eyes, his hands behind his head.

"Damian is weird," Callum said. He stayed standing awkwardly by the door, like he wasn't sure what he should do. He crossed his arms over his chest, leaning against the wall to give off a casual vibe. Furthest from how he actually felt.

"What do you mean?" Ambrose asked, looking at him for a moment before closing his eyes again.

Callum wasn't even sure himself. It was gross the way

Damian looked at Ambrose like he wanted to tear into him, especially since he was well older and knew him as a child. Ambrose seemed clueless about it all.

He didn't know what to say, so he sighed and said nothing. He had instantly disliked Damian. Maybe it was warranted, maybe he was being ridiculous.

"You'll like him soon enough," Ambrose stated confidently. "He's like family to me. Damian is kind. He's just a little eccentric."

Callum said nothing, hardly convinced. He walked over to the door on the other wall and found the bathroom. Shutting himself in, he sifted through his clothes. He wasn't sure what someone would wear to a medieval style party, but he was sure he didn't have it. After a while, Callum settled on his nicer pair of jeans and a plain black tee. He thought it was weird for adults to dress up, anyway. Like, grow up.

He adjusted his overgrown curls, styling his hair to at least be presentable. By the time he walked out, Ambrose was sleeping. Callum grabbed the throw from the bottom of the bed and got as comfortable as he could in the chair.

He was startled awake by a knock on the door. Ambrose groggily wiped at his eyes and called, "come in."

When his gaze landed on Callum in the chair, he made a strange face. He said nothing though because Devin peeked his head in.

"Sorry boss. Damian wanted me to wake you so you could join the party."

"Now worries, we'll be out in a few."

Devin ducked back out, and Ambrose crawled out of bed. It felt strangely intimate to Callum.

"Flying always wipes me out, man," Ambrose said, stretching. His tee shirt rode up slightly, revealing an inch of skin. "I'll change really quick."

He ducked into the bathroom after grabbing a suitcase that was by the door, most likely put there by Devin, unaware of Callum's sigh. Ambrose wouldn't even look at him. Callum wondered if he had made a big mistake, if Ambrose really didn't want him here, if those moments with Rose were less than nothing to him.

He wasn't even sure what they were to *himself*. How could he cherish those moments when he was just being toyed with? Time and time again, Ambrose had confirmed his love for Rose. Why did that make Callum feel so annoyed?

Ambrose came out minutes later looking delightfully current, and, much to Callum's relief, not a drop of his ensemble representing anything medieval. He wore black skinny jeans and a black t-shirt with some red detailing. His shoes were chunky converse hightops, the classic black and white. His hair was combed up and back. Callum felt his stomach tightening as he stared for a beat and a half too long.

When his eyes wandered back up to Ambrose's face, he was looking at Callum. He didn't look away. Even though he had been internally bemoaning the lack of eye contact, Callum was the one to break it.

"I guess we should go downstairs," he said.

Ambrose chuckled, but it was strained. "You couldn't sound less enthusiastic."

Callum couldn't *feel* less enthusiastic. He wasn't expecting to come here and have to mingle with complete strangers, dressing up like the past was something to care about. Callum always believed the past was better left buried. That's where he liked to keep his.

"It'll be fine," Ambrose said when Callum was silent for too long. "Just stick to me. We can have a few drinks and then duck out. I just need Damian to get comfortable with us. With me."

He'd love that, Callum thought, but aloud he said, "Alright." He played with a thread on his jeans before admitting. "I'm nervous around people I don't know."

Ambrose laughed, and said not unkindly, "yeah, no shit." he paused before adding, "stay by me."

It was more of a plea. Callum was startled by it, looking at him directly, but Ambrose was chewing on his lower lip, hands stuffed in his pockets, staring at his sneakers.

When they opened the door, they were met by the sounds of a party, the hall upstairs even a bustle with people coming and going from their rooms. One couple, two women, were already retiring from the party, making out as they eagerly pushed each other into the room across from theirs.

Ambrose chuckled, lighter already. No matter what he might say, Callum knew he fed off energy, could relax in a crowd. "Your ears are as red as tomatoes, Callum."

Callum said nothing because the way Ambrose said his name was different than usual, like softer, richer. It was all in his head, of course; he was self-aware enough to know that, but it still had his stomach flipping.

They wandered down the stairs, passing more people than Callum had imagined. He imagined this was an added stress to Ambrose, making the entire reason they had come here even more difficult. Callum kept purposefully forgetting the real reason they came here in the first place; so Ambrose could kill a man.

The Great Hall was packed and on the far wall, dressed like a knight, was a DJ, spinning music that was so modern as to be jarring in the setting. Some people came dressed up for the theme and others, like Callum and Ambrose, chose not to. It was enough to muddle the mind, the constant contrast throughout the castle of old and new.

Damian waved them over to where he stood with a group of men and one woman.

"You have to meet Ambrose," he was saying as they approached. "He's Tomas

Romano's son."

"*The* Tomas Romano?" the woman asked, a hand to her chest. She was one of the few dressed in modern attire, a tight white sparking gown that hung low, displaying plenty of cleavage.

Ambrose was obviously tense next to Callum, he was standing close enough to him to feel but from his smile, no one could tell.

"That's me," he said brightly.

Damian clasped Ambrose on the shoulder and, to the group, stated, "Much less of a stick in the mud, though." The group chuckled. Damian was wearing the garb of a king, crown, and all.

Subtle, Callum thought.

The woman looked Callum up and down. She was younger, late twenties maybe,

and just as subtle as Damian; that is to say, not subtle at all, "Who is this charming fellow?"

The way she asked it had his hair on end.

Ambrose threw an arm around Callum's shoulder, pulling him closer playfully.

"This is my friend, Callum. His mom is my dad's lawyer."

The lady made a face. "Ahh, the infamous Sia." Callum's pulse picked up. "The woman who caught Tomas's eye."

"Now, now," Damian interjected. "Olivia, let's not make them uncomfortable."

Ambrose smiled at their host. "Hardly, Damian. You've been so gracious; we feel perfectly at ease."

When Damian touched Ambrose's arm, and said, "I'm relieved." His hand lingered. And lingered.

Olivia asked, "How old are you, Callum?"

"Seventeen."

"Ahh," her face fell. "A bit too young for me." She looked at her nails, then back up at Callum. "What a pity."

Ambrose cleared his throat, his arm tightening around Callum's shoulders defensively. Callum felt disgusted at the implications of this woman, so much older than himself, and he felt light with the weight of Ambrose's touch. "Callum and I are going to grab a drink, if you'd excuse us, Damian?"

Damian reached out and touched Ambrose's arm again. It was completely unnecessary contact, in Callum's opinion. He dug his nails into his palm, deep.

"I'm a terrible host! Follow me, I will serve you."

Ambrose casually dropped his arm from Callum's shoulder as they followed their host to a table against the wall. The alcohol was served in medieval style goblets, but there was also a punch bowl by red solo cups.

Damian spoke to everyone he passed, introducing Ambrose here and there–never Callum. It was like Callum wasn't there, invisible to him. Callum might as well start calling him *dad* and be done with it.

He asked them what they wanted, and Ambrose said, "We'll both have a whiskey and coke, if we can?"

He shot Callum a quick grin, stuffing his hands in his pockets and returning his attention to Damian. "So, do you have parties like this often?"

Damian opened a Coke, the *snap* lost in the noise of the party, Lady Gaga thumping over the speakers, bodies pressed together in the center of the floor as they danced.

"No," Damian said, honestly. "Just once or a month or so. I have dinner parties a lot, but I built this stupid castle in the middle of nowhere. It's hard to get up here, and that was the whole point back then, but now I regret it a bit." He handed Ambrose a goblet, eyes falling on Callum for a brief second as if remembering he was still there, and turned to mix another drink. "Honestly, I have your father to thank in a strange way, for my comfort in my own homosexuality. Believe it or not."

Ambrose sputtered mid-drink. "Oh, you have to tell me more."

Absently, Damian passed the now finished drink to Callum. Some of it sloshed onto his shirt. Callum hid his scowl in the rim of the cup as he took a sip. Just as expected, it was absolutely disgusting.

Damian leaned his palms on the table with the drinks. Someone came up to mix their own, and he waited until they had walked away before saying, "The last time your father and I spoke, well, before this time, was when he found out I was gay. I thought we had enough repertoire to come out to him." He chuckled without mirth. "He was actually one of the first people I had ever told. I was struggling with immense guilt, the joys of growing up a Catholic. Your father said I was right to feel disgusted in myself, that I was an abomination. That riled my feathers, I'm a proud man, and he had just taken a swipe at it. Almost as a fuck you to him, I came out to the entire world, I stopped hiding. Once I did, it wasn't exactly like I just became comfortable with it overnight, but it was better. It kept getting better." He spread his arms wide, a grin on his face, solely for Ambrose, all of this for Ambrose. "And here I am now."

Ambrose dipped his goblet in Damian's direction, a little toast, and spoke. "Well, cheers to that. Glad he could be of service in his own fucked up way."

"It must be hard for you," Damian said. "Since he's your father. Maybe he will accept you because he loves you so much."

Ambrose's expression was pinched as he said, "Ahh, you've got it wrong, Damian. I'm actually straight. And madly, stupidly in love with Rose. You've worked with her father before. Been dating for almost four years." He winked at Callum. "Though I've had to share her occasionally."

Damian cocked his head. "I remember Rose. I'm sorry to assume. Ever since I've known you, I just assumed you were gay. My bad."

Ambrose's smile was strained. "No worries."

On a loop in his brain, Callum was hearing *madly, stupidly in love with Rose.* It wasn't like it was some news flash to him; he'd known this. Still, jealousy wrapped its claws around his throat, forcing him closer to acknowledging the feelings that were forming.

Damian was saying, "Though, Ambrose, you know me. We've always had a good relationship, whether your father was being an ass. I'm open to talk to you anytime," He touched Ambrose again, for what, the thirtieth time that night? His eyes were boring right through him. "If you need to get anything off your chest." This man was overkill. Callum found him to be immensely tacky. *Be yourself, love who you are, blah blah*

blah. As if it were that easy.

With his other hand, Ambrose squeezed the hand Damian had on him. "I appreciate that. Thank you. Really."

Callum took a big, long gulp of the hideous drink in his hands. He felt more like a third wheel now than he ever had with Rose. Ambrose was oblivious to what was happening right in front of his face. Who was the clueless one now?

"Ahh," Damian said. "I have to go speak to that man." He inclined his head towards a tall, dark man in a purple suit. "Ambrose, he's associated with the Mangano's, so I won't suffer you to meet him."

Ambrose laughed. "Appreciated."

When he was out of earshot. Callum asked, "He works with the other families too? That sounds messy. What is it he does, exactly?"

"He's a genius hacker," Ambrose said, before taking a sip from his goblet. "He can get into anyone's account, basically." Ambrose's gaze followed Damian as he walked over and greeted the man in the purple suit. He pursed his lips before looking back at Callum. "He can do anything really, but he's eccentric about it. You really have to go through the ringer before he will agree." Ambrose did a quick scan to make sure they were out of general earshot before adding, "I'm here under the pretence of getting him to hack into a Lastra account. Like we have trouble in paradise, that sort of thing."

Callum finished off his drink. At this rate, he might as well pretend to like the stuff; he'd been drinking it enough lately.

"Delightful."

"He's a great guy, Callum," Ambrose insisted. "I don't know why you have to be so rude to him."

Callum scoffed. "Me? Rude to him?"

Ambrose tented his eyebrows. "He's been a perfectly decent host."

Again, the desire to punch Ambrose caught Callum off guard. He sighed. "Okay," he lied, "sorry." He set his goblet on the table. Ambrose picked it up and started to mix another drink for him.

He sighed too. "No, don't apologize. I shouldn't be trying to get you to like him, ya know, given the circumstances."

Callum smiled at the fucked-up-ness of it all.

Ambrose passed him the drink, cocked his head and spoke. "You hardly ever smile. When you do, I feel relieved," Ambrose looked down at his own drink, awkward, "Relieved that I'm able to cause it."

Callum swallowed, unsure of how to respond. Confusion was a natural state of his mind whenever he was around Ambrose, but now, he was sure he was picking up mixed signals; he had to be.

"I'm not a very smiley person," Callum admitted stupidly. The DJ switched over to some obnoxious techno and it was getting louder and louder. Damian had left the room, towards his modern office with the man in the blue suit. "Unlike you."

Ambrose laughed. "Are you saying I smile too much?" He had inched closer during their conversation to hear over the music.

Callum felt his breath quicken. "Is there such a thing as smiling too much?"

Ambrose leaned a palm on the table, his other hand in his pocket. Callum's own hand leaned on the table, mere inches away. "Yes. If they aren't genuine."

Callum didn't bother asking if Ambrose's weren't genuine. They rarely were. Callum could tell the difference now; the less manic smiles were his genuine ones, but they were few and far between. He understood, though. Hiding behind a smile made perfect sense for Ambrose.

He was about to respond when he saw Damian exit his office and head towards them. When he approached, he said, "A few of us are gonna pop into the lounge and partake. Would you care to join?"

Ambrose took another big swig. "You don't have to ask me twice. Callum here doesn't partake much per se, but he'll join since he's good company, regardless."

"I'll take your word for it," Damian said in a flat tone.

Callum felt indignant for himself as he followed them out of the hall down to another room. Inside, it again was a bit disconcerting at how modern it was compared to most of the castle; it was filled with leather couches and row upon row of bookshelves stuffed with very modern-looking books.

A few other men were in the room, two women, one being Olivia, much to Callum's chagrin.

Damian directed them to one of the leather couches, sitting

obnoxiously close to Ambrose. Callum sat on Ambrose's other side. Across from them, a man dressed like a bard leaned forward in his seat to cut lines of cocaine on the small tabletop between them. Damian removed the crown from his head, tossing out behind them.

"How many lines am I cutting here, boss?" the man asked of Damian.

"The occupants of this room minus one." He pointed over at Callum. "We have a moralist in our midst."

Callum felt the tips of his ears go red.

"How adorable," Olivia crooned from the couch across from them.

Ambrose casually patted Callum's knee and defended cheerfully. "Nothing wrong with morals."

Damian chuckled, leaning back. His arm leaned on the back of the couch, precariously close to an embrace with Ambrose. "Morals are a bit out of place amongst our kind, wouldn't you say?"

Callum felt Ambrose tense. Callum himself had never felt so uncomfortable in his life as all eyes were on him, judging him for his lack of a lack of morals.

Olivia interjected, "I think we need a little moral here and there. Keep us grounded." She winked at Callum before leaning over, accepting a rolled a silver straw looking thing from the man who had cut the lines and snorting one in one quick motion. "I like the kid."

Callum said nothing. Ambrose leaned into him slightly.

Damian smiled predatorily. "He's a dear friend of Ambrose, so he must be a charmer." He leaned in, and with the same silver straw that had been in Olivia's nose, snorted his line before passing it to Ambrose. Callum was disturbed that no one was cleaning it in between snorts, but he was not about to say anything.

When Ambrose leaned in to partake, his thigh pushed against Callum's. He snorted it, leaned back and sighed, content. His pupils were dilated, his hair was falling around his eyes, and he looked absolutely wild in a beautiful way. Callum couldn't stop looking. When Ambrose noticed, he smiled, and Callum almost couldn't breathe because it was genuine, it was real.

Fuck, he thought.

The others did their lines and then the man started cutting some more.

Damian was leaning against Ambrose. Ambrose was wildly tapping his own knee, leg bouncing in the restlessness of his high.

"Are you sure you won't try some, pretty boy?" the man asked Callum as he cut.

Callum hesitated. Ambrose placed his hand on his knee again, squeezing. "He's okay," Ambrose insisted, pleasantly. "He doesn't like the way it makes him feel, honestly."

Callum was grateful for the lie. He couldn't believe he had even been considered snorting a line just now. It was not even something he remotely wanted to do. He smiled his thanks at Ambrose, leaned into him a little. Ambrose left his hand on Callum's knee, tapping it restlessly with his long, slender fingers. Callum was grateful for the drink in his hand, finishing it off. He felt the effects of his two drinks. He almost worried for a second that they were fools, losing their sense among strangers and a man they were meant to kill but then he remembered that Vincent and Devin were out mingling with the party. Watching their every move. He relaxed slightly.

Damian was literally whispering something in Ambrose's ear. Ambrose giggled at whatever it was. They passed around the straw, doing their second lines in turn. Ambrose bounced his leg with more fervor, knocking again and again against Callum's thigh, his fingers still playing on Callum's knee.

Olivia leaned across the table to ask Callum, "What are you into, pretty little boy?" She, like Ambrose, was restless. The man next to her was touching her obscenely, and she leaned into it here and there, drug-addled brains just itching for touch.

Callum desperately wanted to leave the room. Two men behind their couch were making out against one of the shelves in a rated R fashion.

"By into, what do you mean?"

"Who do you like to fuck?" she asked. She adjusted herself so that she was half in the lap of the man who was exploring her body with his hands. Next to him, Ambrose leaned his head back against the couch, smiling at the ceiling, oblivious to the turmoil of his friend. Out of the corner of his eye, Callum saw Damian drop his arm so that it was around Ambrose. He shifted,

"I don't, as you put it, *fuck.*"

Olivia laughed, a high-pitched shriek, startling Ambrose. He sat up, to Callum's relief, out of the touch of Damian.

"Did you hear that?" Olivia asked the room. "He doesn't partake in any of the world's pleasures, it appears!"

The man who had cut the lines looked more interested than shocked. "You ace, man?" he asked.

Ambrose's fingers on Callum's knee seemed to tap faster, harder.

"No," Callum admitted. "I'm probably demi if it's anyone's business."

"You are so fucking adorable," Olivia squealed. "I wish you were just a year older."

Ambrose said, his tone deceptively light. "You know, saying that you wish he was of age is almost just as creepy."

The irony was that Damian, who had been well into adult years when Ambrose visited as a child, was obviously trying his hardest to get a taste. Ambrose might be of age now, but Callum thought it was still disgusting and creepy. These people made him feel gross and dirty.

Olivia laughed at Ambrose's remark. She abruptly turned her face on the man she was half-sitting on and started making out.

"Yuck," Damian said with a chuckle. "Take that straight shit somewhere else."

Obediently, they headed for more privacy.

"Hey, Mikey, Nate, take their place," Damian called. The two men who were making out by the shelves grinned, taking the seats Olivia and the man had just vacated. They started making out again and Damian leaned forward, watching with delight.

"Too bad you aren't into this sort of thing," he said to Ambrose, though it ended as more of a question. Then to the two, he demanded, "Ramp it up boys, I need some material for tonight."

Mikey chuckled. He straddled Nate, rolling his hips as he continued to tongue his mouth. Nate moaned. The others in the room were all watching too, like it was some live porn show. Ambrose gave Callum an apologetic look. He returned his gaze to the men putting on their little show. His hand on Callum's knee restlessly moved to his thigh, where he squeezed.

Callum was frustrated. He was always touched by Ambrose in the most awkward, humiliating situations. How could he even begin to parse what his strange feelings meant if it was always like this? Why did Ambrose insist on playing with him like a toy?

Yet, he made no move to stop it. He leaned back awkwardly on the couch. He didn't want to be here, but he couldn't really look away. Morbid curiosity kept him watching. Mikey pulled off Nate's shirt, discarding it in a pile on the floor. He sucked one of Nate's nipples into his mouth. Nate threw his head back, biting back moan after moan.

Ambrose looked at Callum, looked away, looked back. His

hand on Callum's thigh was gripping so tight it almost hurt. Impulsively, perhaps aided by the alcohol, Callum rested his hand on top of the hand on his thigh, delighting in the feel of Ambrose's delicate fingers under his.

Ambrose stared at Callum's hand on his like he might be dreaming.

Next to Ambrose, Damian was taking off his belt, unzipping his pants. Callum looked away, knowing what was coming next and having no desire to see. His face was burning. These people were sick. Who did shit like this?

"This is the part where I jerk off. Fair warning," he told them.

Ambrose flipped his hand over under Callum's, lacing their fingers together and standing. "No offense meant, but we will take our leave then."

Damian had his cock in his hands shamelessly. He raised a brow at their joined hands, smirked, and shrugged. "Off with you then. See you in the morning."

Ambrose pulled Callum along with him, his fingers tapping against his, their palms squished together. They pushed their way through throngs of people, headed to the stairs, then up to their room, hands never separating.

Callum wickedly thought he wouldn't mind Ambrose having a coke addiction if it meant he would touch him. He would forget about Rose for a while. He would *like* touching Callum.

Devin and Vincent were close behind, taking up their spots at either side of the door. Ambrose said goodnight to them, pulled Callum in and shut the door.

He dropped his hand, ran it through his hair. "I don't usually do cocaine. I couldn't refuse, though. He needs to be comfortable with me."

"You don't have to explain to me," Callum said, awkward now that Ambrose had taken his hand away, "or justify it. If you want to do cocaine, do cocaine."

Ambrose tilted his head, pupils still dilated. "I'm sorry if you were—" he cleared his throat, "—uncomfortable back there."

"Which part?" Callum asked, as casually as he could.

"All of it. Olivia was inappropriate with her questions and then Damian just, like, whipped his dick out in front of us all. Cocaine makes you super sensitive to touch, which is beneficial for sexual pleasures but, I mean, that doesn't excuse his behaviour. He... he's so different," Ambrose sighed. "I know it's been years since I saw him last, but fuck, he's so different."

Callum's brain sort of snagged on the part about being sensitive to touch. He cleared his throat. "I'm sorry. This all must be so hard for you."

Ambrose looked at Callum. He moved closer. He was so much taller than Callum's below average height that Callum had to look up to meet his gaze.

Ambrose swallowed and looked away. "C'mon. Let's go to bed."

Callum flushed, turning to look at the bed. The one bed.

Ambrose pulled off his shirt, his chest on full display. Callum felt a surge of anger at the scattering of scars. He could guess who inflicted them. Then Ambrose took off his shoes, clumsily, his socks and his pants, stripping down to his black boxers.

Ambrose was glorious, toned, and slender, with long, long legs that were making Callum feel hot under his t-shirt.

Callum saw the freshly healed scar on Ambrose's thigh, probably three whole inches in length. Leaning on the fact that they were both inebriated, he reached forward, traced it with a finger and said in a whisper, "Your dad is a fucking waste of space." Lucas would surely be proud of the amount of times Callum had cursed on this trip.

Ambrose laughed, breathlessly.

"You knew."

Callum nodded. "Yeah, I knew."

Face to face, they took in each other. Ambrose had plenty of scars scattered across his body. He was the most beautiful person Callum had ever seen. Callum was overwhelmed with these new feelings, feelings he had never felt before and had accepted that he might never. Of course, it had to be Ambrose. The feelings had to be attached to someone impossible, someone messy, someone otherwise taken. It was poetic in a twisted, depressing sort of way.

Ambrose gnawed at his lower lip, insistent on killing Callum slowly. "My dad means well," he said. "He has a sick way of disciplining me, but I think it's out of fear. He's scared that I'll get myself killed or something, so he gets my attention in drastic ways."

Callum shook his head. "It's fucked up, Ambrose."

Ambrose laughed. "It's so funny when you curse."

Callum grinned. "You're changing the subject."

"Let's just go to bed," Ambrose said, wandering over and folding himself onto the mattress.

"I'm gonna change," Callum said, moving towards the bathroom.

Ambrose waved a hand. "Just strip, Cal. We're all friends here."

Callum really had no reason to argue. What could he say, *hey I better not? I'm starting to think I'm attracted to you. Don't say friends, it's like ice water on my skin.*

Ambrose flipped from his stomach to his back. "Well?"

Callum pulled his shirt off, slipped out of his shoes and socks and, hesitant for a moment, took off his pants. He stood in his ocean blue boxers, feeling completely naked.

Ambrose was staring at him.

"Woah," Ambrose said.

"What?" Callum asked, swallowing.

"You..." he patted the bed. "Never mind. Come on. We need to sleep."

Callum went to the bed, careful to keep a space between them, unsure of what was happening. Ambrose winked at him, sitting up. "Watch this," he said as he leaned over to one of the posters, pulling on the ribbon around the curtain. The red bed curtain fell. Ambrose moved around the bed, removing all four ribbons. They were in the dark now, in their own little bubble. Callum was grateful for the dark because he was sure his ears were the brightest shade of red.

Ambrose scooted back to the top of the bed, leaving no space between them, his thigh against Callum's.

"Thank you," he whispered into the dark, "for coming. I don't think I realized how badly I didn't want to do this alone."

Callum stilled. Ambrose found his hand and laced their fingers together again. They were both on their backs, bodies touching in so many places. Ambrose's thumb moved back and forth over Callum's wrist.

"Of course," Callum said, "what are friends for?"

The word *friends* felt so wrong to say. It felt like they were so much more, their connection way beyond friendship. But what did Callum know? Ambrose was a strange person on the best of days. He would probably never fully understand him and there was Rose and there was Tomas and there was danger.

"You're the best person I know," Ambrose stated.

"Easy." Callum brushed it off with a chuckle. "I mean, look at the company you keep."

Ambrose sighed, followed by a yawn. "I forgot to call Rose today," he said sleepily.

"Oh," Callum said blankly. "Will she be upset?"

Ambrose was practically asleep, his response sluggish. "She wants this over just as badly as me."

"What?"

Ambrose didn't respond, his breathing heavier, fast asleep.

Callum was left awake, hand still wrapped in Ambrose's, trying to parse what it meant. What did Rose want to be over?

Callum closed his eyes, trying to sleep. He was restless, still a little drunk, and a lot out of his element. He missed Mick and Lucas, even Asther.

He scooted slightly onto his side, facing Ambrose. He could barely make him out in the dark. After a while, he fell asleep, as he distantly recalled Ambrose saying he usually had a hard time sleeping.

CHAPTER 31

AMBROSE

The next morning Ambrose changed slowly, afraid to go back into the room and face Callum. Damian had called for him to have a meeting later in the afternoon and stressed that he was to come alone.

He couldn't really think about any of that though, the real reason they were here was completely forgotten, replaced by the fluttering in his chest, the stupid shit he did the previous night playing on loop in his mind, his arms around Callum's bare waist, his leg tucked between his thighs. Of course, it was a blatant lie when he said he couldn't remember the night before; he remembered everything in stark clarity.

He had almost told Callum again that the Rose situation was fake, that he was gay, that pretty much since the moment he saw Callum he knew he wanted to touch him.

It was so cruel. Callum was his closest friend, the one he wanted to share all of his secrets with, and because of that, he was the one person he couldn't. It was too dangerous for them both. If Callum were a nobody, then maybe he would have no problem taking the risk, but he wasn't a nobody. He was...

Callum.

After stalling for a decent amount of time, Ambrose ambled out in fresh black jeans and a white button up, only half buttoned. His zippo was tucked in his back pocket. Callum was making the bed, wearing one of Ambrose's oversized black tees over his jeans.

"Nice," Ambrose said, winking at Callum. "This feels domestic."

Shut up, shut up, shut up.

Callum rolled his eyes. "My head is killing me. Remind me never to drink again."

Callum started tying back the bed curtains. Ambrose leaned against one of the posts, stuffing his hands in his pockets to prevent himself from reaching out. Callum's hair was wild this morning, like he had been properly sexed and it was a struggle for Ambrose to keep his thoughts clean.

Not that he was really trying. He wasn't ashamed to say he imagined plenty of filthy things when it came to Callum. Imagining might be all he ever got; he wasn't going to waste an opportunity.

"Did you sleep well?" Ambrose asked, as if he couldn't recall his body flush against Callum's.

The scariest part of all of this was that Ambrose had the best sleep of his life. Perhaps it was a combination of exhaustion and a drug addled brain, but a small part of him was curious to see if he would sleep well again tonight. If it was because of something else entirely.

"Great," Callum said, his whole attention on tying back the curtains, his ears red. "It's a bed fit for a king, really."

Ambrose bit back his grin. "I have to go see Damian. He wants to see me alone."

Callum paused, his brows pinched together, his face contorted in the way that it did whenever they spoke about Damian. "Should you?"

Ambrose felt a reluctant surge of irritation as "I mean Devin will be nearby."

Callum sighed. "In other words, he wants to see you without me."

Ambrose shook his head. "Why are you doing this?"

Callum crossed his arms. "Doing what exactly?"

"You aren't even giving him a chance, Callum." Ambrose wasn't sure why it was bothering him, why he couldn't keep the edge out of his tone. He didn't want to be fighting. Maybe it was that fighting was the easiest way to keep Callum at somewhat of a distance. The thought made him sick to his stomach.

Callum scoffed, staring at his shoes. "Okay. I mean, it's a two-way street. Besides, I think it's super weird you want me to get attached to him, you know, considering."

Ambrose clenched his fists in his pockets. "Why did you come if you are going to be so fucking judgy about it? This is my life, Callum. Shit like this will happen again. And again. This is far from the most fucked up thing I'll ever have to do."

Callum had a look of indignation on his face. "I'm not

judging you at all. I chose to come here!" Ambrose couldn't remember a time Callum had raised his voice since he'd known him. It both terrified him and excited him. "I don't care what you have to do. I *chose* this. But I don't have to like Damian, and I don't have to make excuses for him. I'm technically a minor, Ambrose, and he pulled his... *thing* out right in front of me. The dude is weird."

Ambrose winced. Callum wasn't wrong there, but for some reason, he didn't want to admit it. Damian was like family to him. "Whatever, Callum." Ambrose started to turn, and Callum laughed humorlessly.

"That's right. It's just *whatever* to you, Ambrose. Like everything else. You don't care about anything but yourself, and it's starting to piss me off."

Ambrose whirred back around. "What did you just say?" he demanded.

"You heard me," Callum said with a lift of his chin. "You just get to play around with everyone's feelings and suffer no consequences."

Ambrose froze. "What are you talking about?"

Callum groaned, his hands running through his hair, obviously agitated. "Never mind. Go run off to Damian. I'll be right here waiting for when you get back, like a good little dog."

Callum turned around and headed for the bathroom. Ambrose walked after him, grabbing his arm. "I don't... don't say that," he said, voice soft, "please don't say things like that."

Callum shrugged his arm free of Ambrose's grip with a self-deprecating smile. "It doesn't matter. I make my choices."

He slammed the bathroom door, locking it, locking himself away from Ambrose.

All the agitation and anger had left Ambrose replaced by panic. *Like a good little dog,* Callum had said.

You just get to play around with everyone's feelings.

Ambrose leaned his forehead against the door. "Callum," he said hoarsely. "I'm going. But we'll talk when I get back. Just... Callum? Please."

There was no answer. Ambrose waited a moment, then a hundred more before he sighed and left the room, joining Devin.

***

Ambrose met Damian in the Great Hall.

"I'll show you around the immediate grounds while we chat," Damian said, way too cheerfully for a man who had been snorting coke and drinking all night. Ambrose felt his own head pounding.

Devin kept a respectful distance behind them as they walked. No guard followed for Damian, which, Ambrose noted, was good. He was already blindly trusting Ambrose.

"I'm thinking of installing a moat," Damian said as they began walking around the castle, the grounds impeccably manicured. Ambrose saw that they were approaching a hedge that formed a sort of fencing around what he assumed was a garden. "You know, truly medieval."

"That would be great," Ambrose said, trying hard to care about anything right now other than Callum, up in their room, waiting. *Like a dog.*

"How did you like the party?" Damian asked.

"Delightful," Ambrose lied, a bright smile on his face. "You sure know how to throw one."

"Shame you had to cut your time short," Damian hedged. "Callum seems... needy."

"Hardly," Ambrose returned, politely, "he's... parties are new to him. He's just—"

"Ahh, yeah," Damian interrupted. "Anyway, enough about Callum. I don't want to waste the time we get talking about other people." Damian led them through the hedge-fence and, sure enough, there was a sprawling garden, entirely breathtaking, with a stone walkway winding through and an exquisite fountain in the center. The fountain was topped with a white marbled statue, two men in the nude, one palming the other's generous size in his hand.

"Subtle." Ambrose dipped his chin in its direction with a chuckle.

Damian grinned, straight, white teeth on display. Ambrose dimly remembered he had a gap between his top front teeth the last time he had seen him.

"I had it made. I'm quite done being subtle. Over half my life was wasted in subtlety." His voice was a little pained. Ambrose couldn't relate more, the feeling in his chest sharp and nasty, the strongest desire to follow in this man's footsteps, to just let it all out in the open.

"I'm sorry," he said.

When they reached the fountain, a large pool surrounded it. Damian sat on the marbled edge, Ambrose following suit.

"I admit, that is what I wanted to discuss with you. Business can wait, you are here a whole week, aren't you? Anyway, Ambrose. It's safe here." Damian reached a handout, placing it on Ambrose's arm comfortingly. He stressed the next words. "I want you to understand. You can be yourself here and know that what happens at Damian's stays at Damian's."

Ambrose cleared his throat. It sounded wonderful.

It wasn't like there weren't people that knew. Liam knew, Asther did, Rose did, and even Lucas and Mick knew. The stranger Ambrose had fucked last year at a school party in Atchinson knew.

But it was always guarded. He remembered panicking for a whole month after that party, worried the boy would say something to the wrong person, even though they didn't run in the same city, let alone the same circles. Fear loomed over his head, wondering when the shoe would drop, when his father would come and wrap his hands around Ambrose's neck, strangling the life out of the shame that was his son.

"I'm not sure what you m—"

Damian lifted his hand. "You don't have to say anything. I just wanted to make sure you understood that what happens at these parties is never revealed to the world outside. Olivia is happily married to an upstanding man in New York. The man who cut our lines, well, he's a single parent of three delightful children, all bound for great things. The two that put on that delightful show? They married sisters and have a happy life back in Montana. I'm just saying they can be whatever and whoever they want here, and no one would dare to speak of it beyond my walls."

Something with his words sat uncomfortably.

"Okay," he only said.

Damian grinned. "You must not remember. Ambrose, the time you were here. When you were eleven?"

"I remember a bit. How could I forget any of the times here? I mean, it's a castle. I was a kid who loved fantasy."

With a nod, Damian went on, "Your father had left you in my care while he met with some of the Gambino family a few miles into my grounds. You told me something, then. Can you not recall?"

Ambrose swallowed. Devin stood, a distance away but a comfortable dot on the horizon. "I remember him leaving. You let me see the swords, even let me swing at one of the dummies in the armory. I'll probably never forget. It was so kind of you."

"Kindness to you came easy for me," Damian admitted. "You were so like me. I knew it right away. You don't remember the rest?"

Ambrose chewed on his lower lip. "I'm so sorry. I don't think I do."

Placing a hand on Ambrose's knee, Damian said good-naturedly. "No need. You found some... paraphernalia of mine, shall we say? While we were in the armory. Snoopy little kid that you were."

At that, Ambrose barked out a laugh. "I had no boundaries."

"But I'm glad. It was a little box I kept underneath the scabbard chest. It was filled with shots of men with men, men and men, men on men. You get my drift."

Ambrose cocked his head, racking his brain for the memory. He remembered the scabbard chest, but had a hard time remembering the rest.

"I see you don't remember," Damian said, almost disappointed. "Odd. But you especially liked one of the shots. The more innocent one. Two men kissing, tenderly holding each other's faces. You told me you wanted that. You wanted something like that."

Ambrose let out a deep breath, fingers tapping the stone of the fountain pool. He had noticed boys when he was eleven and he had noticed his lack of notice for girls. He couldn't remember this, no matter how hard he tried. He did remember snooping, scouring the whole armor like he had owned it.

Dimply, he remembered a little locked box under the chest. He felt his face drain of blood.

Damian squeezed his knee. "Don't panic. Your secret has always been safe with me."

Ambrose angled his body towards Damian and blurted, "Callum doesn't know. Callum can't know."

Damian smiled, his eyes shrinking a little in size. "Of course, Ambrose. I understand."

"It—it does feel nice. To have one less person to hide it from," Ambrose admitted, suddenly wondering if there was any way he didn't have to kill Damian. There had to be another way. Someone else. Anyone else.

"Be yourself around me. All you want," Damian leaned in conspiratorially, "I'm whatever you need this entire week." Tension seemed to seep right from Ambrose. "That means a lot," he said, resolving in his mind to call his dad, to try and find another way. There had to be a way to appease their rivals without killing this man. "Thank you, Damian."

"You can pay me back by being more present at tonight's party," Damian responded with a grin.

CHAPTER 32

CALLUM

Callum called Mick when Ambrose had left and talked for hours, the phone being passed between Mick and Lucas and once even Asther. When Asther said goodbye, he added, "Make sure Ambrose isn't stupid. Well, not extra stupid anyway."

It was good to hear Mick and Lucas's voices. When he was done talking, he felt a little less annoyed. Then he saw that three hours had passed since Ambrose had left.

He shot him a quick text.

Callum: *Everything good?*

Ambrose: Y*es!*

Callum rolled his eyes, tucking his phone into his pocket and leaning back in his chair. He had debated strolling around the castle, but the place was still bustling with guests and the talk of another party tonight.

He drifted into a fitful sleep, only waking when Ambrose returned.

"Hey," Callum said, from where he sat, cocooned in a blanket on the chair. He took in Ambrose whose hair was windswept, his cheeks pink.

"We rode four-wheelers," Ambrose said, pointing at his hair, "helmet head."

He peeled his shirt off, tossing it to the side and flopping onto the bed.

"That was his business talk?" Callum asked.

"Please, Callum, don't start," Ambrose said with a sigh.

"Okay then." Callum reached for his bag by the chair and dug out his book.

After several moments, Ambrose spoke, "Another party tonight."

"Nice," Callum said, not looking up from his book. He flipped the page rather roughly, tearing off a tiny corner piece.

"Will you come?" Ambrose sounded hopeful.

"This is a really good book," Callum answered, before amending. "Maybe."

Ambrose sat up on the bed, stretching a little. "You're still angry."

Callum kept his eyes on the words on the page, far from actually reading, simply using the book as a buffer, a prop. "I had hours cooped up in this room to stew. Sounds like you had a great time, though." Callum hated the pettiness that he had resorted to, but he couldn't even help himself. He experienced attraction and feelings for a person for the first time in his life and it was going epically, disastrously, wrong. He could not help feeling bitter about it.

"Callum, this *is* business. I have a week to know my target's ins and outs."

"Right."

"Could you at least look at me?" Ambrose huffed.

Callum did, and immediately regretted it. It was hard to be angry at him with those wicked scars on display, the knowledge of how he got them even more wicked.

"Let's not fight," Ambrose pleaded.

Callum closed his book with a sigh, dropping it back into his bag. He wasn't even exactly sure why they were fighting in the first place; he just knew he wanted to keep doing it, he wanted to never do it again.

"Alright," he agreed. "We can call a truce for now."

Ambrose grinned, hesitantly. "Look at you. Stay in a castle for a day and you're already saying shit like *truce.*"

"I think I'll skip the party tonight, though," Callum admitted, picking at the arm of his seat. "I want to sleep."

Ambrose's face fell. "Are you sure?"

Callum thought of last night. The touches from Ambrose, the remarks from everyone else, Damian with his private parts in his hand. He was never surer of anything when he answered, "Yes."

Another night like that and he knew he would do something stupid.

CHAPTER 33

AMBROSE

Ambrose joined the party, dressed in a classic black three-piece with a pink tie for a pop of color. Damian had forewarned him that tonight's party was more of a modern dress-up than a medieval thing.

He had casually asked Callum one more time before leaving the room if he would come. He was trying not to seem desperate. Callum had taken one look at him from where he was half asleep on the bed, swallowed and shook his head.

Ambrose was trying not to let it sting his pride. But after the comment about Callum feeling like a dog, he didn't press the issue.

There were plenty of people, even more than the previous night, dressed to the nines. The alcohol table was decidedly classier too, wine glasses and whiskey glasses; no solo cups in sight.

Ambrose poured himself a whiskey, neat.

Damian waved to him from across the Hall, motioning him over. He was in a group again, of new people. Ambrose realized, with a start, that he recognized some of them from

Boston.

One of them had his back to him, but when he approached, turned and grinned.

"Hey Ambrose," Sean said.

"Sean," Ambrose wondered if Sean's presence had anything to do with his father. Damian grinned and motioned to his own tie, and then back to Callum's. The group around him *oohed* obnoxiously. They were both pink ties. In fact, they were both pink Rubinacci ties.

"A man of excellent taste," Damian said fondly.

Ambrose felt glad, briefly, that Callum had decided not to come.

Damian made quick introductions of the rest of the group and then led them to the same room from the previous night. Damian himself started cutting lines on the table.

"None for me tonight," Ambrose remarked from where he stood, leaning against one of the couches. He loosened his tie, unbuttoned the top buttons of his shirt, already feeling sweaty and stuffy.

"That moralist is rubbing off on you," Damian said with a chuckle. "Suit yourself."

Damian took the first line, passed the straw down. Ambrose noticed when it was Sean's turn he took the straw, and it seemed like he snorted the line but, quick as a flash, he tapped the straw over the edge of the couch and Ambrose saw the cocaine flit to the floor where it was lost to the threads of the carpet.

Sean winked at him, lifted a pointer finger to his lips and passed the straw back to an oblivious Damian.

Ambrose tilted his head in question.

Sean pulled out his phone, shot out a few texts, and a few moments later Ambrose felt the buzzing in his pocket.

Sean: *We need to talk.*

Sean: *Wait until fuckface is good and high. Then I'm gonna get really touchy with you. And you're gonna take me to your room.*

Ambrose pinched his brows together. Sean watched him.

Sean: *Relax, Princess. It's about the business.*

Ambrose pocketed his phone after shooting Callum a warning text and then subtly nodded in Sean's direction.

Assuming *fuckface* referred to Damian, Ambrose took a seat on the nearest couch, next to a stranger, and waited.

"You look really good," Sean called over to Ambrose, again tapping the straw after he snorted, the cocaine falling to the ground. No one but Ambrose sober enough to be aware. "Last time I saw you, you were skinnier. Been hitting the gym?" he finished it with a wink.

Damian watched them intently. Too intently. Ambrose wondered if Sean's presence here was a red flag to him. So he leaned forward. "You too, Sean. I like the long hair."

Sean flipped said hair that was now shoulder length, eyes practically fucking Ambrose from across the table.

He's good was Ambrose's first thought, but his second thought was of another man, up in their room, alone.

Damian looked displeased. He cut himself another line, took it, and leaned back.

"Ambrose," Damian said.

Ambrose waited, but Damian said nothing else, his left leg bouncing a cocaine-addled rhythm, his head leaning on the back of the couch, eyes on the ceiling. The man next to him, Xavier if Ambrose remembered correctly, leaned into him. Damian cupped the nape of Xavier's, neck.

Ambrose wondered what Xavier had beyond these walls. If he was like Olivia or the men that had married sisters, or if he was a single parent, leaving behind everything for a night of debauchery.

He suddenly had a terrible taste in his mouth.

He downed the rest of his whiskey. There was a bottle on the table of Redbreast and he poured himself a few more inches.

Sean whispered something to the man who was seated next to him. Ambrose recognized the man as another one from Boston, but the name was lost to him. The man nodded at Sean, stood, and started ambling around the room.

Sean eyed Ambrose and patted the now empty space next to him. Steeling himself, Ambrose painted a flirtatious grin on his face and ambled over. Damian had said that what happened here would stay here, and now Ambrose was about to test the truth of those words very foolishly.

Damian watched.

Ambrose felt sick, wondering if they were expected to be the entertainment of the night.

Sean wasted no time getting to touching Ambrose. His fingers walked up his arm, his voice sultry. "That night in Boston, I really wanted to fuck you," he breathed, quiet enough that it felt like it was meant just for Ambrose, loud enough that Damian, seated a few feet away from them, could hear.

Ambrose swallowed. It sounded too believable. Though Ambrose himself was an excellent actor. Perhaps, between the two of them, it was simply a product of the life they were raised in. It was do or die. You learned to be a good actor pretty fast.

"I noticed you," he lied. "If my circumstances were any different, I'm sure you would have been able to."

Sean laughed, his fingers slipping through Ambrose's hair. "Don't lie. You strike me as the one who does the fucking." He pulled a little at Ambrose's hair, all sensual touches.

Ambrose chuckled, aware of Damian watching them like a hawk. Ambrose did a horrible thing to make the acting come easier and pretended like Sean was a certain other brown-haired boy. He leaned in closer to him. "Perhaps you're right."

Sean matched his lean, inch by inch, till their noses were just barely touching. "I guess we should find out," he breathed, pulling at Ambrose's suit jacket.

Ambrose faltered momentarily before letting Sean pull it off, letting him loosen his tie till it hung open on either side, letting him begin at the buttons of his shirt.

Sean raised an eyebrow, leaned in and nipped at Ambrose's ear before whispering, truly only for him, "You look terrified.

Sell it, man. Then ask to take it to your room."

Ambrose slid his hand up Sean's thigh, squeezing gently when he got precariously close to a certain spot.

Sean moaned, arched his back, inched his face closer before his lips were on Ambrose's. Ambrose kept his hands busy, pulling at Sean's jacket, busy while Sean explored his mouth with his tongue, busy until Sean was shirtless, and they were both breathless.

"Let's—let's take this to my room," Ambrose said.

Sean stood, pulling Ambrose up, kissing at his neck. "You don't have to ask me twice," he murmured against his neck.

"Leaving? I was so enjoying that." Damian's tone was icy, or Ambrose was imagining it.

It seemed like Damian was a drastically different person from the one he had spent the afternoon with.

Ambrose smiled at him. "Tempting as that is, I'm more of a private guy with these matters. You understand why."

Damian sighed. "What happens at my castle stays at my castle." He pointed at the man who had been touching him. "He's here to get some time away from his partner." He pointed at another. "He's here because he hates his wife and generally prefers dick, anyway." Then Damian pointed at Sean. "He's here because he's depraved and enjoys the company of other depraved souls, feels right at home when he's surrounded by the other muck." Damian paused, then pointed at Ambrose. "And you're here hoping that your father never finds out that you like to fuck men. We all have secrets that can't be shared."

Ambrose flinched. Sean's hand that was at the nape of his neck squeezed gently.

"Damian," Ambrose said, as calmly as he could, "why would you say that?"

His host just rolled his eyes. "Get out then. Go fuck the little pretty boy behind closed doors."

The man next to Damian spoke up, "Really, Damian had the last guy who spoke outside the walls of another's secret shot right in the head. It's not worth it to any of us."

Ambrose felt the floor practically tilt, the room spinning around him. He looked at the man seated on the couch, the man he had practically adored, and wondered what led him to become like this. Callum had been right.

"Or," Damian continued, unaware of the turmoil happening inside Ambrose, or completely aware and just too selfish to care, "you can come fuck me." He patted his own lap. "There. You know *my* secret now."

Ambrose swallowed back a gag, Sean's firm grip on his neck reminding him to tread lightly. Suddenly, all those seemingly innocent touches from the past few days made Ambrose want to throw up. His secret was that he liked them young. Ambrose realized with a startling clarity that killing this man would be much easier than he had anticipated.

The other memories from his past that he held so fondly in his heart were now tainted, sullied, with the fear of *how young does he like them?* The story Damian told him of Ambrose finding the porn was so disgusting now that he could scream.

"Well, a simple yes or no," Damian insisted.

"No," Ambrose said, turning from the room, hand slipping into Sean's as he pulled him after him.

He stopped when Damian called, "maybe you should send Callum down. I'm sure he'd rather not listen to you fuck. Now that I recall, he is rather pretty. Maybe I'll pay better attention to him tonight. Oh, and didn't you say he couldn't know about your preferences? He's such a pious little shit. Would he judge you? I've never been with someone so... pretentiously moralled. Perhaps it's time I tried it out. Goody on the streets, freak in the sheets perhaps."

Ambrose spun around. Sean tugged on him, a warning.

"What the fuck, Damian?" Ambrose said. "Leave Callum alone. Just leave him alone."

Damian grinned, feral. "It was all in jest. Calm down. Don't feel like you must defend your little shadow's honor. Truly, he's a prude. I prefer a bit of a bad boy when it comes down to it. It's not my style to force, either."

Ambrose lunged for him.

Sean laughed, pulling him back. "Come on Ambrose, he's just ruffling your feathers." Sean let a hand fall to Ambrose's ass, squeezing. "Let's go have some fun and forget about this, huh?" His voice was sultry, tempting.

Damian sighed. "Damn it, Sean, you ruin all the fun. I quite looked forward to being tackled by Ambrose." Damian's eyes twinkled. "If that's how I have to get him on top of me, then I'll take what I can take."

Ambrose left the room, Sean close behind, hand in his, to the laughter of the room. He had tunnel vision, pushing through the people without a care, Sean's lack of a shirt causing catcalls and profanities from the crowd. The crowd. Everyone here had a secret, but Ambrose's secret was innocent. He was hiding his sexuality from a homophobic father. Their secrets were fucked up and sickening. He couldn't even look at anyone as he pushed and barrelled his way up to his room. He felt, unashamedly, like he was better than every person here. He felt like he was even *good* when surrounded by these monsters.

Vincent dipped his chin at Ambrose from his post, ignoring Sean entirely. Inside, he dropped Sean's hand, scanning the room for Callum. He wasn't in the bedroom, but Ambrose heard the shower running and breathed in relief.

"That must be Callum?" Sean asked, inclining his head toward the door. "I heard about the boy who followed you here."

"What are you doing here?" Ambrose asked. He was shaking from the revelations of the night. His pulse was erratic. He wanted to go home. He wanted Callum to get out of the shower so Ambrose could see something *good and* could be reminded that truly good people existed. Then he regretted ever letting Callum come here, as if these people could sully him in any way. Damian's comments made him sicker and sicker, and he was almost looking forward to fucking ending him.

"Calm down," Sean demanded, not unkindly. "Were you not briefed on Damian? He's a fuck-creep and everyone knows it."

Ambrose shook his head. "My dad conveniently left that part out."

Sean smirked. "Not really surprised. Anyway, let's be quick. Damian needs to be taken care of before Wednesday."

"I thought I had the week?" Ambrose said. He heard the shower squeak off. "And anyway, why is my father sending you to tell me this?"

"Oh, no. The Campano's sent me."

Ambrose stared blankly, waiting for an explanation.

"They really don't tell you anything," Sean said with an impatient shake. "I'm a cousin of the Campano's. I'm a double agent if you will. Haven't you ever wondered why Mr. Lastra would keep me around? He only ever keeps his own. But I'm worth it to him. He's been a better father to me than my own, so he's worth it to me."

"Wow," Ambrose breathed. "You're quite the handy one."

"Back to business. Damian is set to hack into an account that would be damning to the entire Campano branch on Wednesday evening, with the help of a hacker friend of his—equally creepy, by the way, so if you want the debt settled you need to kill him fast."

Sean rummaged in his pants pocket, pulled out his wallet and slid a thin vial from an insert.

"This has a few drops of pure, untarnished Maitotoxin. I can't stress enough how careful you need to be when handling this." He passed the vial over to Ambrose. He followed suit, pulling out his wallet and slipping it in. "And I can't stress enough how lucky you are that the Campano's are aiding you this much."

"That account must be pretty fucking important.," Ambrose stated.

The bathroom door opened. Callum froze. He was shirtless, with gray sweats riding low on his hips. Ambrose swallowed.

Callum was pink as he asked, awkward as ever, "Oh my g—oh shit. Am I interrupting something?" His eyebrows were pinched together, confusion painted on his face.

"No," Ambrose said, too quickly. "Oh God, no, Callum. This is Sean, he's... here for business. God, nothing else."

Sean raised a brow, an amused expression on his face. "So those kisses meant nothing to you?" His tone was playful.

Ambrose wanted to use his gifted poison on *him*.

Callum said, "sorry, I can, uh, I can leave the room."

"No!" Ambrose rushed over to his suitcase, grabbed a t-shirt, and threw it at Sean. With a chuckle, Sean obliged. "Callum, we had to get away without raising suspicion that it was for anything other than pleasure. We... I mean... that's all this is."

"Yes," Sean agreed, unhelpfully, "that's exactly why we had our tongues down each other's throats. Strictly business, absolutely no pleasure at all."

"Shut up," Ambrose hissed.

Callum looked completely out of his element. He shrugged. "Okay. I mean, it's none of my business." He walked over to the chair, grabbed his book from his backpack and sat on the bed, starting to read.

"The book is upside down," Sean stated, delighted.

"I know," Callum said defensively, flipping the book around.

Ambrose turned to Sean. "Well, if you are quite done here, you can get out. I got the message, loud and clear. I'll do what I can."

Sean nodded. "Well, after defending your little friend's honor here, you are going to have your work cut out for you. I don't think you are in Damian's good graces right now."

Callum looked up from the book he was too obviously pretending to read. "What?"

"I'll leave him to explain," Sean said, nodding at Ambrose. "I'm going to hop in your shower so we can keep the appearance up of a good fuck. Any objections?"

Ambrose groaned, waving a hand. "Yes, yes, do whatever, man."

Once Sean was in the bathroom, Callum asked, not making eye contact, "What did he mean by that?"

"Nothing." Ambrose rubbed at the back of his neck. "Just, you were right about Damian. God, you were so right. He's a fucking creep."

Callum stood. "Are you alright?"

"Nah," Ambrose admitted, surprised by his own honesty. "None of this is alright. It's all so completely fucked up, Callum." Ambrose looked down at his shoes before adding, "you being here, with me, means... it means..." Instead of trying to use any words, because words just wouldn't cut it, Ambrose crossed the distance between them and wrapped his arms around Callum's neck in a tight embrace. "Just, thank you," he whispered.

After a moment, Callum's arms came around Ambrose's waist. The stark difference between their heights, Callum so much shorter, was doing wonderful things to Ambrose's stomach.

"Of course," Callum murmured into Ambrose's chest, "of course."

CHAPTER 34

CALLUM

Callum listened while Ambrose conveyed the events of the night, tuning out the parts where he put his hands all over Sean as a cover. When he finished, Callum blew out an angry breath. "Wow," he said.

"Yeah."

They were seated on the floor in the center of their room, face to face, cross-legged, Sean long gone.

"I'm sorry," Callum said, simply. "I know you held him in high regard."

Ambrose huffed. "It just makes it easier."

"I should have gone to the party with you," Callum admitted, properly ashamed. "I knew Damian was gross. I shouldn't have left you alone."

"Nah, I was a complete ass. I wouldn't have gone either, in your place."

"I was a bit of an ass myself."

"Look at us," Ambrose grinned, "a couple of asses."

"So, what?" Callum asked, leaning back on his palms. "You poison his drink and then we bounce?"

Ambrose gnawed at his lower lip. He'd changed out of the suit and opted for black sweatpants. Callum had thrown on a shirt, Ambrose was shirtless, scars again on full display.

"I've been texting with my dad," Ambrose explained, "and maybe I should make the move soon. Like as soon as possible, when the guests are starting to leave, little by little. If this gets blown up investigation-wise, they will have their hands full with a suspect list. Perhaps so many people will be a blessing after all." He paused. "Though I know it's fucked up, I'm pretty safe from consequences, regardless. The rich in America can get away with anything, even murder, if you know what I mean."

"What can I do?" Callum asked.

"Absolutely nothing," Ambrose said with a smile. One of the genuine ones, the beautiful ones. "Leave this shit to me. You're more of my moral support."

"Like the moralist that I am," Callum said lightly.

"Fuck that guy and every stupid thing he ever said," Ambrose responded firmly. "Though having morals is nothing to be ashamed of. Everyone who comes to this fucking place could benefit from some." Ambrose made a face. "I used to love this castle. Now I'll always associate it with these perverts."

Callum took in the room around them, the grand bedroom, a piece of the past brought to like. "Same," he lied.

Callum would always associate this castle with Ambrose, with himself admitting his feelings, with Ambrose, Ambrose. So how could he hate it entirely?

***

The next morning, the two of them searched the castle floor for Damian. Guests were loitered everywhere, passed out in the most inconvenient of places, some just right on the floor, bodies upon bodies.

"How wonderful," Callum deadpanned, taking in the mess.

"I think so too."

Both boys were startled as Damian seemed to appear out of nowhere, materializing beside them. He looked like he had a full ten hours of sleep, fresh and bright.

Ambrose struggled to smile. "I was looking for you," he said, voice even, pleasant.

"Really?" Damian asked, his gaze flitting up and down Callum's body once, twice. "I thought you would be upset. About last night."

Ambrose made a confused face. "Last night?"

"Do you not recall?" Damian hedged, almost sounding hopeful. Callum looked at the man, imagining in his mind the pleasure he would get from gutting him.

Moralist indeed.

"I'm afraid I must have ingested more whiskey than I thought. Last night is a bit of a blur. What would I be upset about?"

Damian seemed to ponder over a response. "I was being unkind. I had a bit of a rough day, no excuse, of course, and

I said things I should not have. Though, you can rest assured, anything I won't get past these walls."

Ambrose grinned, his acting effortless. "Ahh, what happens at Damian's stays at Damian's."

Callum was told the events of the night, but he knew Ambrose had left out something important, something that was bugging him personally. He figured it was whatever Damian revealed to the room, something personal to Ambrose. Though he was disappointed Ambrose didn't share that part with him, he was angrier at this stupid man in front of him. What gave him the gall to mess with someone like Ambrose?

Damian addressed Callum directly, possibly for the first time since they had arrived. "Were you not feeling up to the party, then?"

"I hope you'll forgive my absence," Callum felt gross, even pretending to apologize. He swallowed down his desired response, something Lucas would be proud of like, *fuck you to hell,* and tried to act as smoothly as Ambrose. It was rather jarring how easily Ambrose could pretend.

"I rarely fly. I think some sort of flight sickness was catching up to me. Paired with the drink of the previous night, I was hardly feeling up to anything much but sleeping."

"How in keeping with your character."

Callum laughed before Ambrose could defend him. The whole point of this was to kiss up, get close enough to kill him, and get out. He could deal with a few more snide remarks if he had to.

"What is it you were needing me for?"

Ambrose shifted, playing at uncomfortable. "I feel rude, but I would really like to discuss the reason I am here. Maybe we could have dinner together tonight?"

Damian placed a hand on Ambrose's arm again. "Of course. I'll have a menu prepared. Don't for a minute feel rude. I want you to feel at home here."

Ambrose smiled. "I always have, Damian."

It caused Callum severe turmoil to hear Ambrose have to say those words. He couldn't imagine what it was doing to Ambrose.

CHAPTER 35

CALLUM

Callum borrowed some of Ambrose's clothes again for dinner; skinny jeans that he had to cuff because Ambrose had eternally long legs and a button-down shirt. He followed Ambrose to the smaller dining room, where Damian said he would be waiting.

Tonight, it was especially comforting knowing that Devin and Vincent were close by.

Harry was on high alert; he was staying on a Lastra estate nearby in California, ready to fly in and get them out at a moment's notice. They had already packed up their things as best they could in case they needed to grab and run like the wind.

But when they entered the dining room, Damian was not alone. Security guards peppered the room, more than Callum had seen together in one room since they had arrived. He couldn't look at Ambrose in case it gave anything away, but he was sure that Damian suspected... something.

Ambrose was a god at acting, casually ignoring the presence of so many guards, the epitome of at ease. He slid into the chair to Damian's right, grinning at the man. Callum took his seat next to Ambrose, relieved that Damian disliked him enough not to care.

"Lovely for Callum to come along with you," Damian said to Ambrose, never even sparing Callum so much as a glance.

"Ahh," Callum interjected, "I hope you don't mind. It's just that I'm famished."

Damian's smile was tight. "Of course, I don't mind." He waved a hand,

encompassing the room. "I hope neither of you are offended by my increase in security. A certain guest here was said to be in possession of a lethal dosage of poison. Until we know for sure who it is, I'm being extra cautious."

Ambrose's words oozed with concern. "Goodness, Damian. Who have you pissed off recently?"

Damian leaned over, pouring some wine in the glass at Ambrose's setting. He

was about to set the wine bottle back down, but Ambrose took it from him, pouring some for Callum.

"You know the business," Damian said dismissively. "Get in bed with the Mafia, you pay the price."

He pointedly looked at Callum. Callum nodded politely in agreement.

Servers, all younger men, brought out food on rolling trays, placing a covered

plate before each of them. When Callum removed his, he

was faced with a meal keeping in theme of the castle, a whole pheasant it looked like, on a bed of greens.

"Impressive," Ambrose said, immediately cutting into his.

Callum saw no opportunity for Ambrose to make his move here. He hated to

admit the only way the poison could work is if Ambrose got alone with Damian. How he would have to do that made his stomach sour.

Damian grinned at Ambrose digging in. "Your father always made everyone pray first."

Ambrose chuckled, mouth full of the bird meat. Callum was struggling to take a first bite. He was a fan of the most basic foods; anything remotely exotic didn't appeal to him.

"Daddy dearest does love his prayers."

"He's an odd man, I hope you don't mind me saying."

Callum noted, with some unease, that Damian had not touched his food. Callum put his own fork down, resolving to not take a bite. He watched Ambrose, warily.

"Nah," Ambrose said, eating, oblivious to the fact he was the only one. "He is odd. This is delicious, by the way."

Callum's whole body went on high alert when Damian said, "Excellent. It's a special recipe for a special guest."

"Excuse me," Callum said, standing. "I need to use the restroom."

"Take your time," Damian called after him.

Vincent and Devin were right outside the door. Callum hissed under his breath, "I am almost positive he drugged the food or poisoned it. Ambrose needs help."

Devin nodded, immediately heading for the door.

"Wait," Callum said. "There are like six guards in that room alone."

Callum was eerily calm, panic leaving him like an empty shell. He couldn't afford to panic. Not right now, not until he was sure Ambrose was safe.

Devin spoke in low tones to Vincent, "send a quick message to Harry. Regardless of whether the mission is completed tonight, as soon as we get Ambrose out, we leave. His life is more important."

Vincent nodded, pulling a flip phone from his back pocket and sending Harry one word.

"Alright," Devin said, scanning the hall around them. "Callum, are you familiar with any weapons?"

"No," Callum said, a little horrified.

"Then stay on this side of the door until I call you. You'll only be another mark to worry about in there, and you could jeopardize our position. Understood?"

"Yes."

"Vincent, are you comfortable with our odds?" Devin asked.

Vincent was practically bouncing on his heels, a glint in his eyes. "We've overcome much worse."

A loud clang came from the other side of the closed doors. Callum felt the breath leaving his body. Devin had a pistol in his hand, quickly snapping on the silencer. Vincent went to open the door.

"Locked and fucking bolted," he stated.

Devin cursed, pushing Callum back, before shooting at the door, once, twice, and then kicking it down.

Devin either didn't realize his own strength or he wanted Callum winded because when Callum's back hit the wall, he felt his breath go out of him, and his body sank to the floor. On all fours he heaved, and heaved, any previous keeping of his cool long gone. He heard shouting, and he knew it was only a matter of time before every guest and guard in this house made their way over.

It felt like only moments before Devin shouted, "Callum, get Ambrose!"

Callum forced himself to stand, to move. Devin and Vincent had made quick and impressive work of the six men, dead and scattered around the room, blood pooling everywhere Callum stepped.

Vincent was dragging Damian away from a dazed Ambrose, still in his seat. Damian had been hovering over him, *touching him*. Before Damian had much of a chance to shout, Vincent had him gagged.

Callum knelt in front of Ambrose. "Fuck, fuck, fuck, Ambrose are you okay?"

Ambrose smiled, lopsided, swaying a little. His hands were folded neatly in his lap. He giggled.

Half relieved, Callum thought, *drugged, not poisoned.*

"Callum," Ambrose said, reaching a handout and tugging at one of his curls, "on your knees for me?" His voice was sultry.

"What a sight."

Devin approached. "An aphrodisiac then," he spat, "in his wine glass." Devin dropped the wine glass; it smashed on the floor. He leaned over to inspect the plate of food. He took a small bite, spat again, "In the food too, I think."

"Oh my god," Callum said. Without giving himself much time to think about it, he reached into Ambrose's pocket. The first one he searched had the zippo Callum had gifted him for his birthday. Ignoring how that made him feel for now, he stuffed it back into his own pocket, moving onto Ambrose's other pockets.

"Wow," Ambrose said, leaning back a little, "this is not how I expected the night to go." He giggled again and Callum felt sick.

"I need his wallet," he said,

"Back pocket," Devin supplied, immediately aiding Callum by leaning Ambrose forward slightly. Callum reached into the back pocket, grabbing the wallet.

"Whatever you plan to do, you need to hurry," Devin said. "Vincent can only stall the others for so long."

"Callum, if you wanted to touch my butt, you should have just asked," Ambrose said, delighted, his eyes hazed over. "Who am I to tell you no?"

Callum smiled at Ambrose. "You're gonna be okay," he said.

He turned. Ambrose had mentioned the poison was in his wallet. Callum found the vial and walked over to where Vincent had bound and left Damian on his side on the floor.

"Callum," Devin warned.

He ignored him. With his foot, he kicked Damian onto his back. He crouched down next to him and smiled. "You've underestimated me," he whispered, for Damian's ears only. Damian shouted; the sound muted by the gag. His eyes were wide with hate and maybe a little fear. Callum delighted in it. He wasn't even a drop ashamed that he did either. Certain people deserved death.

He waved the vial in front of Damian, moving it back and forth, teasing.

"Fucking with Ambrose was a mistake," Callum whispered, "of the *fatal* variety."

Callum removed the top of the vial, holding his breath. In one hand, he gripped Damian's chin. With the other, he adjusted the gag, stuffing the entire vial into Damian's mouth before clamping his mouth shut with the hand on his jaw.

Damian writhed in desperation.

"Swallow," Callum demanded.

He didn't even know who he was now, blinded by anger, taking pleasure in death he was dealing with his own hands.

Damian didn't need to swallow. The damage was done. His writhing slowed; life started leaving his eyes. It only took moments. Blood started oozing from his mouth. Callum shoved the gag aside. Pieces of glass from the vial cut into Damian's cheek. Damian started choking on his own blood as Callum clamped back down on his jaw, keeping it all trapped inside.

"I wanted to say this earlier," Callum went on, as Damian's eyes lost light, as he took his last breaths. "Fuck you to hell, Damian."

Hate was the final emotion locked in the dead eyes of the man.

Callum stood, dusted his hands off on his pants. When he turned, Devin was staring at him, eyes wide. He had Ambrose slung over his shoulders. He was sleeping.

"Damn," Devin stated, "that was... that was..."

He couldn't finish his sentence. Vincent flew into the room, panting. "Guys, we need to fucking fly."

PART THREE
By My Own Hands (Seven Years Ago)

CHAPTER 36

CALLUM

Callum woke up in a panic. They had made it to one of the Lastra's estates near Morro Bay the night before, and Ambrose was immediately locked in a room to see a physician. Devin arranged Callum in one of the bedrooms and told him to go to sleep.

Callum was surprised he got any sleep. Now, awake, the weight of what he had done was slamming into his chest, feeling like he was hit by a train. He stumbled out of the bed, sticky with sweat, and barely made it to the bathroom to throw up in the toilet.

"What have I done?" he asked himself over and over, rocking back and forth where he sat on the bathroom floor.

A while later, he pulled himself up to answer a knock at the bedroom door.

Vincent said, "Ambrose wants to see you."

Callum let loose a deep breath, relieved. "Let me change first."

Vincent cleared his throat before adding, "we also need to discuss what happened. Tomas will be here sometime tonight.

Until then, I suppose it's pretty obvious, but I still have to tell you that you can't tell anyone."

"Of course." Callum ducked back into his room to change. Who would he dream of telling? He was so ashamed, so disgusted in himself, remembering how much pleasure he took taking someone else's life. A life, a whole life. Worthless though it may have been.

He threw on his sweats and Ambrose's oversized t-shirt and found Vincent waiting for him, followed him down the hall to a set of stairs that led to the lower floor.

Ambrose had been set up in a guest bedroom near the office, where he was seen by a physician who worked with the family.

Vincent stopped at the closed door, knocked lightly. Devin opened, called something back to Ambrose and then stepped out.

"Go ahead," he told Callum.

Nervous, excited, relieved, Callum shut the door behind him. Ambrose was lying on the bed, but he lifted himself onto his elbows when Callum entered. He looked exhausted—Devin had given him a heavy sleeping pill so he could sleep through the aphrodisiac, but aside from that, he looked well.

But Callum's pulse quickened again when he realized Ambrose was looking at him, angrier than he had ever seen him.

"What the fuck did you do, Callum?" he snapped.

Callum flinched. "What?"

Ambrose pulled himself out of the bed, with some effort, ran a hand through his hair, "Damian. *You* fucking killed him! Do you get it? He has friends in high places, Callum. You pretty much just put a big red target on your head!"

"Are you kidding me?" Callum asked, voice raised, matching Ambrose's. "You were gonna have to do it, anyway! You would have been the one with the target. What difference does it make?"

Ambrose's chest was rising and falling with his angry, heavy breathing. "News flash, Callum, I was fucking born with a target on me. I am used to it, it's just part of my life! Part of who I am!"

Callum took a step back. "Well, I'm part of your life too now," he said, voice quieter, trying to keep the hurt from his face. "He tried to hurt you, Ambrose. He *did* hurt you. An aphrodisiac... he was going to..."

Ambrose's face contorted; he winced like Callum's words were fresh pain. "I get hurt. It's normal in this life. It's not your fucking place to do anything about it, though. It's too dangerous."

Callum huffed. "That isn't fair. You don't have to do everything alone. You're being ridiculous right now."

Ambrose closed the distance between them, so close to Callum, his words vicious. "Don't ever fucking do something like that again, Callum. I woke up terrified. Don't ever fucking do it again." Ambrose fisted his hand into Callum's t-shirt, tugging slightly, "Okay?"

That last word was desperate, pleading.

Callum looked up at Ambrose and sucked in a breath. He looked afraid; he looked wild.

"Okay," Callum lied. "Why does it matter, anyway?"

"Why does it matter?" Ambrose was manic now. He tugged harder on the shirt that Callum wore. "Because if you get hurt, I don't know what I would do."

Ambrose released Callum's shirt, his hand cupping the nape of Callum's neck. Callum couldn't breathe with the *want* he was feeling.

Ambrose pulled him close, his mouth angrily, hungrily meeting Callum's. Callum's lips parted almost instantly, letting Ambrose slip his tongue inside. Everything was angry and so, so, hot. When Ambrose pulled slightly at Callum's hair, Callum moaned.

"Fucking shit, Callum," Ambrose murmured into his mouth.

"Agreed," Callum said breathlessly, his hands restless, moving from Ambrose's neck to his chest, to his stomach. Ambrose wasn't gentle, he was angry, but Callum didn't care. He was shamelessly hard. Never in his life had he experienced a want like this.

Callum's tongue danced with Ambrose's, Ambrose slid an arm around his waist pulling him close, when Callum moaned it seemed to undo Ambrose. He pulled Callum even closer, and Callum delighted when he felt Ambrose was just as hard.

A knock on the door startled them both apart. Ambrose ran

a hand through his mussed hair, his breathing heavy. Callum adjusted his pants quickly.

Devin poked his head around the door. "Sorry," he cleared his throat. "I just wanted to warn you that your dad has just left. He'll be here in a few hours." Devin exchanged a meaningful look with Ambrose. "With Rose."

Callum looked at the ground, staring at his shoes like they fascinated him, his

stomach sinking. Ambrose wandered over and took a seat on the chaise at the foot of his bed. He crossed an ankle over his knee, cleared his throat, and nodded. "Thanks, Devin."

Devin dipped his chin/ "You have total privacy until then," he said as he closed the door.

Callum couldn't look at Ambrose. The mention of Rose surely was like a bucket of ice water poured over his head, dousing the hot flames. When he finally did look, Ambrose had his arm thrown over the back of the chaise. He was looking at Callum warily. He stood and walked closer.

"Are you okay?" he asked, his eyes flicking briefly to Callum's pants, then back

up to his face.

"Yes," Callum said, his voice still a little hoarse with desire.

Ambrose definitely picked up on it because he came even closer, a little grin on

his face. With a palm on Callum's chest, he pushed him back, back, until he was up against the wall. When Ambrose brought his mouth to Callum's ear he whispered, "shall we pick up where we left off then?"

Callum groaned softly. "Definitely," he agreed, in that moment not caring about Rose or Ambrose and Rose as a whole or anything at all except this. Who cared if he was being toyed with again when it felt like this?

Ambrose leaned in, resting his forehead on Callum's. "Fuck, should we? God, Callum, you're so hot."

Callum swallowed, suddenly insecure. "Sorry about my... inexperience."

"Shut up," Ambrose demanded, pulling at the hair at Callum's nape again, pulling him closer, kissing him.

Ambrose knocked Callum's legs apart at the knee and slid one of his in between, his tongue exploring Callum's mouth with vigor. Instinct had Callum grinding up against his thigh, too turned on to feel embarrassed. Ambrose pushed into him, moving his mouth to kiss along his neck. "Fucking hell... fucking hell."

Ambrose slipped his hand under the hem of Callum's shirt and pulled it up and over, tossing it to the side. "While seeing you in my shirt is one hell of a turn-on," he drawled, his voice husky, "I prefer when it's off."

Callum bit at his lower lip, feeling more exposed and vulnerable. Ambrose had seen him shirtless several times before, but never when both were hard for each other.

"Callum, you're fucking gorgeous," Ambrose said, his slender fingers sliding up and down Callum's chest, his mouth falling to the little crook at the base of Callum's neck. He bit down lightly, sucking. Callum lost his mind. He tugged on Ambrose's shirt, urging him to remove it. Ambrose obliged and tossed it on the floor.

Callum's fingers immediately traced the large scar on Ambrose's left side, right below his nipple. Ambrose snatched his wrist, moved it away from his scars, and let it settle on his waist.

"I fucking hate your dad," Callum said, squeezing where his hand was placed.

Ambrose laughed, kissing Callum's neck, then moved to his jaw, then he murmured into his mouth. "Let's not talk about my dad when we're occupied like this."

Callum smirked, pulled Ambrose in closer, his inexperienced kisses wild and hungry. Wild in a way that meant Callum worried this was his only time, this was his only chance to feel what he wanted to feel with Ambrose, to touch him however he desired.

A slender finger slipped into the waistband of Callum's sweats and tugged. "Take these off," Ambrose demanded into his mouth.

Callum clumsily obeyed, kicking them to the side. Ambrose tugged on his maroon boxers. "These too."

Stalling, Callum chuckled, his hands exploring Ambrose's bare chest. "You're so bossy when you're aroused."

Ambrose tugged impatiently at the boxers. "Less talking, Cal, more doing. I want to suck you off."

Callum practically whimpered, lifting his hips, rubbing

himself against Ambrose's thigh.

"Don't be nervous," Ambrose whispered into his ear, bracing a hand on the wall above his head. "I'm going to make you feel fucking good."

Callum had no doubt in his mind. He started, almost shyly, to remove his boxers. "I just want you to feel good, too. I don't know what I'm doing."

Ambrose shook his head, took Callum's hand temporarily away from the boxers and brought it to his dick. "Feel that? Stop worrying. I'm fucking hard for you."

Callum felt a heady rush with Ambrose's sex in the palm of his hands, wickedly hard with his desire.

Ambrose pulled Callum's boxers down, with a "now get these off," and Callum kicked them to the side with the rest of his clothes, completely naked. Ambrose's eyes rolled back in pleasure, and he wasted no time getting to his knees. The height difference meant he had to lean back on his ankles slightly. He pinned Callum's hips against the wall with his hands. He looked up at Callum, and the sight of Ambrose on his knees pinning those sex-crazed eyes on *him* made Callum weak.

When Ambrose's mouth took him in, paired with the sensation of his thumbs digging sharply into Callum's thighs as he pinned him in place on the wall, it was so much pleasure that Callum leaned his head back, swallowing his moan. He had to stop himself from thrusting into Ambrose's mouth.

Ambrose pulled back for a moment, looked up at Callum, and removed his hands from where they were on his thighs.

He lifted them up. "Alright then, baby," he said with a smirk. "Don't be afraid to fuck my face," he winked. "I don't mind."

Ambrose had a filthy, filthy mouth. Callum adored it.

When Ambrose sucked him in again, Callum did lift his hips, let his body take over, thrust in deeper. Ambrose groaned around his cock. Callum ran a hand through his dark hair and used the other hand to support himself on the wall.

I want to do this every day, he thought, brain addled with pleasure.

His stomach muscles tightened as he got closer to coming. He wanted to hold it back. He didn't want Ambrose's warm, wet, experienced, and so-fucking-sweet mouth to leave him.

Callum frantically tapped Ambrose's head to warn him. Ambrose knocked his hand away, shook his head and kept going. He raised his eyes, so he was watching Callum, spit dripping from the corner of his mouth. The sight finished Callum, and he came right in Ambrose's mouth, stuffing a hand in his own to stop the sounds he would make.

He pulled out. "Oh my gosh, I'm so sorry."

Ambrose grinned up at him, pinned him back to the wall and deliberately and obviously swallowed. He released Callum, wiped his mouth with the back of his hand, and pulled him down to the floor, where they sat side by side.

"That was a fucking pleasure," Ambrose stated.

Callum leaned his head back, closed his eyes as he caught his breath and grunted his agreement. After a few moments, he looked over at Ambrose.

"I want to..." he paused, chewing on his lower lip, suddenly embarrassed again, "I want to do that for you."

Ambrose leaned his clothed thigh against Callum's naked one, his hand gently traveling up and down Callum's leg. He smiled. "Trust me, Callum, I want it too. God, I can't fucking wait." He sighed. "But my dad is going to be here soon. We should clean up. You know if he even had the slightest suspicion, we were fucking around..."

"Yeah," Callum said, both disappointed and stupidly hopeful. *I can't fucking wait,* Ambrose had said. Like they *would* do this again.

Ambrose leaned his head back too, his fingers tapping a rhythm on Callum's thigh.

Callum teased. "You talk like a whore."

Ambrose chuckled. His hand came up to Callum's cheek, angling his face and kissing him. "You fucked my mouth like a whore," he retorted, eyes twinkling.

Callum's gaze fell to Ambrose's pants, where he was still hard.

"Don't worry about it," he told Callum, standing up in a smooth motion, pulling Callum up by the hand. "I'll take care of it in the shower."

Callum swallowed.

"Are you panicking?" Ambrose asked, a hand on Callum's shoulder. "You don't have to panic. I—I'm not expecting a single thing."

Callum chewed the inside of his cheek, Ambrose oblivious to

the fact that he voiced the very reason Callum *was* panicking.

"Right," Callum said, plainly, "because... well, Rose."

Ambrose was bent over, gathering Callum's clothes. He passed the bundle to him with a strange face. Callum started changing.

Ambrose watched him for a few moments before asking, softly, "you still don't get it?"

Callum pulled the shirt over his head, the fact that it was Ambrose's felt more intimate now that he had just been blown by him. "Get what?" Callum asked, a little bitterly. "I get it fine. She fucks Lucas. You play around with me. You don't expect anything from me because you have her, no matter how weird your relationship is. Am I right?"

Ambrose seemed to be biting back a smile. Callum was growing increasingly more frustrated.

"No." Ambrose finally said, firmly.

"No?"

"Callum, you idiot," Ambrose said fondly, brushing the hair aside that had fallen in disarray into Callum's eyes. "Rose is not real. She... I do love her. But not in any romantic way. She's just a beard."

"A what?"

"Like, I'm fake to her too, don't get me wrong. Her dad is a terrible person and her dating me makes him feel important because I'm Tomas's son. He stopped beating her when we started pretending. And on my side, I had just witnessed what happens to anyone in this branch who is openly gay. I was terrified. I *am* terrified. So Rose was a great way to keep my dad thinking I'm straight," he paused. "Callum, I'm gay. Gay, gay, not a drop straight. When I have to kiss Rose, it's actually torture." He winked before amending, "unless you are there for me to grope, of course."

Callum looked away. "Oh," he said lightly. "Does Lucas know?"

"Lucas, Asther, Liam. Probably Mick since Asther becomes a Chatty Cathy around him. Everyone knows, you were the only person who couldn't know."

Callum reared back slightly. "Everyone knows? Why couldn't I know?"

Ambrose placed two fingers on Callum's cheek, pushing his gaze back to him. "Isn't it obvious? Pretty much the day I met you, I knew I wanted to jump your bones. Callum, it's dangerous." He waved a hand back and forth between them. "*This* is dangerous."

Callum was quiet, taking the new information in.

When Ambrose spoke, his voice was pained. "I can't expect anything from you because it's unfair. You would always have to be a secret. I'm gonna marry Rose one day and you will always be the secret."

Callum felt sick. "It's unfair for you too," he told Ambrose. He leaned into him a little, their foreheads against each other.

Ambrose breathed in. "I can't live another life, Cal. I'm not even just saying that. It's not like I can just be born into a new family."

Callum thought to himself that there surely had to be a way. Somehow. But he only sighed. "I want..." shy again, he paused before saying, quickly, before he could change his mind, "I want to do this again, Ambrose."

Ambrose brought his hand back to Callum's nape, squeezed. "Fuck man, me too." Ambrose stepped back. "We can talk later. I need to get ready to see my dad now."

Callum's face fell, causing Ambrose to grin. "Don't give me that face." He reached over, and flicked Callum's nose.

"I'll collect what I'm owed, don't you worry."

Ambrose walked backwards to the bathroom and with a smirk he said, "now I'm gonna jerk off really quick."

CHAPTER 37

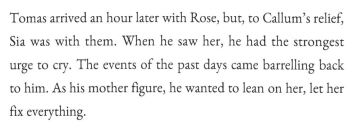

CALLUM

Tomas arrived an hour later with Rose, but, to Callum's relief, Sia was with them. When he saw her, he had the strongest urge to cry. The events of the past days came barrelling back to him. As his mother figure, he wanted to lean on her, let her fix everything.

When she saw him, she didn't hold back *her* tears, wrapping him in a hug. "Callum Brecker, you are never leaving my sight again." She didn't let go, and he was glad for it. He didn't say a word, preoccupied with holding back his tears.

Tomas embraced Ambrose, though it was stiffer and much quicker. Then Sia pulled Ambrose into an embrace, too.

Callum watched as Rose impatiently waited for her turn, concern, relief and love in her eyes as she looked at Ambrose. When she finally had an opening, she rushed into Ambrose's arms, sobbing into the crook of his neck. *"I'm so glad you are okay. I love you, I love you, I love you."*

Ever the superb actor, he held her like his life depended on it. *"I'm here Rose, I'm safe. I love you."* Rose kissed his face; he kissed her back.

Callum knew the whole truth, yet still his stomach soured. They were so excellent at making it look *real* that even now Callum doubted that it wasn't. Ambrose briefly locked gazes with him, conveying a look of... Callum didn't know. Regret. Pain, maybe.

After their hellos, they sat comfortably in a living room, Sia next to Tomas on a

blue linen couch, Callum and Ambrose each in a recliner across from them, separated by a victorian-style coffee table. The table was a comfort to have there, like a buffer. Tomas, after his initial, short-lived relief to see his son alive and well, was lived.

Rose was noticeably absent; Tomas had sent her to Ambrose's room to wait.

Again, Callum felt his stomach sour.

"Devin briefed me on the events," Tomas said. Gone was the temporary tenderness he had shown Ambrose earlier at the relief that he was alive, replaced with a dangerous edge, anger, and disappointment. Sia placed a hand on his knee, in solidarity or to calm him down. "But we are definitely changing the narrative when I report back to the Campano's."

Callum pinched his brows, confused, but Ambrose nodded. He was freshly

showered, hair neatly combed. Gone was the more punk, relaxed way he had dressed the past few days; in the presence of his father, he wore crisp jeans and a black button down.

"I killed Damian," Ambrose stated, "to the Campano's it was

me. Damian drugged Callum, and I was the one who killed him."

Sia made a pained face. Callum could hardly look at her. He wondered how ashamed she was of him, how disgusted. He knew that, for the rest of his life, he would struggle with that night. With the look in Damian's eyes as he died, with the pleasure it gave Callum like he was some monster, delighted by death.

"Exactly," Tomas said. He shot a frustrated look at Callum. "I'm touched that you protected my son like that. But if anyone present at the castle somehow witness what actually happened, we are, quite frankly, fucked."

"I'm not sure," Callum said, as respectfully as he could manage, "why it matters which one of us did the killing."

Ambrose subtly shook his head, begging Callum to remain seen and not heard.

Sia explained, before Tomas had a chance to speak. "Callum, it's all about mind games, asserting dominance, damaging pride. Ambrose killed an important Campano family member. They want him to be the one to make up for it."

"Right," Tomas agreed. "We are currently finding out names and positions of everyone present at the party, in case we need to... take care of talkers."

Ambrose said, confidently, "no one will say anything. The whole motto there is 'what happens at Damian's stays at Damian's.' I have so much dirt on every person there, they wouldn't dare speak."

Tomas seemed to glow at this new information. "That could come in handy for other jobs."

"Well, then my secrets would be out too," Ambrose deadpanned.

Tomas ignored the comment, in favor of more business talk. "We have another

Problem."

"Wonderful," Ambrose said, cheerily.

Tomas looked at Callum again, then back to Ambrose. "The Campano's are always one step ahead of my jobs. Whenever I am about to get an important client, or open a larger account, they get there first. We are always in competition with each other, so the first few times I let it roll off my shoulders, chalked it up to coincidence." He leaned his elbows on his knees, steepling his fingers under his sharp chin. "But it's happening every time now. In fact, Lastra is growing tired of my failures. Someone is targeting me and me specifically. And I think we have a mole, right in our Kansas company."

Callum watched Ambrose out of the corner of his eyes. He tensed.

"You'll notice," Tomas said coolly. "Rose is not present. Everyone is suspect at this point."

Again, he looked right at Callum. Callum had the startling realization that Tomas included *him* in that, but would never admit it, not with Sia seated at his side.

Ambrose barked out a laugh. "I know Rose, Dad, better than I know anyone. She's innocent in this. Also, think of her dad and how he climbs up your ass and makes home there. They would suffer most from your downfall, that's a fact."

Tomas scowled. "Must you speak like that?"

Ambrose sobered up quickly. It was shocking how he went from his smart-mouth, languid self to a stiff, respectful child in a flash at the tone of his father's voice. Like he was frightened.

Callum bit the inside of his cheek hard enough to bleed.

"I just want you to be aware," Tomas explained. "It's more inconvenient than anything at this point. I have my most trusted men on it and we *will* find the spy, whoever it may be, but exercise extra caution until then. Understood?"

"Yes, sir," Ambrose responded.

There was an awkward silence. All eyes were on Callum, Ambrose's squinted in warning.

"Oh, yes. Yes, sir." Callum said.

Sia seemed to deflate with relief.

I hate you, Callum thought and then almost jumped out of his own seat, startled by it. He didn't hate her. He could never hate her. He just understood, in that moment, Lucas and his anger... his frustration.

Tomas waved a hand. "You boys are dismissed. Ambrose, I know Rose will be wanting to spend some time with you. But go in for another check up with the physician. He's waiting for you now."

Callum followed Ambrose out, followed by the sound of Sia and Tomas, speaking in low tones.

Ambrose stopped in front of his door. Awkwardly, he said,

"Rose is in there."

"I get it," Callum replied with a forced smile. "I'm gonna go up to my room."

He turned As Ambrose grabbed him by the wrist. "Don't lock your door tonight," he whispered. "Please."

He didn't need to sound so desperate. It's not like Callum would ever refuse him.

CHAPTER 38

AMBROSE

"Ambrose." Rose looked concerned. Ambrose told her everything that transpired between him and Callum. He wanted to be fair, even though she had hidden Lucas from him. He wouldn't hide anything from her. "I knew that Callum would be a problem. You need to be careful."

He almost preferred it when Marco hit him. He was sure Marco, very subtly, did not use all his strength. His father, however, did not spare the rod. Ambrose bit down hard at the first strike, the second, the third and the final, searing pain lancing through his body.

"He's not a problem," Ambrose said defensively, even though he knew perfectly well what she meant. They lay side by side on the bed, fingers interlocked. It was comforting in a platonic sense. Rose *was* real to him, in a sense. She was a steady shoulder to lean on. They were brought together in desperation, both with abusive fathers, both with something to prove and everything to lose. She had always been his friend and she probably always would be, despite the circumstance they found themselves in.

She squeezed his hand. "I knew you liked him. You are hardly subtle about it. You basically dress him down with your eyes every time you see him."

Ambrose scoffed, but a grin played at the corner of his mouth. "But he's so fun to dress down with my eyes. He becomes so squeamish."

Rose laughed lightly. "You have to be cautious, Ambrose. God, your dad will kill you. My dad will probably kill *me.*"

"Don't you think I understand that?"

She sighed. "Sorry. Of course, you do."

Devin knocked, stuck his head in with a quick apology. "Your dad wants to see you, Ambrose. In his quarters."

Ambrose immediately felt clammy. Rose stood with him, wrapped him in a hug. She was thinking the same thing he was. He knew that much. When she pulled back, her eyes were wet. "I'm so sorry," was all she said before turning away from him, slipping back into the bed, pulling the covers over her as a shield. She hated to see people cry and especially hated to show any sort of empathy. She was one of the most empathic people he had ever known; her tears right now because she knew what was coming for him.

He had to pass Callum's room to get to his fathers. He trailed his fingers lightly on the door as he walked by.

He knocked on his dad's door, entering only when he was called for. Sia was nowhere to be found. That was the only confirmation he needed. Especially because Marco was there, standing by his father in the center of the room, a whip in hand.

Anger had Ambrose forget about caution and respect.

He smiled, nodded at the whip. "Am I interrupting sexy time?" he started for the door. "I can come back."

"Get over here," his father demanded.

Ambrose obeyed, because in the end he always did.

"Take off your shirt," his father said. He had one arm crossed over his chest, the other hand rubbing his chin. "The physician informed me that you are cleared."

Ambrose tossed his shirt to the side with a sigh. *Stupid fucking physician.*

"Knees."

Ambrose got on his knees. To Marco's credit, he had the decency to look uncomfortable. Or at least, like he didn't enjoy this. Ambrose was rather fond of the guy, all things aside.

His father said, from above Ambrose's bent head, "I don't want to do this to you, Ambrose. You respond best to pain, and I need you to respond now. I need you to learn from this."

"Sir, I'm not even sure why I'm being punished," Ambrose admitted, respect oozing from his voice so much that it could be interpreted as nothing but fake. "The events of the past days were, quite frankly, out of my hands."

Tomas crouched in front of Ambrose, gripped his chin in a hand, squeezing roughly until Ambrose looked at him. "That is exactly the problem, you damn fool. You almost died." His father stressed the words, squeezed tighter, his voice raising, a little manic. "You almost died. The *events* should never be out of your hands."

Ambrose's tears could have been from the pain but were more likely a disturbing sort of relief that his father cared in his ultra-fucked up way. That his father was panicking because he almost lost his son. Love wasn't always non-toxic, his father's love dripped with toxicity, but it was love nonetheless and Ambrose wanted to cling to it. Desperate in the same way he had been as a child, just wanting to know that his father cared.

Tomas's own eyes were wet. He reached his hand back and Marco placed the whip on his palm. Ambrose might have imagined the sympathetic wince he shot his way.

His father stood. He tossed Ambrose a balled-up cloth. Ambrose was no stranger to any of this. He placed the cloth in his mouth, biting down. He clasped his hands in front of him.

CHAPTER 39

CALLUM

Sia brought Callum back to their house. Lucas and Mick were waiting, restless, on the front steps. They were shivering—Kansas winter was wildly different from California's—but when they saw Callum get out of Sia's car they rushed him, practically tackling him to the ground.

"Callum, what the hell?" Lucas said, roughly, but he was pulling him in close. Mick wrapped his arms around them both, shamelessly sobbing.

"I can't believe you killed a man," Mick said. "I'm so sorry, Callum, I'm so sorry."

Callum pulled away and smiled at his cousins. He hadn't really thought that they would know. Sia explained, "I called them Callum and told them everything. No more secrets between the four of us. Not ever again."

Except Callum had a secret now. He couldn't find the energy to be annoyed that Sia had not even asked him if it was okay that she told them.

He only nodded, ruffling Mick's hair as they all went into the house, Lucas taking Callum's bag.

"I thought you might be angry with me," Callum admitted to his aunt. Mick was hanging onto Callum for dear life, and he felt like he might cry when he looked at his little cousin. After being around filth and trash, Damian, and his ilk, coming back to someone like Mick was a breath of fresh air. It was hope.

Sia looked at her boys, unmistakable sadness in her eyes. "How could I be angry? The only person I am angry at is myself. I did this to us. I should never have taken the job; I should never have come here. How did I ever think I could keep you boys away from it all?"

Maybe just a few weeks ago, Callum would have wished the same thing. That Sia had never moved them all to the middle of nowhere Kansas, that none of this had ever happened. Now he couldn't imagine a different life, as horrible as this one could be. He wanted to throw up, thinking of existing without knowing Ambrose. Of Mick never knowing Asther. Even Lucas and Rose, since he understood the dynamic much better now.

"Mom, it's not your fault," Mick said sweetly. "You really had no choice."

Lucas, his grip firm and steady on Callum's shoulder, the three of them all

holding on to each other, added, "Dad really pushed you into a corner. If we must blame anyone, I think it should be him."

She laughed a little. There was a time when she would try to defend their father to them, for their sakes. At least she wouldn't badmouth him. But everything was different now.

"I want you boys all to know that Tomas and I... being a thing... happened much

after I took the job. That played no part in my decision."

"Of course," Mick nodded vigorously.

Lucas, always brutally honest, "I wish you could have chosen literally any other man. What is it about Tomas? He's..."

"Terrible," Callum filled in for him, startling them all. It was so out of character for him to speak up. Especially when it went against Sia.

Sia seemed to be choosing her words carefully. "He is terrible. But he's also wonderful. He's worth it to me, because under everything he is a kind man who was handed a life he may not have otherwise chosen. He was just like Ambrose once, though he wasn't lucky enough to have such supportive friends, to have good people around him. Most of the terrible things he does are out of love. I'm not defending him; I'm just saying I think he can be saved."

He was just like Ambrose once.

Callum swallowed his next words. He wouldn't argue with her. He just remembered the fear he saw in her eyes; she was afraid of Tomas, just as afraid as she was in love.

She ushered them into the kitchen so she could get some food together. She added water to a pot, setting it to boil on the stove. Reaching into one of the cabinets, she pulled out six packs of ramen—Lucas always ate an obnoxious amount of it.

"Callum," she hedged, gently, "will you want to see a therapist? Tomas has one that comes to the estate twice a week for anyone who needs it."

"No," Callum said immediately. He didn't want to think about what happened, let alone talk about it with a stranger paid off by Tomas. "I'll manage."

Three sets of eyes were pinned on him, full of doubt.

"Callum," Mick started, but Sia shook her head.

"Tell me when you are ready," she said, salting the water. "Until then, I'm here if you need me."

Lucas made a face at Callum when the others weren't looking. He didn't believe Sia, and Callum didn't really either. She hadn't quite been there for them for some time now. Understanding passed between the two of them with that look. And a promise. They would always have each other.

"I like this," Mick said from where he perched on the counter, hand on Callum's back. He wondered if Mick would ever let go of him again. "The four of us, having dinner together like old times."

"Yeah," Lucas said acerbically, "except now Mom works for the Mafia, and Callum's a murderer."

Sia made a horrified sound, opening her mouth to scold her son. She stopped because Callum was laughing. He couldn't stop laughing. Lucas grinned. Mick looked confused, but he grinned too.

"It's good to have you back," Mick said. "You belong with us."

Ambrose: *Miss me yet? ;)*

Callum: *not quite yet.*

Ambrose: *You wound me, Callum Brecker, you wound me.*

Ambrose: *I seem to be missing something.*

Ambrose: *Do you have my zippo?*

Callum: *Yes. I was surprised. You kept it.*

Ambrose: *Why the fuck wouldn't I?*

...

Ambrose: *It was from you <3*

CHAPTER 40

CALLUM

Callum awoke in the middle of the night, a hand covering his mouth. He widened his eyes in terror, trying to adjust to the dark to see his attacker. A phone flashlight went on, momentarily blinding him. Then he saw Asther. He relaxed slightly. Until Asther urgently put a finger to his lips, silencing Callum. His mind immediately went to Mick or Ambrose, thinking someone had to be in trouble.

"Don't make a sound and follow me," Asther whispered.

There were tears in his eyes. Confusion had Callum rushing after him, silently.

Unease prickled at his spine. "Do we need to get Mick and Lucas?" He asked as they crept quietly out the front door.

Asther guided him to a sleek black Mercedes parked on the side of the driveway, engine so quiet, lights off. "No," Asther said over a cracked sob. "This is about Ambrose."

Callum had been trying to buckle, but when he heard those words his hands slipped, the buckle jerking back. He felt immediately dizzy, his panic taking over.

"I have to get you to Ambrose," Asther said, urgently, his

hands tightening on the wheel, his eyes wet with tears.

"Fuck," Callum said, burying his head in his hands, leaning forward, seatbeltless for the very first time. His mind spun to the worst possible outcomes; the Campano's found out about the castle events. They retaliated and hurt Ambrose. It was all Callum's fault, it was all his fault.

"His dad, Tomas," Asther started, but broke off with a sob.

The phrase, *seeing red,* suddenly had meaning to Callum. He understood. His fists clenched at his sides, he found himself imagining that it wasn't Damian that night; it was Tomas, Callum stuffing the vial down Tomas's throat, the pleasure of his death tenfold.

Disgusted by his own thoughts and terrified for Ambrose, he kept his head tucked between his knees, trying to regulate his breathing.

"Fuck shit," Asther swore, slamming on the brakes. They were on the backroads leading to the estate. Callum looked up to see a car blocking the road, men in black in a line, guns pointed right at them.

"Fuck shit... fuck shit... fuck shit," Asther kept saying.

Before Callum could tell him that was completely unhelpful, one of the men came over to the driver door, wrenched it open and pulled a screaming Asther out of the Merc. Callum immediately dove for the driver's seat, instinct taking over, grabbing Asther by the ankle and stupidly, naively trying to hold on.

Another man sauntered over, knocked Callum on the wrist

with the butt of his pistol and snarled, "Get the fuck off, if either of you want to live."

Callum reared back, screaming as the pain shot up his entire arm. His wrist hung limp. Through the tears, he watched as another car pulled up and two men stuffed a kicking, screaming Asther into the back, tapped the hood, and then the car pulled away.

He couldn't breathe. Callum couldn't breathe. His first thought was, *what do I tell Mick?* but his next thoughts were all about getting away, getting out, getting to Ambrose.

The man who had hit him, tall and dark, came around and pulled Callum out by his hair.

"This sniveling shit is really the one who killed Damian?" He called over to another man, who approached them.

"That's right," he said, looking at his phone, then back to Callum, then back to his phone, "here's his photo D sent us."

The dark man smirked, hands still in Callum's hair. He pulled him up so that he was standing wobbly and crouched low to look him in the eyes. "Aren't you a dumb-fuck?"

"What's this about?" Callum asked in between heaving breaths. Though the mention of Damian told him enough.

"It's about your dumb-fuckery," the man said, pushing him to the ground, kicking him to stay down. Callum cradled his wrist, the pain still blinding. "Sticking your nose in where it doesn't belong."

"Diego, stop talking." The other man said. "Just knock him out and get him in the car."

"Wai—" Callum started desperately, but it didn't matter. This time, the butt of Diego's pistol met his temple, and the world went black.

CHAPTER 41

AMBROSE

Ambrose couldn't sleep, so he decided to go on an early morning run. He slipped into his joggers and Nike running shoes and quietly crept downstairs.

When he opened the door, he screamed.

The two men who stood guard during the night were dead, bullets through their heads; blood seeping around them in little pools on the porch. But at Ambrose's feet, bound and gagged, was Asther, a note stapled to his chest. Ambrose couldn't tear his eyes away from the horror of it, immediately feeling weak and dizzy.

Ambrose knelt to help his friend, barely registering his own actions, but Devin was there, pulling it off.

"Get inside!" He demanded, as he started shouting orders into his earpiece.

"Asther," Ambrose started weakly, but his father's hands were pulling him back.

"Ambrose, follow Sia. Go to the safe room." The shock of hearing his father use such a gentle tone had Ambrose about to comply. The estate was in an uproar, their men rushing everywhere, weapons at the ready, speaking through their earpieces, preparing for...

"Wait," Devin said. He passed Asther's body; *oh God, was he dead?* to the man nearest and held up the bloodied note he had removed. "This is addressed to Ambrose."

Ambrose hardly heard. He watched as one of his father's men took Asther and walked towards the safe room, saying something about the physician in his earpiece. If Asther was dead, if he would die, *no, no, no.*

"Ambrose, focus!" Tomas boomed, snapping his fingers in his face. Gone was any previous gentleness, in its place the father he had always known. Tomas shoved the note at Ambrose. "Now we have a fucking mess to clean. You had *one* job, dammit, Ambrose, one job!"

Ambrose opened the note, his hands shaking. At the top was a phone number. But the rest of the note.

If anyone were to ask him when he started to break, when he started to embrace who he was and welcome the dark parts of his life, this would be the moment. Because he was angry. Angrier than he had ever been. An icy cold settled over him as he pocketed the note and turned to his dad.

"We are going to fucking kill them," he seethed. His father looked disturbingly proud as Ambrose continued. "Whoever they are, we are going to kill them and everyone they fucking love."

***

Ambrose Romano,
We have your little boy toy, Callum.
Call the number above and prepare to comply. You have 24
hours before this pretty little brat gets to decorate my walls

with his brains.

END OF BOOK ONE

***

Acknowledgements

I have so many people I would like to thank for helping me get to this point. My partner, Mat, for all the help he provided and all the times he left me the heck alone so I could write. (Haha) My lifelong best friends, Celia and Angelika, I would truly be nowhere without them and their unfailing support. Emma Rossi, a valuable critique partner and friend, who pushed me and encouraged me to do hard things. My sister in law, Teresa Bordelon. Thank you always for your encouragement. To all the wonderful friends I've made in the bookstagram community for encouraging me, supporting me and cheering me on, especially @karens_books and @reading_with_chloe. I wish I could mention all of you. Thank you so much for reading my book. You matter, each and every one of you.

About The Author

Marilyn Bordelon is a twenty-seven year old woman with a passion for all things books! Born and raised in Kansas where she now resides with her spouse and two children, she spends all of her free time reading and writing.

Becoming an author has been a dream of hers. Since she was old enough to hold a pencil she has always been writing fiction stories. She hopes to build a little "found family" through her books that have strong themes of acceptance, love and belonging.

Excellent LGBTQ+ fiction by unique, wonderful authors.

Thrillers

Mystery

Romance

Young Adult
& More

Join our mailing list here for news, offers and free books!

Visit our website for more Spectrum Books

www.spectrum-books.com

Or find us on Instagram

@spectrumbookpublisher

Printed in Great Britain
by Amazon

17320927R00207